USA TODAY BESTSELLING AUTHOR

SARA
NEY

AND

MEGHAN
QUINN

~~Sincerely~~ LOVE

Yours

Published by Hot-Lanta Publishing, LLC

Copyright 2018

Cover Design By: RBA Designs

Cover Model: Fabian Castro

Photo Credit: Rafa Catala

PROLOGUE

PEYTON

Vivian: *God, why is he such an asshole?*

Kimberly: *Don't you think the better question is, "Poor George, why is he never prepared?"*

Peyton: *George spends more time at the latte machine than his computer. That's why. And look how jolly he is. Like a cute little Santa Claus . . .*

Vivian: *Sigh. George's wife makes the best apple pie.*

Kimberly: *Oh crap, Vivian, look out. He's coming for you.*

"Vivian, what came out of your test study?" A man's voice cuts into our group chat and, unprepared, our coworker stumbles to pull her notes up on her iPad.

Kimberly: *Shit. Viv is a goner.*

Peyton: *Oh I feel bad. She's turning red.*

Kimberly: *Yeah, Viv. You're turning SO red.*

Peyton: *Viv, you should see your ears . . .*

Kimberly: *Maybe if the devil himself wasn't breathing down her neck, she wouldn't be sweating so much.*

Peyton: *To be fair, we are in the middle of a meeting. She should be prepared, not pretending to take notes white chatting online.*

Kimberly: *Look how irritated he is. His nostrils are flaring.*

Peyton: *Yeah . . . look at his face. He looks like a dragon tempted to light the entire room on fire.*

I turn to study him from my position at the conference table, the long wooden slab a monolithic buffer between my boss and me. He's at the head of the table, brandishing control and his silver tongue over the room like a sharp sword.

No one is safe from his contempt.

I watch as he reprimands my friend from the marketing department—her small office is two down from mine—laying both palms on the desk and leaning toward her.

"I have no new ideas to work with here. How the fu—" He stops himself from cursing mid-sentence, pausing to take a deep breath and starting over. He then runs one of those large, masculine palms through his dark hair. "What the hell is it you do in your office all day? Stare out the damn windows waiting for inspiration? I want you outside for fuck's sake. Go climb a goddamn mountain. This is an *outdoor* adventures company, for fuck's sake. Go outdoors."

He pins a mammoth, brawny guy named Branson with a hard, emotionless stare. "Innovation is one of your jobs, Branson. Take a tent out, set the fucking thing up, and find a way to improve it."

He's breathing hard. Pissed off.

"Look. I know we've just come off the holiday season and everyone is beat, but if we don't get some advances with our designs to boost sales, this fiscal year will end up being complete shit."

He drones on, his deep voice reverberating off the walls as we all sit silently, holding our breath.

Vivian: *Uh, hey guys? Do you think he still wants my notes?*

2

Kimberly: *Fuck your notes, Viv. Don't say another word unless your "notes" are actual notes.*

Peyton: *Pretty sure you lost your moment before he stood up and starting pacing like a tiger at the zoo.*

Vivian: *Thank God. I had nothing new to add.*

I watch across the table as Vivian slouches with relief, a sly smile playing across her bubblegum-painted lips. Her lithe fingers tap away at the iPad propped up on the table, and I know her next message isn't to us.

Kimberly: *Do you not have notes because you were so focused on flirting with the guy online that has—how did you put it . . .*

Peyton: *Meat steaks for pecs?*

Kimberly: *Yeah, that guy. "Meat steak guy."*

Vivian: *I can't be accountable for my actions. I have to flirt.*

Peyton: *You don't even know if he's real.*

Vivian: *Who cares if he's real? He's the perfect distraction.*

"I want everyone to crawl back to their hole of an office and pull an idea out of their ass by noon. This is the summer of 'roughing it.' Our target demographic—Harry can provide the data —is the millennial and the yuppy. If you don't know what a yuppy is, google it. If you can't figure out how to do *that*, clear the shit out of your desk."

At the mention of his name, Harry blanches, an unattractive contrast to the muddy-green color of his short-sleeve plaid shirt. His neck turns a muddy burgundy, which only serves to highlight the stubble his razor missed when he shaved this morning.

Kimberly: *Did you guys just see that? Harry wiped his brow. He's legit sweating.*

Peyton: *Yeah, I saw that—gross. He looks like he's about to barf. You heard what happened though, right?*

Vivian: *No, what happened?*

Peyton: *Rumor has it, the ad copy he proofed for Mountain Man Magazine had three errors in it.*

Kimberly: *NO IT DID NOT*

Vivian: *THREE?? Ohhhh shitttttt . . .*

Peyton: *Yes, three.*

Our boss levitates Harry with a pair of eyes so grey I squirm, though they're not directed anywhere in my direction.

Thank God.

Bossman holds up three fingers.

"How could you let three god—" He stops himself again, pushing his large hand through his thick, ruffled hair. "How could you let three errors get through proofing? You had one job, Harry. One. Keep us from looking illiterate."

He has a point; an ad has no more than one hundred words in it.

"I'm so sorry, Rome. I, uh, had a headache that day." Harry fidgets with the handkerchief in his hand. It was given to him by his wife, embroidered with his initials and a heart that's gag-worthy sweet. Too bad he's using it to wipe the nervous sweat pouring from his temples.

It's not a good look for Harry—or anyone for that matter.

"You're giving *me* a headache." Bossman surrenders to his chair, head in his hand.

"I'm sorry, Rome, I—"

"No, Harold, I'm the one who's sorry." His meaning couldn't be more clear: *I'm sorry I hired you. I regret it. I intend to fire you if you fuck up one more time.* "There will be no second chances."

He straightens to his full height, addressing the room of minions.

"For the love of all that's holy, someone give me something by noon."

My fingers, about to tap out another message to my friends, cease their mission.

It's ten fifteen.

He wants ideas by noon.

I have an appointment with him at *eleven.*

Shit.

When my eyes go up from the small screen cradled in my

hands, they connect with a set of steel-gray ones. Dark brows, an expressionless line. Full lips, impassive.

He is so good-looking.

Beautiful, even.

Such a waste on a man so emotionally unattached.

Still.

When our eyes lock—a little too long to be coincidental—heat rises up my chest, neck, and then cheeks. It colors my entire face and has me reaching to press a palm there.

It's warm, too.

I shiver.

I have an appointment with him at eleven.

And he isn't going to like what I have to say.

CHAPTER ONE

ROME

W*hy the fuck is she staring at me like that?*
She hasn't said a goddamn word in—I check my watch —three minutes.

Allowing the seconds to tick by despite her discomfort, or possibly because of it, I let the silence stretch in front of us unpleasantly long. Uncomfortable and challenging situations are what I do best, and I thrive on them.

Tic.

Tock.

No worries, my sardonic smile says to her. *I have plenty of time.* An entire twenty minutes penciled in just for her, per her request, to sit here pissing away my precious time. Waiting for her to open that pretty mouth and speak her mind.

Instead, she shifts in her seat, the gray skirt she's unable to tug down hugging her hips. It's tight and prim, complemented by a stark, white button-down shirt. Black glasses rest primly on the tip of her nose, the dark slash of eyebrows above their rims, raised in surprise.

7

She doesn't look like any marketing coordinator I've ever met, and I certainly had no idea there was someone who looked like her working for me. *Under* me.

Four floors down.

She looks like a goddamn accountant. Or secretary. Or the principal of an East Coast prep school.

I swivel in my leather chair before plucking a pen off my desk and pinching it between my fingers, studying it with half-hooded eyes.

Feign boredom.

I'm anything but.

Click the end cap once, twice, watching this woman's large brown eyes track my movements from the other side of my mammoth desk. Her brows pinch, thinly veiled patience wearing thin.

Peyton.

Shit, when I saw her name in my appointment calendar, I assumed the person walking through the door would be male. Imagine my surprise when the delicate wrist gently knocking on my doorframe belonged to the woman seated at my conference table this morning.

She was on her cell phone during that meeting. I'll bet my right nut sac on it.

I glance at the sheet of paper and stare at each letter of her name; I've never had a sit-down, or meeting, with this woman since she's been with my company.

Five years.

Even with a solid track record for results—according to my secretary's snooping—she's never been in my office. Peyton some-thing-or-other, whose last name I can't fucking pronounce and won't bother to try.

Why bother? She has one prissy foot out the door of the company *I* built.

I part my lips and put us both out of our misery. "Does your supervisor know you're here?"

"Not yet," she begins, spine straightening, breasts straining against the starched shirt. "I wanted . . ." She pauses, inhaling a nervous breath.

"Why didn't you go to HR first? That's protocol."

I like being direct. Favor bluntness over candy-coated bullshit, no matter what flavor someone is trying to feed me.

"I wanted to give you my two-weeks' notice in person. I thought it would be personable."

Personable.

Is she fucking serious? Who does that?

"You're *quitting*. Do you think I give a shit about being personable?" Or polite? Or her trying to be *considerate*?

Those traits have no place in this office.

It's an office, not a daycare center; we're here to make money, not pander to hurt feelings.

Another pause from Peyton before she shakily says, "I thought since it was *your* company, it would behoove me to not burn any bridges."

Behoove.

Isn't she just fucking adorable? I suddenly imagine her from a small town in the middle of nowhere USA, where parents teach their children manners and spend quality time together on the weekends. Family movie nights and all that feel-good bullshit.

I snort, clicking my pen.

Peyton. What kind of a name is that?

A *man's* name, that's what.

"You didn't want to burn any bridges," I repeat with a sneer, thumbing the cream-colored paper she set on my desk when she waltzed in. Her letter of resignation printed on résumé paper. "I don't just burn bridges. I drain the rivers and fill them with concrete."

Then I go camping along the banks of the rivers remains; I own an outdoor adventure company, so finding a tent would be easy.

SARA NEY & MEGHAN QUINN

Peyton's mouth puckers, surprised or shocked or disgusted by my candor, I can't tell.

I skim the paper in my hands. "It doesn't say where you're headed next. Do you not need a letter of recommendation? Because I must say, Peyton"—I lean back in my chair, letting it squeak on its rusted, old hinges—"quitting is a piss-poor way of wringing one out of me."

Her head shakes, and the dark hair pulled back in a tidy bun at the nape of her neck doesn't budge an inch. All it's missing is a hairnet.

I let my eyes drift from the tips of her shiny leather heels to the collar of her starched dress shirt as she sits across from me.

My eyes narrow. "Do you always dress like that for work?"

She glances at her blouse, touching a pearl button fastened against her throat. "When I have an important meeting, yes."

"It's a goddamn *out*door adventures company and you have a librarian bun in your hair."

She stiffens, eyes falling to the blue silk tie knotted around my throat, the broad shoulders of my suit coat, no doubt labeling me a hypocrite. Tough shit; it's my company. I do whatever the fuck I want, and I too have an important meeting this afternoon with advertisers. I'm not about to show up in a goddamn lumberjack plaid shirt with the sleeves rolled up to my elbows.

Peyton fiddles with a gold hoop earring. "I thought our meeting warranted a little extra effort this morning."

"Well, you could have saved yourself the trouble. When someone quits on Roam, Inc., I no longer have use for their time."

"But Rome, I was hoping . . ." She uses my first name instead of my last, lifting an arm, brushing a lock of hair behind her ear that isn't there; a nervous habit I've seen her do several times already. She can't rake her fingers through her hair though because it's pulled back in that damn matronly bun. "I came in to suggest that though I'm striking out on my own, my services could still be of use to you."

"Your services?" A chuckle escapes my lips despite myself, lips settling into a sneer.

When I think *services*, my mind goes immediately into the gutter: escorts and blow jobs and loose women. Sue me for immediately thinking about sex.

She must read my thoughts reflected in my eyes, because hers flutter and the skin on her exposed neck ignites to a hot red.

"My *design* services, yes. I'm finally—"

"We'll manage just fine without you, I'm sure." Agitated by the excited glint in her eye, I cut her off. She's leaving and has the balls to begin a pitch for her subcontract work?

I don't fucking think so, sweetheart.

I lean forward, hands folded on my desktop, sleeves of my dress shirt cuffed and rolled to my elbows. "I'm not successful because I spend my time sensitivity training the shit out of everyone who needs it. This is a business, not a hobby. And since you insisted on this little meeting, let me fill you in on something; a valuable lesson that might come in handy for your next job, if you will."

"I-Im listening."

I level Peyton with a hard stare. "If you think for one second you're going to work for a competitor, think again."

I shift the papers on my desk, jabbing my finger at her non-compete contract; the one she signed the first week she came onboard at Roam, Inc.

It's ironclad and irrevocable for one year after the termination of her employment, and I'm not afraid to enforce it.

Yup. I'll take her for everything she's worth if she works for the competition.

Her chin lifts a fraction. "I would never."

My lip curls into a smile. "That's what everyone says."

She stares at my mouth a few heartbeats before shaking her head. "I won't be working for anyone again. I'm finally going to work for myself. And if you can't respect that, I guess I underestimated you."

I lean forward, clasping my hands on my desk. "Underestimated me?"

"I thought you were progressive. As someone that started their own company from the ground up, I thought maybe you'd give me a chance." She stands, handing me a manila folder. "My graphic design work is good. Fantastic even. If you can't see that, then, well. You . . . you're a . . ."

My brows rise into my hairline. "I'm a what?"

"An ass." After getting the last word in, she rises with a huff and leaves my office. *An ass? Please, I've heard worse.*

When she's gone, I fiddle with the mouse of my laptop, scrolling through the company contacts. I need to know more.

Peyton Lévêque.

I spell her fucking last name wrong three times before finally getting it right.

Hit enter.

~

PEYTON

The sound of Rome Blackburn's door closing behind me startles me out of my stupor. Out of the haze of *delusion* I'd somehow created and been surrounding myself with the past few weeks, thinking maybe—just maybe—he'd want to hire me on as a contractor once I left the company.

I was betting on him giving me a chance.

What the hell just happened in there?

Did I just march into Mr. Outdoor Adventure's office to resign with an envelope full of designs? To pitch him my new company? To *stare* at the strong set of his jaw while he rattled off insults?

I did.

Oh God, I did.

And I called him an ass—to his face. Honestly, the look on his face will be burned into my brain forever. And I doubt insulting him will bode well for me in the slightest. Talk about not wanting to burn bridges . . .

But he didn't even let me get a word in edgewise.

Well, maybe a few—a stutter here and there.

Good job, Peyton. Way to represent the future of Fresh Minted Designs by losing your backbone when you needed it the most. How is that going to help you succeed?

"How'd it go?"

I breeze past Lauren, Rome's assistant, but her stage whisper stops me. She's leaning over the cold stone counter, glancing up and down the hall—then back at me, crooking her finger so I'll come closer.

"Well? How did it go? You weren't in there long."

I glance toward Rome Blackburn's office, my face defeated. "*Not* as I expected. And now I know where he gets his last name from."

His personality is as *black* as his soul.

Wincing, Lauren motions with her finger for me to come closer, still. I have nothing better to do since I just *quit*, so I follow her little command, resting my hip against her granite counter with a loud sigh.

She grimaces. "That bad, huh?"

"*Worse.*"

"I didn't hear any shouting. How bad could it have been?"

My brows shoot up. "Shouting?"

"Well, yeah—you're *leaving*. You quit. Rome Blackburn doesn't take kindly to people leaving the company."

As if I needed to be told; I just witnessed it firsthand.

"Were you able to give him your two-weeks' notice?"

"No. The conversation tanked when he started talking about my non-compete."

Lauren laughs, clicking away at her keyboard. "Yeah, he usually has people clean out their desk on the spot when they intend to leave. Don't be surprised if there's a box already packed by the time you reach your desk."

"Oh really? I never would have guessed." The words drip from my mouth, coated in sarcasm I can't conceal, but my stomach drops.

I hope he lets me stay; I *need* these last two weeks.

"He's built this company on blood, sweat, and tears from the ground—"

"Sweetie, I know." I lean over to pat Lauren on her shoulder. "You don't have to defend him. I get it. It's nothing personal. It's business. I just wish he'd have given me more of a chance to—"

Down the corridor, a door opens.

His door.

Lauren's back goes rigid; her fingers immediately begin flying faster across her keyboard.

I freeze.

My shoulders stiffen, back straightens, senses kick in, and I'm suddenly on high alert.

His cologne is sharp and masculine—with an air of power— mixed into one unmistakable and ridiculously intoxicating scent, *and what the hell am I even saying?*

Rome Blackburn is woods and rivers and adventure.

He is excitement.

He is an asshole.

Rome Blackburn is a freaking prick.

The energy in the air shifts in the hallway. Commanding steps move toward Lauren and me, stopping just behind me.

"Ms. Lll—" The tool isn't even going to attempt to try and pronounce my last name. Like it'd be too hard? "What are you still doing here? Don't you have two-weeks' notice to give to your supervisor?"

He's not making me clean out my desk. *He's not making me clean out my desk.*

"It's Lévêque." It's pronounced le-veck.

"What is?"

"My last name."

Sharp, intense silver eyes narrow, five o'clock shadow covering his strong, chiseled jaw. Rome crosses his arms, biceps straining against the expensive fabric of his blue button-down shirt, feet a shoulder-width apart. The stance makes the room feel smaller, tighter, sucking all the air.

"Le-veck," he repeats, testing it on his lips. His gorgeous, pouty lips.

"Yes."

"Then why the hell don't you spell it that way?"

"It's French."

His eyes narrow even farther—if that were possible—jaw ticking, thrumming an irritated beat as he sticks his hand in his pocket.

"Lauren, please show Ms. Fancy Pants Le-Veck to the elevator. The clock is ticking on her time here."

"Yes, Mr. Blackburn." Flicking an apologetic look my way, his assistant stands, hastening to do his bidding, guiding me hastily to the elevators twenty feet in front of her desk, hands on my shoulders, propelling me forward.

"I'm so sorry. We'll talk more later," she whispers, her ruby-red nail poking at the down button; the doors automatically slide open, revealing the interior black and chrome walls.

Stepping in, I turn around and press my floor button, four levels down.

"Human Resources first, Ms. Fancy Pants," Rome calls out the reminder with a smirk. "It's that way."

He points toward the ceiling.

Jerk.

Tall, with wide shoulders and a tapered waist, the best part about him is his broody demeanor. I am attracted to it like bees to honey; it intrigues me to no end.

As the doors of the elevator begin to shut, Rome steps into view, hands tucked into the pockets of his perfectly pressed trousers as he watches me, scowl etched across his beautiful dark brows.

Just because I feel the need to be pleasant—despite how rude he's treated me—I mouth the words, "Thank you, Mr. Blackburn," as the door slides closed in front of me.

I smile to myself, knowing I had the last word.

Smile as the door shuts me in.

Only when they close do my shoulders slump, and I lean against the wall for support, letting out a ragged breath.

Giving your two-weeks' notice is difficult enough—giving it directly to a man like *that*?

Harder.

That could have gone better.

It went nothing like I imagined when I played out the scenario in my mind. Or when I rehearsed the speech I was going to give to my dog, a rescue mutt I named Scott, because I think it's hilarious giving my pets people names.

"*Scott and Mr. Blackburn. Thanks so much for seeing me today, I know your time is valuable.*" I cleared my throat. "*Oh, what's that? You like my skirt? (giggle) Thank you so much. I picked it out just for you.*"

But he hadn't liked my skirt; he'd made fun of it. I'd stuttered over myself, hadn't been able to give him my pitch, and fallen flat on my face.

I had visions of how much better that could have been. Dreams actually.

Praise and gratitude were supposed to be thrown my way. Excitement for a new partnership. For growth. Maybe some high fives, a few professional handshakes, or a fist bump to seal the deal.

I adjust my tweed tight-fitting pencil skirt, feeling the hug of the fabric—and slit up the back, allowing for some breathing room—then I pluck open the top two buttons of my stifling shirt.

Embarrassed from the gauntlet I just ran through, I make my way back to my small office, which is really just a glorified cubicle, passing many onlooking and incredibly nosey coworkers.

Leave the door open.

Squeaky wheels adjust against the plastic chair mat that protects the carpet of the office, rolling forward as I sit down.

Leaning forward, I grip my forehead with one of my hands and replay the meeting over and over in my head.

Rome Blackburn's casual, yet intimidating stance. The pinch of his long fingers as he fiddled with that damn pen. The taper of his waist of his well-tailored pants as he watched the elevator doors close on me. The simple *mess* of his hair, pushed in all different directions, as if moments ago he was pulling on the silky brown strands, making a decision for the Fortune 500 company he's created from the ground up.

And those eyes.

Dark brows hooded over pools of complex silver—not blue, not gray . . . *silver*—that for once, I'd been close enough to discover the color of.

They grew a darker mossy color as he became more irritated with me.

With me.

Ugh.

Rome Blackburn is callous, brash, and calculating. Yet, in that brief moment we stared at each other, I saw it—a fleeting look of vulnerability behind his tough exterior.

A glimmer of—

Knock, knock.

Before I even look up to see who's tapping on the wall of my cubicle, I know it's my best friend, Genevieve.

"Well. How did it go?" Genevieve works in IT, the technical side of Roam, Inc and has been incredibly supportive of me leaving the company to start my own branding and consulting firm.

Gen sits on a small filing cabinet in my office, smooth legs crossed and ready to listen.

Spinning slowly in my chair, I angle toward her. Purse my lips. "How do you think it went?"

Her face contorts. "I'm going to guess not so well?" She phrases it like a question. "Mr. Blackburn doesn't seem like an understanding guy. He's too pissed off all the time."

Understatement of the year.

"God, Gen, I wussed out so hard. I'm so embarrassed—and I didn't even get to talk about my idea or my plans." I shake my head. "What the hell was I thinking? Rome Blackburn legit cut me off before I could even get my words out of my mouth." I laugh some more, finding the meeting more comical with each passing breath.

"At least it's a pretty mouth," my friend teases.

"He didn't even know my last name, which means he had no idea who I was. Awesome."

That gathers a chuckle from Genevieve. "He seems so refined. How could he mess up your last name?"

"He couldn't pronounce it, so he didn't bother saying it." I shrug. "Or maybe it was his way of jabbing me with one last insult before I left."

Dutiful and supportive, my friend rubs my back.

"All it did was make him look like an ass." Her high-heeled shoe bounces up and down. "Hey. Listen. Forget about him. You're leaving, and you're going to kick some serious ass when you're out there, hustling all these companies, making a name for yourself, that he's going to be sorry he passed on you."

I shake my head mirthfully. "He is not. You're so stupid."

Genevieve considers that a compliment. "I'm telling you, he'll be sorry."

Picking up a paperclip, I play with the metal and undo its shape—a nervous tick of mine. When I was younger, I used to shove the metal in my mouth against my teeth and pretend I wore braces. I'm older now, so I set the bent metal back on my desk. "Any gossip lately I need to know about?"

Genevieve knows *everything*. And, in my opinion, has the best job in the company.

She monitors the instant messaging accounts, watching for any kind of misconduct or misuse of time. Creates new employee accounts and emails. Deletes old ones. Takes random screenshots of coworkers' desktops.

Basically, she is the eyes and ears of Roam, Inc.

The best part of her job? No one knows exactly what she does; they think she sets up work phones and fixes their computers every now and again, which means she can dig up some real dirt on people.

"Hmmm," she hums, tapping a finger against her chin. "Calvin in finance has a girlfriend getting implants this Monday, and he's paying for the entire thing."

"You're lying."

She shakes her head.

I quietly laugh, slightly jealous, my shoulders shaking. "What about Rose and Blaine?"

She takes a mint from my candy dish and pops it in her mouth, the crinkle of the wrapper rolling in her fingers before she tosses it in the trashcan next to my desk.

"Still in a standoff. He won't admit to crushing on her, and she won't admit to kissing him when they were drunk at the last office party. Looks like good old-fashioned stubbornness is going to get in their way of true love."

"Such a shame." Tossing my paper clip in the trash, I grab another one. "And Sally in payroll? Is she still talking shit about me to Jessica?"

Genevieve rolls her bright blue eyes. "*Always*. Said you were dressed like a tramp today and went to the boss's office to try and fuck him." She emits a soft snort. "As if anyone would want to go near that icicle dick."

I bite the corner of my lip, eyes cast down. *Some*one might want to fuck him.

In fact, I could name one person off the top of my head in an instant.

Me.

Me, me, me.

I would do *Rome Blackburn in a heartbeat.*

My friend chatters on, oblivious. God, if she knew the thoughts I've had about our boss? She would die.

"Hey!" She perks up, sitting up ramrod straight on the filing

19

cabinet. "Are we all still on for tomorrow night? Thirtieth birthday celebration?" She claps her hands, excited.

Some people might dread turning thirty, but not me.

I'm excited to be out of my twenties, and I'm ready to be taken more seriously. I'm ready to have my own business. I'm ready for this new chapter in my life, despite the slightly negative start to it.

"We're on. I need a stiff drink."

My friend snickers. "A stiff drink and a stiff cock inside you."

"Trust me, that's not going to happen."

"Why not?"

Because. For some unknown reason, my vagina and I want one man. The man who most definitely doesn't want *me*: Rome Blackburn.

CHAPTER TWO

ROME

"Can you get your feet off my desk?" My friend Hunter rolls his eyes, not giving a shit that his muddy boots are leaving gravel on my carpet and desktop.

He ignores me. "What's got your panties in a twist? You're bitchier than usual."

I ignore that, too. "The meeting this morning was a joke; I could have used you there."

"What would *I* have done?"

"I don't know. Lent moral support? Kept me from losing my shit?"

Hunter O'Rourke is the CIO: Chief Innovations Officer, and it's his primary function to test the new ideas our development team create. Innovate. Or in this case—fail to develop. Create a new tent? He'll take it into the wild and sleep in it. Invent a new rock-climbing tool? O'Rourke is the guy who will scale the wall.

Jump from a bridge on a new cord? O'Rourke.

He's my best friend and voice of reason.

Fucked up, but true, since he rafts down raging waters for a living.

"You lost your shit in a meeting? That's so unlike you." He rolls his eyes, then leans forward and digs into the stash of Brach's candy I keep in a small silver galvanized pail. Unwraps a caramel loudly, crinkling the paper—on purpose—to annoy the shit out of me.

I narrow my eyes. "Fine. That might be a slight exaggeration, but I swear to fucking God, I don't know who hired some of these people . . ."

He smirks, popping the candy in his mouth and chewing. "Uh. You?"

I make the sound of a buzzer. "Wrong. Human Resources. These are supposed to be the best of the best, and none of them had a single fucking idea."

"Then I had a meeting with Peyton Lévêque, which was another fucking disaster to my already shit day." Obviously it doesn't escape my notice that I pronounce her damn last name *correctly*—fluidly—each syllable rolling off my tongue the way it rolled off hers. Silky. Exotic.

"You've just cursed four times."

Jesus, he's a pain in my ass. "Would you listen?"

"I'll try, but I have no idea who this Peyton dude is."

"Peyton is a female. And she quit this morning."

Resigned. *Quit.*

Same thing.

"Damn, dude, that sucks. Did you pack up her shit and have security escort her out?"

"No. She'll receive her full two weeks'."

My friend's dark brows rise. "Do you have a fever? Should I take your temperature?" He rises half out of his seat, reaching across the desk, aiming for my forehead with his palm.

I slap it away. "Knock it off."

O'Rourke laughs—popping another one of my candies—chews, tilting his head to study me. "I have to see this chick."

No, he does not. "Why?"

His brows go up at my tone. "She's obviously affected you, or you'd be kicking her ass to the curb like you've done with anyone else who bailed."

I scoff, turning my attention to the computer monitor. "What the hell are you talking about?" She has not affected me. I don't even know her. "This is a business, not a goddamn dating service. Don't shit where you eat—that's what the no fraternizing policy is for." I narrow my eyes at him. "Have you read it?"

His hand waves through the air. "That policy is bullshit and you know it."

Now my eyes narrow. "Why? Because you're breaking it?"

Another laugh. "Trust me, if there was someone here I wanted to screw, no stupid *No Banging* policy would stop me."

Charming.

But Hunter isn't done; not with stirring up shit and not with the idiotic comments. "So this chick left you hanging . . . you had no fucking clue who she was before your meeting. So you're keeping her around because *why?* She'll be done in two weeks, why not just kick her ass to the curb?"

I sigh, leaning back in my chair, loosening the tie I only wore to impress my investors. It's shocking blue against my blue shirt with its sleeves rolled and pushed to my elbows.

Shoving my keyboard to the side, I lean forward, resting my forearms on the wood surface in front of me. Clasp my hands.

Shoot Hunter an impatient glare.

"I have no one to replace her with. Have you not been listening? This morning's meeting was a fucking shitshow. If she leaves, I'm fucked. We've been pitching to Outdoor Ecosphere, and I need her for marketing."

"But you said the marketing people sucked."

"She's not on the marketing team; she's been doing all the social media, and she's good." I admit this last part begrudgingly, my lip actually curling.

How would I know? I stalked our online presence the better half of an hour, like a moron, clicking through our website, Instagram, and Twitter. Clean, branded, and timely, her posts are clever and funny—yet professional.

Just as her personal pages are.

And I would know, because I scoped those out pretty damn hard, too.

Shit.

Shit.

Shit.

"So you're just going to let her stay." *Chew.* Swallow. *Chew.*

The squishy sound of gooey caramel being masticated makes me want to reach across the desk and strangle him.

"Yes." I flip a pencil to occupy my hands until it rolls off the desk and falls to the floor.

"And you have *zero* interest in banging her."

I raise my eyes and glare. "Why are you like this?"

Hunter O'Rourke shrugs beneath the plaid flannel of his shirt. "Why are you being so bitchy?"

Hunter and I have history; only he gets away with calling me bitchy, mostly because I'm aware I'm acting like an asshole. I am, in fact, being bitchy.

It's no secret that I'm an unrelenting asshole; I don't like cheerful people. Or *being* cheerful.

Or people.

Yeah—*definitely don't like people.*

But I love O'Rourke like a brother, even though he's nothing but a giant asshole most of the time.

We met in middle school when his family moved in next door, a big moving van pulling up to the front of a house that had been empty an entire four months a few weeks before school started.

He climbed out of the cab with the movers, stood on the curb, shielding his face with his hands, staring at the house. Climbed inside the cab and came back with a baseball mitt.

He pounded the leather a few times before catching my eye, then he raised it up, shrugging.

I had a ball and ran to retrieve it.

Lobbed it at the little bastard hard as I could.

And when he caught it?

The rest was history.

In high school, we both played baseball. Got in trouble for all kinds of shit, ranging from busting our parents' windows to sneaking out, to getting shitfaced and staying out past curfew.

In high school, Hunter broke up with my girlfriends for me; in college, I broke up with his. He became the sensitive one—giving an actual shit about people's feelings. But me?

Didn't give a shit at all. *Still don't.*

I worked my ass off in school, carrying a full course load of credits and working one crap job after the next. Saved. Invested.

I was the levelheaded one.

I was the stiff collar.

I was the buzzkill while Hunter partied. *Fucked anything with a pulse.*

Business minded, I went on to get my master's, while he dabbled in random, shitty side jobs. Honestly, I think he was waiting for me to hatch a plan that would put us both into business.

And I did.

Roam, Inc.

A play on my name—O'Rourke's idea (sometimes he has good ones)—I spent the two years busting ass on my postgrad, restless as shit. Wanted adventure but needed to fucking *work.* Loved the outdoors. Testing boundaries and limits and seeking an adrenaline high.

Roam around the world is what I wanted to do.

Rome.

I'm synonymous with my brand; it's who I am. The company is me, and I am the company. That's why it pissed me off that little

Miss Goodie Two Shoes quit without a care. To my fucking face. Who does that?

"Why am I like what?" Hunter is staring at me, head cocked to the side, fingers steepled in front of his mouth, waiting.

"Huh?"

"You asked why the hell I'm like this." He uses air quotes around the words "like this." "Get your head out of your ass." The bastard laughs, tipping his head back. "Who the hell is this girl?"

Girl?

Hardly.

Peyton is all woman; a bashful, but somewhat ballsy woman.

"Why is everything about women and sex with you?"

"It's not. I just know you're not getting any. Maybe we should go out this weekend; get the lead out. Dude, I can see the sperm retention bulging out of the veins on the side of your temples. You need to get laid, man."

He's right. I do.

But unlike O'Rourke, I'm the discriminating sort. I require someone more polished than the cheap women he picks up at the bar. Someone classy, who won't demand anything in return but a quick ride on my cock. A one-way orgasm to the front door of my townhouse afterward.

Someone that not only rolls out of my bed immediately afterward but does it without *talking* to me.

Try finding one of those in a town where everyone knows my name.

My goddamn face is plastered on the side of a city bus with the company's slogan. Last year, one of the marketing geniuses wanted to capitalize on my good looks, complete with a globe, a heart circling it, and my face. I must have been shit-faced when I signed off on it because, Holy Christ. The women.

They've been relentless.

I run one of my giant palms down my face, swiveling in my chair, face my best friend, and snort. "Do me a favor and don't talk about sex at work. It's unprofessional."

"It's unprofessional," he mimics, pinching the bridge of his nose so it sounds like he was sucking on helium. "Where is that in the code of conduct, anyway?"

"Page eight," I remind him with a straight face.

"That's right. You wrote the damn thing." I've never seen a grown man roll his eyes more than he does.

"No. The *legal* department did."

Hunter's shoulders rise and fall as he inspects his nails. "Same thing."

"Not the same thing," I grind out. "Why are you arguing with me?"

He ignores me completely and plows on to a new subject. "When do you want to go out this weekend? Let's head to Skeeters. I hear they have a band playing."

The last thing I want to do is listen to a fucking band play when I have voices screaming inside my head about deadlines. All I want is some damn peace and quiet, and he's determined to make my fucking life miserable.

"I'll think about it."

"Think harder." He pauses. "Better yet, think with your dick."

I snort.

I haven't let *that* appendage lead me around in years. Not since college, and only during a phase where I'd take study breaks to drink, party, and slake my sexual appetite.

Hunter used to deliver willing girls to my dorm room so I wouldn't have to leave; girls who willingly got down on their knees and blew me off. Efficient. Emotionless.

"How long has it been?"

Months.

Who has the damn time?

I scoff. "I'm not discussing this with you."

Hunter laughs again, and the sound grates on my last nerve. "Months, I bet."

He's relentless.

Which makes him the perfect business partner.

Which makes him an aggravating friend.

My hands go behind my head and I lace my fingers together. "Oh, and you have so much free time you're getting banged on a regular basis?"

His cocky grin falters. "I've been getting laid more than you have."

True.

My thoughts drift to Peyton Lévêque and the last photo she posted of herself on her Instagram account. Hair in a messy pile atop her head. Smile wide. Hiking in the woods with a godawful-looking mutt, with a Roam, Inc. signature walking stick.

I nodded with satisfaction at that small detail. Brand loyalty, I like it.

"Are we done here?" I'm close to grinding my teeth.

"Not until you agree to hit the bars with me this weekend. It's been forever."

It has been.

"I'll think about it."

"I'll pick you up tomorrow at nine."

"*Nine?*" Do I sound horrified? I'm in *bed* by then.

"Jesus Christ, Rome, quit acting like a seventy-year-old."

I feel like I am sometimes, as the weight of responsibilities pile up on my broad shoulders.

"Bro, admit it. You could use a drink."

I hate when he's right, so I argue. "I have beer in the fridge under my desk."

"A *real* drink."

My mouth twists at the corners. "Fine."

Hunter cackles, finally removing his fucking boots from my walnut desk. "Man, that was easier than I thought."

Cocky dickhead.

"Get the hell out of my office."

His loud laugh follows him out, and I catch Lauren hiding her smile as she ducks her head behind a file folder.

Shit.

CHAPTER THREE

PEYTON

"To the birthday girl!"

Clink.

"To being single and ready to mingle!"

Clink.

We raise our shot glasses, brimming with a red concoction known as a Swedish Fish. I don't know what's in it, but after shot number two, who the hell even cares?

I wouldn't mind downing a few more.

I throw up my finger to the bartender, ordering another round.

"To Peyton."

Clink, clink, clink . . . and down the gullet they go. Smooth. Hot. Burning just enough to make it worth the while.

My cheeks pucker; my lips smack together. I squeeze my blue eyes shut, the liquid washing down my throat, skin tingling—all inhibitions getting ready to fly.

This is my night and after the week I've had, I'm going to enjoy it.

The shot glasses hit the tabletop with the resounding glass-on-wood plunk, my little circle of friends grinning back at me as my gaze roams the table.

Ugh, these girls—I love them so much.

And . . . okay. So I'm feeling emotional tonight.

Sentimental even?

Definitely drunk.

Drunk as a damn skunk.

I giggle, watching Gen, Vivian, and Kimberly, three girls I feel like I've grown up with at Roam, Inc.

Not just professionally, but personally.

In the few short years I've been with the company, we've become close friends. Fast friends. Even closer confidants.

God, I love these guys.

Girls. Guys.

Guh!

You know what I mean . . .

Genevieve and I started at the company at the same time, quickly followed by Viv and Kim, who both work in the marketing department—one of the toughest departments at Roam, Inc. Rome is very demanding about being innovative, thinking outside the box, and being at the forefront of promotion rather than being a follower.

He's up their ass constantly.

Rome's strict and vigorous demands is one of the reasons we spend our girl nights in the same red-leather booth in the back of Skeeters in SOHO, snacking on their world-famous smoked sea salt popcorn, and sipping our overpriced handcrafted cocktails, high heels piled into a mountain under the table.

But today is different.

Today we celebrate my thirtieth birthday. The big three oh.

God, I wish I had more Os in my life.

More sex. More banging.

More orgasms.

Thank God my loud sigh is drowned out by the noise of the bar. *I don't want to be* that *girl on my birthday night.*

"Welcome to the dirty-thirty club," Gen says, snagging a few pieces of popcorn from the center of the table and popping them between her ruby-red lips. "You're going to love it."

The margarita I ordered off the cocktail menu is pinched between my fingers, and as I drink it, cherry rhubarb bitters hit the right spot, filling my flat stomach with a wave of warmth.

There is a limit when I drink—three shots, one drink—and I've definitely exceeded it.

My limit is a happy place; I can sit back, take in the people who are drunker than me and be entertained. My limit stops me from getting plastered.

And from making poor choices.

"I think thirty looks good on me." I smooth my hands over a tight-fitting black dress, one that turned a few heads at work today. Unfortunately, the one head I wanted to turn never made an appearance on my floor.

As usual.

Man, do I have shitty luck.

Why would he show his face though? He only calls us to his office if he wants to speak to us. Or reprimand us, and in the five years I've been at Roam, Inc., I've never been called to his office once.

Maybe I'm a little bitter because I looked freaking good today. Would it have killed him to split from his office and catch a glimpse of me?

"Thirty is the new twenty-five." I give my dark hair a flip.

"Thirty looks really good on you, babe," Kim agrees, lifting her glass toward me. "So do your boobs, if you don't mind me saying."

My chest pops out.

Popcorn kernels fly every which way when Viv gestures toward my breasts—she doesn't hold her liquor well—her sassy grin staring holes into the front of my chest.

I raise my brows expectantly; waiting.

Vivian's next words do not disappoint as she slurs out loud, "Now we just have to get you laid for your birthday."

"Our gift to you."

Their gift to me . . . Oh shit, no.

My already hot face burns. "You did not hire me an escort."

I'm hissing, leaning over the table so they can hear me, horrified.

They are talking so loud, and now I am, too.

"Shh, relax." Vivian's inebriated hands wave me off. "God, no—I don't have the money for that—"

"But if we did have the monies, we totally would have," Gen adds.

A wobbly nod. "Totally would have."

"We're going to find you a man in here to bang."

Viv claps her hands, hopping on the seat of the booth, making the whole bench bounce. "Yes, yes. We love that idea." She pops her head up over the booth, determined to assess the pool of men flooding the overcrowded bar. "Let's see, there's a guy over there with some heavy-duty sideburns that could be promising."

"Sideburns are for werewolves," Kim announces, sitting on her knees so she can get a better view of the perimeter. "What about Mr. Sunshine State there with the blond hair and sunglasses? He looks fuckable."

Oh. My. God. "Would you keep it down?"

"Relax." Viv pats my hand. "No one can hear us."

"Sunglasses in a bar?" Genevieve scoffs, watching the guy wearing a pink polo and shades. "He's either a total douchebag or he's high as a kite and doesn't want people to know. Next."

Vivian's shrewd eyes hit the bar . . . move toward the pool tables . . . scan the tables along the back of the room. Then she raises her hand and makes an "ooo, ooo" sound like she's waiting to be called on in class.

Deadpanning, Gen says, "Yes, Viv, can we help you?"

"What about that guy? The one in the dark suit?"

She points; I push down her arm.

"There are twenty guys here wearing dark suits, you're going to

LOVE SINCERELY YOURS

have to be more specific." Kimberly takes a sip of her drink, rolling her eyes.

"You guys . . ." I begin weakly, defenseless against them.

See, the thing is: I don't like hooking up with random strangers —that's Vivian's gig, not mine. Another thing? I'm stupidly holding out for one passionate night from a *certain someone* who didn't know I even existed until yesterday when I quit, despite the many times we've been in the same room together, no fraternizing policy or not.

I glumly recite the rules from the Employee Handbook in my head:

"No employee of Roam, Inc. may date another employee who is separated by more than one level in the heirarchy. This includes an employee who reports to their boss's counterpart in another department."

And it got better, via an addendum memo send round only thirty days ago:

"No employee of Roam, Inc. may date an employee who reports to their boss's counterpart in another department."

I've read these rules no less than one hundred times.

Wishful thinking.

Daydreaming.

"Employees of Roam, Inc. who disregard this policy will be subject to disciplinary actions, up to and including immediate termination."

Termination: that was slightly sobering.

I drink from the glass in front of me, disregarding my limit, and then shake my head when Vivian elbows me in the rib cage, knocking me out of my stupor.

"Huh?"

"*That* one." Her tone is stalwart. Absolute. "The one with the tailor-made suit jacket, messy hair. Drop-dead gorgeous jaw—"

"Holy—"

"*Shit.*"

It's a collective gasp from my friends. Collective cursing.

Collective covering.

33

All three of my friends fly back on their asses and duck for cover.

"What the ever loving . . . What the hell is *he* doing here?" Kimberly breathes, putting a napkin in front of her face. *To mask it?*

"The nerve of him." Viv ducks under her cardigan like it's a cloak of invisibility. "This is our drinking hole, not his."

Gen's eyes are narrowed into dangerous slits as she stares at me, hiding behind the bowl of popcorn. "Cover your face, or he'll see you."

They must be really drunk.

"Who are you three yammering about?" I take another sip, blissfully unaware.

"Pey, cover your damn face." Kimberly scowls at me, tossing her drink straw in my direction. "It's moody boss pants."

Moody boss pants?

"It's freaking Rome, you drunken idiot," Gen says with a whack to my leg under the table.

His name leaves her lips, igniting a gleeful spark deep in my belly.

Rome . . .

Rome is here.

I turn around and spot him.

There he is.

All two of him . . .

Both of him are so good-looking, I can barely stand it.

Wait. *Two of him?*

That can't be right, and *oh God, I'm so drunk.*

Planted on a bar stool, Rome has one foot propped on the wrung, while the other is rooted firmly to the floor. A glass tumbler is suspended from his hand; grip firm, yet casual. His tie is nowhere to be seen, leaving the top few buttons of his crisp white shirt undone.

Guh.

God, he's so ridiculously hot. *Why do I have to find the one man in the world I* cannot *have so freakin' gorgeous?*

A rigid set in his jaw, lips pursed, he peruses the crowd, a crease in his brow, his eyes never really pausing, just observing.

Is he waiting for someone or just enjoying the atmosphere?

"Why aren't you hiding?" Kimberly asks me, true fear in her voice. "Are you nuts? He's going to see us."

But that's the thing you don't realize, I want to say. *I want him to see me. I'm practically desperate for it.* Which really isn't like me—not at all. Yes, it has been a while since my last *bang*, as my friends so eloquently said earlier. But there is just something mysterious about Rome Blackburn that gets my heart beating. That sends my skin tingling. *He's an enigma, and I want to unwrap his many layers.* I admit that his clothing is the first layer I wish to unwrap . . . but still.

I want him to see my little black dress, designed with a deeper neckline than I ought to have worn to the office today. Deeper than what's considered workplace appropriate.

I want him to notice the length of my hair; how the wavy ends reach the swell of my breasts.

I want him to see the bright red lipstick I wore and reapplied often, hoping and praying that maybe, *just maybe* he'd come to my floor and catch a glimpse; wonder what my mouth might look like planted and smeared all over his body.

Red kisses on what promises to be a beautiful, powerful chest.

Abs.

Collarbone.

I sigh—*drunk*, eyes wavering—and watch as my boss scans the crowd critically. He takes everyone in, sipping slowly from what looks like rum or brandy on ice, his head slowly swiveling toward our direction.

My body freezes; lips part. Chest puffs with bated breath, willing him to give me *one* glance. Just one.

Look at me.

See me sitting here.

Look at me.

But he doesn't.

His eyes miss me completely—of course they do—as his cool, assessing gaze passes me by as if I meld with everyone else in this place. Nothing special, never standing out amongst the crowd.

Just like at work.

Downing the rest of his drink and slamming his glass onto the bar top, Rome tosses a few bills on the bar and buttons his suit jacket before heading toward the door, leaving me in an aroused and embarrassed state.

Staring after him like a puppy dog stares through the window at its retreating owner.

So dramatic.

God, I'm drunk.

It's the alcohol, I tell myself.

Still hiding and trying to blend in with the booth, I let out a heavy breath and take a sip of my drink. "He's gone, you guys. No need to hide anymore."

Peeking over their pitiful excuses for cover, my friends confirm the coast is clear before resuming their normal positions.

"I thought he'd never leave," Gen breathes.

I hoped he'd stay . . .

"Close call. He almost saw us." Vivian wipes at her forehead.

I wanted him to see me . . .

"Yeah, no thanks to Peyton," Kimberly snaps, tossing popcorn in her mouth. "She was staring."

I couldn't help myself . . .

"Maybe I wanted him to see me," I blurt out, and it seems the booze is making my lips loose.

"What did you just say?" This from Gen.

A flush of red stains my cheeks.

I just hinted toward one of my deepest and darkest secrets: *I have a majorly inappropriate crush on Rome Blackburn.*

"Holy crap. You have an inappropriate crush on Rome Blackburn?" Viv repeats my drunken confession verbatim.

"Did I say that out loud?"

Kimberly laughs. "You did."

"Wait . . ." Vivian holds up her hand to silence the rest of the group. "Do you like Rome, Peyton?"

And there it is, the truth has been revealed. Even though I have a good amount of liquor coursing through my veins, I still feel raw and exposed.

Because when I say no one, I mean no one in the office likes Rome. He's not there to make friends; he's there to make money, to grow his company.

Playing with my napkin on the table, pushing it around, my eyes cast down, I answer, "Well, you know . . . he's really handsome."

"Handsome?" Viv is incredulous. "I mean—he's hot, but . . . he's *Satan.*"

He can be an ass, yes.

But maybe that's what I like about him.

In unison, not having the decency to take turns, my friends get loud, shouting to be heard, brandishing me with opinions how horrible Rome is:

He is rude.

He is an arrogant prick.

He is a tyrant.

Yup, well aware. But there's also something about him that no one else sees—a vulnerable side that I want to know.

I gravitate toward him like a moth to a flame, and for the sake of me I cannot figure out why.

But I do.

I don't just have a crush on him; I have the hots for him. *And God, I hope that stays inside my mind—please don't let me word vomit secrets out of my mouth.*

"Let's just drop it, okay? And drop the guy search as well. I don't want to sleep with anyone in this place."

"Because you want to sleep with the boss," Gen practically shouts.

"Maybe." My answer is delivered shyly, receiving a round of grumbles from the peanut gallery—they cannot help them-damn-selves. *Ugh.*

"Look, I think he's hot, and one passionate night wouldn't kill either of us. God, his hands . . . I want them all over my body . . ." Fueled by alcohol and wishful thinking, I blab on. "I want to know what it feels to be gripped by those powerful giant paws. *Ugh.* I want to feel his lips sucking on the side of my neck, right? What it's like for that asshole to command my body." I glance around at everyone's stupefied expressions. Shrug. "I don't think that's too much to ask, do you?"

No one says a word.

Gen's mouth falls open. "You want to bang the boss?"

I nod.

I do want to bang the boss.

So hard.

"Wow." Vivian gives me a dreamy look, Kimberly's lip is caught up in a very unladylike snarl, and Gen . . .

What the hell is Gen doing?

Head down, typing away on her ever-present iPad, she's got the biggest grin on her face, smiling to herself and no one else. A tech geek, she pounds away at the pad, tapping quickly on the screen, the warm glow reflecting light on her red lips and pretty face.

Seconds pass.

Until.

She turns the screen toward us, presenting us with a blank email ready to be typed up.

"I don't get what you're doing," drunk me says. "Why are you sending work emails on my birthday?"

"It's *for* your birthday. Your gift from me. So, happy birthday," she announces, handing me the iPad.

Drunk me looks in my lap, seeing the iPad glaring up at me. Blinding. I blink, focusing my eyes.

"Uh, what's this?"

As I stare her down, the screen lights up her way too pleased expression. "I set you up with an anonymous email address at Roam, Inc." I get a nudge with her forefinger. "Go ahead, Pey, tell him how you feel."

"What?" My eyebrows shoot up to my hairline. "Are you insane?"

"Yeah, that is one bad idea." Kimberly downs the rest of her drink. "Like, really, really bad."

"Why?" Gen crosses her arms, affronted.

"Because she could get fired, that's why."

Gen pops a piece of popcorn in her mouth. "She gave her two weeks'—who cares? He's not going to know who it's from, and that's the best part." More popcorn gets stuffed down her gullet. "Besides, it's not like he's going to give her his business once she's gone—not that asshole. He's too stubborn."

Kimberly nods slowly, warming to the idea. "Yeah . . . yes. I love it. Yes. Do it, Peyton. Send him an email. Tell him you want to screw his brains out."

"I'm not—I don't want to screw his brains out." I want him to screw mine.

My fingers trace the cursor blinking on the screen, just waiting for a command. I stare at it, biting on my bottom lip, then glance at the door.

The one he just blew out of without a backward glance.

"Do it, Pey."

"Do it."

Do it.

I want to.

I want him to know how I feel.

My finger hovers over the keyboard; I inhale a steady breath, again biting on my red bottom lip.

Skin warm.

Brain muddled.

And type.

CHAPTER FOUR

ROME

Fucking O'Rourke.

I'm going to kill him the next time I see him.

I'm going to shove one of those stupid fucking caramels down his throat and force him to choke on it.

Come out with me. Come hang out. You need to get some action. Let me help you get laid.

Not that I need help, but I fell for it, for O'Rourke's crap, and then the prick stands me up.

Me.

Fucking leaves me at the bar, looking like a chump as I scan the less-than-stellar establishment he chose, searching for my friend.

But nothing.

No sign of the bastard.

Instead, I got a text saying he met some woman at another bar and was on his way to her place. Suggested a raincheck. His exact words: *Dude, you'll never believe this, but I met a twin and she's DTF. Have a drink on me. Take it out of my next paycheck.*

Out of his next paycheck? Over my dead body.

Instead of going out, I could have been at my desk, tackling the mounting pile of papers and figuring out how to stay ahead of the curve; ensuring my company creates the next best thing for the outdoor world.

Once I got home, I sent a text to my assistant, Lauren, telling her to come into the office early, to bring coffee, and to be prepared to work.

Lauren wasn't happy—that was clear by the way she abruptly placed my coffee on my desk, brown liquid spilling out the little hole and onto the white lid—then narrowed her eyes before turning her back.

Fake, tight-lipped smile and a nod of her head, she was out the door, leaving me to my overflowing emails.

Fuck, I'm not in the mood for her attitude today.

I massage my temples with my forefingers, scanning my monitor.

Scrolling my inbox, I delete all the crap email messages. Spam. Mark a few urgent that I already know need replying to, skim down the column, new and unfamiliar emails getting my attention first, subject lines varying to stand out:

Looking for your next big marketing ploy?

Let me have your business.

Check out this new investment.

Rome, I want to bang you so bad.

Denver: the new adventure hot spot.

Stocks are high.

My lips sneer as I begin deleting all the spam that infiltrates my inbox every day, eyes skimming back up the subject column so I don't accidentally delete anything that's an actual priority.

Hold up.

Rewind.

My hand hovers; ceases clicking delete.

I scroll back up and scan the subject lines again, as coffee passes the taste buds of my tongue, searing down my throat.

I want to bang you so bad.

Did I read that shit right? It's addressing me specifically, from a Roam, Inc. email address.

My eyes narrow on the subject line again, unable to get that one word out of my head. Bang.

Bang.

Screw.

Fuck.

Jesus, I'm hard up.

Leaning back in my chair, I casually glance around my office as if someone is watching me, then lean forward, still debating if I should click on the email.

From the preview, all I can see is To Whom it May Concern.

Twist my lips to the side, debate, should I open it?

Far too curious, I chew the inside of my cheek just as I click the email open, scooting in closer to get a better look.

To Whom It May Concern:

You don't know how nervous I am writing this, but it has to be said. Because I can't stand it anymore. Can't go another day without telling you how I feel when you walk past me.

But . . . full disclosure, I would like it to be known that I have consumed an adequate amount of alcoholic beverages to intoxicate myself tonight. Three margaritas, two shots, and one beer—because it was free, and because it was a celebration. Not that you care.

But I think it's important to be open and honest with your coworkers, don't you? And full disclosure, Rome?

I work for you.

And I'm finally being honest. Drunk but honest. Or just drunk with lust? You decide.

I like you so much, and it's clouding my judgment, making me do things I never would sober. Like write this ridiculous email.

I have a hopeless, foolish crush on you, when you are the last person on earth I should be crushing on. Did you know people around the office call you a sadist? An egomaniac? An insensitive, arrogant prick? Your bark is worse than your bite, and you don't scare me. The fact is, I'd love that bite of yours to nip at my bare skin while we're both wearing nothing but sheets.

For once, I want you to look at me as more than one of your employees.

And as long as we're being honest, that navy-blue suit you wear? With the crisp white shirt? It really makes me want to loosen your tie and show you who's boss.

I want to bang you so damn bad I can taste it.

~~*Love,*~~

~~*Sincerely,*~~

Yours.

I do a double take.

My lips press into a hard line. What the hell is this, some kind of joke? If so, it's not one damn bit funny. I have rules in place for this sort of misconduct.

I read and reread the email, glancing up from my desk, I pivot my chair so I can stare through the large picture window on my far wall.

Push back in my chair and rise, walking to my door and locking it. Pull down the shade to the glass wall that's the only thing separating myself from everyone else in the office.

I don't need anyone to see the shocked look on my face right now, and I don't want any of the women out there watching me . .
.

Shit.

Someone out there has been watching me.

Could it be Lauren? I narrow my eyes into slits, examining her irritated movements. Still salty from this morning.

Definitely not Lauren.

I think she's more likely to twist my balls off with one swipe than write me a love letter.

Wait, was that a love letter?

I want to bang you so hard.

Most certainly not a love letter, unless that's how millennials wax poetic now.

This is why I have a no fraternizing policy. This shit right. Here.

Indignant, I sit and lean back in my chair, making the font

larger so I can read it reclined with my hands behind my head, eyes dragging across one ridiculous line after the other.

What the shit is this?

Did you know people around the office call you a sadist? An egomaniac? An insensitive, arrogant prick?

Yeah, I fucking knew that, thank you very much.

I'm not deaf, I'm not blind, and I don't give a shit what anyone thinks about the way I run my company. I am who I am, and no one is going to change me.

And as long as we're being honest, that navy-blue suit you wear? With the crisp white shirt?

I drag my hand down the lapels of said navy-blue suit—another meeting this afternoon requires it—my fingers straightening the starched collar of my dress shirt. Bright blue tie.

I want to bang you so bad.

My eyes dissect that little sentence; the cock in my pressed trousers stirs.

Bang you so bad.

Bang.

Jesus Christ, this is not happening to me right now.

I rake a hand through my hair, an exhausted breath expelling from my lugs. A few more lingering stares and I'm reaching forward, finger hitting the intercom button for Lauren's desk.

"Yes, Mr. Blackburn."

How many times have I asked her not to call me that?

Dozens.

"Can you come in here with a notebook? I need you to take a memo."

This email is so highly inappropriate, bordering on sexual harassment, it needs to be addressed company-wide. No. No *bordering*—it is. And if this has been sent to anyone else in this company, heads would roll.

Heads *will* roll.

Someone will get fired.

I give the email address a hard stare. HandsRomingMyBody@RoamInc.com

Not only is it unfamiliar, it's bloody internal. Fabricated. Entirely sexual. Hands roming my body. Rome—not roam.

And a familiar play on my first name.

This is how companies get sued. The last thing I need is bad publicity because of a bad joke bankrupting my company.

It only takes Lauren a few minutes to bustle into my office—attitude adjusted—*thank fuck*. She closes the door behind her and perches on a chair, just as she's always done when she's about to take dictation, iPad in hand ready.

"I need you to take a memo."

"Ready when you are, boss."

My eyes momentarily rake along my glaringly white computer monitor, nostrils flaring.

I want to bang you so bad.

Lips part. "Uh..."

Lauren waits.

I clear my throat. "I recently received a very disturbing email—"

Lauren's mouth falls open and she interrupts, leaning forward conspiratorially. Lowers her voice to a near whisper. "You did? Was it a bomb threat?"

"No." My lips press together. "As I was saying . . ." I give the iPad a glance. "I recently received a disturbing email, one that not only compromises several of this company's policies, but also the integrity of Roam, Inc. as a whole."

Lauren's eyes widen, but she keeps silent.

I want to bang you so bad.

I haven't been banged in months.

"Our integrity is being compromised," I repeat.

"You . . . just said that."

"I did?"

"Well, not in those exact words but, yes. You're being redundant."

"Clean it up for me, then. Shoot me the draft."

A quick nod. "Got it."

"As I was saying . . ." What the hell was I saying? My eyes won't stray from that one fucking line—it's both driving me crazy and pissing me off simultaneously. "As I was saying."

"As you were saying." Lauren is biting back a grin.

This is pointless. I can't concentrate.

"You know what? I'll jot something down and get it back to you."

Now her grin is a full-blown smirk. "Sure."

Is it Lauren?

No. I shake that thought out of my head. Definitely not Lauren. She has a boyfriend, doesn't she? I should really pay attention to this shit more. No I shouldn't, Goddammit—it's not my job to know about anyone's personal life once they're gone for the day.

My forefinger drums the desktop. "I'll also need to speak to someone in IT. Can you send up the supervisor, uh . . ."

I have no idea whose name to supply.

Hunter was right—I *do* let human resources do most of the hiring and really need to be more hands-on so shit like doesn't slip through the cracks. I have no fucking idea who is handling my technical department.

"Vivian Taggert, sir."

Sir.

I suppress the urge to roll my eyes. "Get me Mrs. Taggert this afternoon please."

"It's Miss."

"What is?"

"Miss Taggert is unmarried, sir. She's single."

Jesus Christ, why is she telling me this? "I'm not interested in Miss Taggert's marital status, Lauren. I need her intelligence."

And to give me a name. And to solve this fucking problem: who created this fake account?

"Yes, sir. I'll let you know when she's available."

I need a fucking drink and it's only nine in the morning. Shit.

CHAPTER FIVE

PEYTON

S weet.
  Jesus.

What is that godforsaken sound? Make it stop. Please, someone, make it stop.

"Gerrrrrrr," I groan, rolling to my side, last night's curls
sticking to my face. "Stop the incessant ringing."

Face planted into my pillow, I shake my fist in the air, asking
for help from the heavens above.

Ring.

Ring.

Ring.

"I'm going to kill someone," I grumble into my pillow. Last
night's alcohol breath hits me hard, tossing my head in the air, hair
curtaining the sides like blinders.

"Whoa, toothbrush, stat," I say to no one in particular.

Pounding out of control, my head throbs with every ring.
Pound. Pound. Pound, tossing my stomach into unwanted somer-
saults. And just when I think the noise will never end . . . it does.

"The Lord has risen," I praise, sticking my head back into my pillow, a muffled hallelujah followed shortly after.

Too much booze last night. Way too much.

So much that I can't remember a damn thing other than shoving two pieces of popcorn up my nose and snot-rocketing them across the table into Gen's drink.

God . . .

Welcome to thirty.

Ring.

Ring.

"Oh, for the love of God." I lift my head trying to find the noise when I spot my phone on my nightstand.

Who the hell is calling me?

I reach over and attempt to yank my phone from the charging cord, but end up pulling the entire cord out of the socket. At least I had the sense to charge it last night.

Pushing the accept button, I bring it to my ear and mumble, "What?"

"Peyton?" Gen's voice rings through the other side, worried. I don't blame her, my "what" sounded like I grew a pair of balls overnight.

"Yeah, what do you want?"

"Uh, did you call in sick today?"

"What? No . . . what are you—"

Oh. Fuck.

"Oh Fuck! What time is it?" I scramble out of bed, my strapless dress pulled down on one side, exposing my right breast to any neighbor who might be looking through my windows. The phone cord dangles, hitting me in the stomach.

"It's . . . nine?"

Oh no.

Oh no. Oh no. Oh no.

Being late to work is not tolerated. It's in the detailed and very well-laid-out employee handbook, and right now, I'm looking at being at least half an hour late.

Running around my apartment, I strip down, not caring if anyone sees me naked at this point, and run to the bathroom where I turn on the faucet and start dousing my body in water, letting it cascade down to the tile floor, an impressive feat since I'm still on the phone.

"Has anyone noticed?"

"A few people asked where you were. I told them you were in the bathroom with tummy troubles."

"Jesus. Okay. I'll be out in ten."

"Pey, we have to—"

"Can't talk, need to drag the dragon off my tongue that's lighting up my breath. See you soon. Have coffee at my desk, I pray you."

I hang up and wet a washcloth, soaking it quickly and rubbing it all over my face. No time for anything else.

I throw my hair up in a messy bun, dab my eyes with some mascara, and then put on the first thing I see in my closet.

Headache or not, I need to be to work, NOW.

～

"Holy hell, did you even look at yourself in the mirror?" Gen asks me, walking beside me with my cup of coffee as we make our way to my cubicle.

"No. Why? Do I have bags under my eyes?" With my index finger, I dab under my eyes, bringing life back to my face. I looked in the mirror for a second, saw I resembled the day of the dead, and decided looking in the mirror wasn't for me this morning.

From Gen's reaction, maybe I should have taken a second gander.

Gen's eyes widen, pure horror all over her face. "I think you should go to the bathroom."

I pause, scared not only from the way Gen is looking at me but from the way everyone around us can't take their eyes off me.

Swallowing hard, I ask, slightly panicked. "Is it bad?"

Whispering from the side of her mouth, Gen says, "I've seen prettier women of the night."

Women of the night? What the . . .

Is she talking about . . .

Hookers?

Shit.

Taking a detour, we both head to the bathroom, Gen trailing closely behind as I duck my head, trying to avoid everyone's stares.

It can't be that bad, right?

When I turn the corner into the bathroom, the first thing I see in the reflection is the *Working Girl* costume I bought two years ago, a brown belt cinching the oversized suit dress to my waist.

Horrified, I move my gaze to my face. A ripple of shock shoots up my spine when I take in last night's lipstick smeared across my cheek, mascara dotted all over my cheekbones, and a fake eyelash plastered across my forehead.

How the hell did I miss that?

"Oh dear God, it looks like I fell asleep in a dumpster."

Cringing to the side, trying to shield her eyes from the hot mess in front of her, Gen says, "You've had better days, that's for sure."

"What do I do?"

"Burn that dress, first of all. I mean, where the hell did you find it?"

"I don't have anything else to wear, Gen."

Sizing me up, she taps her chin with her index finger, finally able to fully look at me, a look of disgust written all over her face.

"Okay, well, I say for starters, we remove last night's fake eyelash." She plucks one from my forehead and tosses it in the trash. Eyes wide, I run my fingers along the skin there. "Then I think we go the whole *True Lies* route."

"*True Lies* route? What are you talking about?"

"You know, when Jamie Lee Curtis's character rips her dress to make it sexier and then throws a vase of water over her head to slick back her hair. Worked for her, might work for you."

Counting to ten and exhaling, I say, "That was a movie, and that dress was supposed to rip perfectly. This thing is made out of trench coat material, so we'll need scissors to make it decent."

Gen nods. "Yeah, I see what you're saying. At least roll up the sleeves, douse your head in water, and do a tight bun at the top of your head. And for the love of God, wash your damn face."

Starting thirty off with a bang.

It takes another ten minutes to make me look somewhat presentable before we're both walking back to my cubicle, still drawing attention from coworkers. As if I'm on a parade float, I kindly nod and wave to those who choose to stare.

Eat your hearts out. I won't be here for much longer.

Plopping into my chair, I fire up my computer and let out a labored breath. "That was a close one." I halfheartedly laugh, looking around one more time to make sure the coast is clear. "Why are you still here? Don't you have work to do?"

Looking guilty as hell, Gen says, "Uh, do you happen to remember anything from last night?"

I shake my pounding head and take a sip of the coffee Gen gave me . . . needing a refill stat.

I think it's best that we all forget about last night . . . and this morning.

When my computer screen comes to life, I type in my password and open my email, thirty new ones popping up immediately. Ugh, can't a girl catch a break?

I casually look through the emails, not really paying attention to any of them as I talk. "Did I say something stupid to Kimberly? It's not my fault she has a stick up her ass most of the time."

I continue to scan through the emails, one from Rome catching my attention. Oh goody! A memo.

When he sends those, they're usually juicy and full of pent-up tension.

What kind of tension do we have in store for us today?

Mentally twiddles fingers.

"No, you didn't offend Kimberly."

I point to the screen, ignoring Gen. "Did you read this one? It's a memo from Rome, the big boss man himself."

She blushes. "Uh yeah, about that."

Last memo we got was about using copy machines for business . . . not pleasure.

God, that was great. All the copy machines had to be washed down by a professional cleaning service due to high concern for sexual germs on the buttons.

"We should read it." I hope it's about someone being caught for doing something massively inappropriate.

"Peyton, wait."

"What?" I turn to face Gen who's had a permanent cringe on her face since she greeted me. Growing concerned, I ask, "What's going on?"

She twists her hands together and says, "Remember how we were drunk?"

"Yeah, the pounding in my head hasn't let me forget that one." I tap on my skull.

"Do you happen to remember confessing your undying lust for . . ." Her voice trails off and with a guilty look, she leans forward, whispers quietly, "For Rome?"

Say what now?

Undying lust for Rome?

I would never.

I might have been drunk, but I wasn't that—

My eyes widen, mouth goes dry, a sinking feeling of dread taking root in the pit of my stomach.

Swedish fish shots.

Lots of them.

Three margaritas.

Beer.

Manhunting.

Rome at the bar in a suit.

His darkened gaze skipping over me.

Irritation and desperation consuming me.

Confessing about my crush . . . typing out that email on Gen's iPad . . .

HOLY SHIT. THE EMAIL.

"Oh my hell." I grip my head and spin back to my computer opening the memo immediately, clicking rapidly on my mouse until the damn thing pops up on my screen ten times. Multiplying with each click. "Stop it," I yell at the computer as the final one pops up.

I scan the contents of the memo, as my heart beats out of my chest.

From: Rome Blackburn, President and CEO

To: Roam Inc. employees

Memorandum RE: Conduct

Good morning. Attached you will find the employee handbook, an updated Section 7 emphasizing inappropriate behavior in the workplace. Please watch your inbox. Miss Taggert, from IT, will be sending a brief inquiry today regarding Section 7 contents; all employees are required to re-sign/acknowledge the agreement regarding sexual harassment, boundaries, and fraternizing. And as a reminder, inappropriate conversations, instant message chats, and emails will not be tolerated—i.e., grounds for termination.

The memo goes on. And on.

"Do . . . do you think this has anything to do with that email I sent him last night?" I chew on my thumbnail nervously, a terrible habit I've always had.

Gen rolls her eyes and hands me her phone. "Of course it was about your email, dumbass. I *dare* you to re-read the email you sent him last night. And try not to piss yourself."

Taking her phone, I focus my blurry eyes on the email in her sent folder and read, wanting to turtle in on myself with each sentence that stands out in my mind as utterly humiliating—which is most of them.

I work for you.

I have a hopeless, foolish crush on you when you are the last person on earth I should be crushing on.

*For once, I want you to look at me as more than one of your employees.
I want to bang you so damn bad.*

I sink into my chair, the shoulder pads of my dress reaching my ears.

"This is bad, isn't it?"

Still twisting her hands in her lap, Gen says, "Well, as long as they can't trace it back to you, you're good, which will be virtually impossible since we didn't use your name." *Virtually. Virtually impossible does not give me confidence.*

"What about you? You created the email address."

She shrugs. "Don't worry about me. I have ways around all of that."

Taking a deep breath, she says, "What's important here is that we silence Kimberly and Viv, since they were there when you wrote it, and act as cool as possible."

"Silence them? What are you, the mob?"

She shrugs. "You can never be too careful."

"Genevieve." I laugh, the action hurting my temples.

I cringe.

"I forgot about Viv and Kimberly, but we're not going to silence them."

"They gossip about everything. Which is why we need to make sure they don't remember anything from last night."

"You're really scary right now. Knock it off, you weirdo." Nonetheless, I sit up and right my suit dress, smoothing down the *many* wrinkles. "I'm going to grab some more coffee and swing by Viv's desk. Will you check with Kimberly for me?"

"On it." Standing, Gen turns to leave when she says, "What if"—she pauses and bites her bottom lip—"what if he writes you *back?*"

I laugh at the absurdity of the thought. Rome Blackburn emailing me back? As if. "Trust me, Gen, he's not going to write back." I snort. "That's not anything we have to worry about. It's never going to happen."

CHAPTER SIX

ROME

"What the hell was that memo about?" Hunter barges into my office without even knocking—not all that unusual, but still pretty damn obnoxious.

He has no fucking manners.

Frantically, I click out of my email inbox and adjust my tie, doing my best to appear normal, as opposed to the way I feel.

Disgusted.

Intrigued.

Casual and businesslike—that's what I am—not someone trying to figure out who sent me the email. No fucking way. I won't even dignify that piss-poor excuse for an email by giving it any more attention. Sure as hell haven't been dissecting it, word for word, line by line.

This has nothing to do with me being turned on by it and everything to do with the welfare of the company. Not one fucking bit.

I cough.

Divert. "When are you going to learn to knock?"

Instead of being affronted, Hunter plops his ass down in the chair across from my desk and takes up his usual position: boots propped on the edge of my desk, hands behind head, brows raised, and mouth curved into a cocky smirk.

"Tell me what the deal is with that memo."

I straighten an already straight stack of paperwork. Move a pen into place. Click my mouse.

My lips purse. I tap the desktop with an index finger. "Do you have the data for the beta testing done on the new tents? Why are you in here?"

"*Pffh*, nah." He laughs. "Didn't have time last night to put it in a spreadsheet. I was otherwise occupied." Hunter wiggles his dark brows.

The holes in his jeans and the dark coffee stain on his plaid shirt—coupled with the work boots—break the dress code, and should have me sending him home to change, but right now I couldn't care less.

"I need those beta tests, Hunter."

"Yeah, yeah, I know." He waves me off. "I'll get to them to you. Relax, man. Did someone get caught looking at porn?"

"No." Thank God.

"Did someone *sext* someone?" Wiggles his eyebrows.

"Not exactly." Leaning back in my chair, I grumble unhappily. "But close enough."

Fascinated, Hunter claps his hands in front of him. Rubs them together gleefully. "Tell me more."

Hunter is my best friend and confidant; I know if I show him the email, he'll keep his loud mouth shut—at least to other people —but there is no doubt in my mind he'd give me a giant rash of shit about it if the opportunity arose. Dirt on me doesn't come along often, and this is solid roasting material.

Fuckin' A.

I adjust my shirt collar. "Someone sent me a *high*ly improper message through company email. *Very* out of line."

I sound like a goddamn prude.

Like—my *grand*mother.

"Improper?" Rising to his feet, my best friend rounds the desk in two seconds flat, leaning greedily over my shoulder to see my screen. "Show me. Show me right fucking now."

"Quit breathing down my neck."

Excited, he ignores me. "Who was it? Show me."

"The email is anonymous."

"Even more fun. Let me see, let me see."

He shoves me with his elbow—begs like a five-year-old—probably because the two of us don't have secrets.

"This stays between us," I warn sternly.

He nods. "Yeah, yeah, yeah."

I level him with one more hard stare before cracking open my laptop and giving him room to ogle the glowing screen and the inbox displayed.

Gleefully, Hunter's gluttonous eyes bounce back and forth just as mine had, a smirk forming on his face as he reads. I read along with him, and there's that sentence I keep getting stuck on: *I want to bang you so hard.*

Jesus Christ, who even says that anymore?

Fuck. Screw. Have sex.

But bang?

Hunter practically vibrates beside me. "Well, shit, this is—"

"Appalling? I know. I'm going to have to—"

"Fucking *awe*some." Standing back, Hunter lets out a howl. "Dude. How lucky are you?"

I can't with him right now . . .

"Jesus, go sit down."

For once, the asshole listens. Thank. God.

His hand scratches the stubble on his jaw as he walks back to his chair. Dumping his giant body into the leather seat, he crosses one leg over the other and studies me.

"You're going to reply." He says it casually, yet it detonates the statement in my office.

"Reply? Are you nuts? No. I'm not dignifying that with a response."

"Why the hell not?" His voice raises an octave; an impossible feat given how deep it is. "Are you insane?"

I give my eyes a healthy roll. "Yes, O'Rourke, I'm the insane one here."

"Yeah—you kind of are."

"You're crazy if you think for one second I'm going to message back an employee." I'm hissing and I don't care.

He has lost his damn mind. I literally just sent a company-wide memo warning people about offensive behavior; I'm not going to fucking perpetuate the behavior myself.

His hands go up in retreat. "Relax. Relax. Just hear me out for two seconds, okay?"

"You have two seconds."

"Well. What if it's that girl in logistics who wears that pink cardigan every Wednesday? She's kind of cute in a 'I have cats and no boyfriends' way."

"I have no clue who the fuck you're talking about."

"*That,* my friend, is your problem. You don't spend any time on the lower floors. You have no clue who any of your employees are."

"And I suppose you do?"

Hunter snorts. "Of course I do."

"I know who the important ones are." Even to my own ears, I sound like a complete asshole.

He chuckles. "You're such a pompous windbag."

He's not wrong. Not even a little.

"I don't have time to know all my employees or to respond to inappropriate emails."

"Right, I get it." He nods knowingly. Patronizing? I can't tell.

"*Get* what?" A dull ache starts to throb behind my eyes.

"You're afraid it's a guy."

Oh shit.

I hadn't even considered that, but now he's mentioned it, a seed of doubt pricks at my brain.

59

Brow pinched, I narrow my eyes at Hunter. "Are you fucking mental? That note was not written by a guy."

"It could easily be a guy. Haven't you ever caught an episode of Catfish? Someone could be catfishing you. That's all I'm saying. Like, a dude. Oh." He snaps his fingers and sits a little taller. "Could be one of your competitors trying to throw you off. Write them back, ask to see a dick pic."

I rub my temples, willing this nightmare to end. "You can slither out of my office now."

"Okay, okay, let's not ask for a dick pic just yet. There's an easy way to discover if it's female. Read me what the drinks were again?"

"Are you serious?"

"Yes, hit me with them." He makes a gesture with his hand, asking for the info.

Sighing, I scan the email and say, "Uh, three margaritas, Swedish fish shots and a beer . . . because it was free."

"Bingo." Hunter holds up his finger. "Total chick. No self-respecting gay man would pack on the sugar with Swedish fish shots, and women are the only ones who get free drinks. You're in the clear, probably not a catfish situation." He looks smug. "Although, now we're in a whole new ballgame. Who's the sex-acholic who wants to bang you? My money is still on pink cardigan. She seems like she'd be kinky out of the workplace."

"Based on what?"

"She makes eye contact every time I walk past."

"How often do you walk past?"

"Often enough."

"And she's kinky because she looks you in the eye," I deadpan.

"She doesn't just look me in the eye—she *looks* me in the eye, if you know what I mean."

"Can you stop talking for a goddamn minute?" He's giving me a fucking headache. My head is pounding.

Elbows on my desk, I rub my temples back and forth.

I want to bang you so hard.

I can't imagine someone who wears a pink cardigan every Wednesday sending me a note like this.

"You're definitely firing back a note. It's the only way to find out who she is."

Oh, someone is getting fired all right.

"How about I don't and instead get back to my fucking job."

"Nah, I like my idea better."

Of course he does, because he's a horny *moron*.

Once again, he gets up and crosses to my desk, shoving me aside and strong-arming his way to the computer. Once on his knees, he jacks me in the rib cage until he has room to type. Fingers poise at the keyboard, hovering.

As he begins typing, he talks out loud.

"Dear Foxy Lady—"

"What? No. I would *never* fucking say that." I try to move him out of the way, but he stays put and continues to type.

"Dear *Yours*. Thank you for your correspondence."

My nostrils flare. "Are you fucking serious?"

He ignores me. "As you've noticed, my underwear is twisted tightly and shoved *so far* up my own ass that I'm often rather unpleasant to be around."

Rolling my eyes, I sit back and let the douche have his moment, but there is no way in hell I'm sending an email.

"But let me assure you," he pauses, "my sensible cotton briefs (probably in a boring white) are untwisted because of your email, and I've never felt so free. Freeballing, one might say." Okay, that part makes me laugh. *Idiot.* "Your email might be the thing I need to *bang* the bastard right out of me; I'd like to return the favor. How about a seat on my lap during the Staff Update meeting— which are a complete waste of everyone's time when an email would serve the same purpose." He gives me a sidelong smirk and I flip him off. "Please RSVP with a Xerox copy of your ass so I know whose ass to park in my lap. Respectfully yours, Romey Bear. P.S.: Let's fuck."

With a wide, satisfied grin, Hunter reads over *his* email and is

SARA NEY & MEGHAN QUINN

about to move the cursor toward the SEND button, when I leap out of my chair and smack his hand away.

"What the fuck were you about to do?"

"Hit send. Duh." He shakes his hand, cradling it to his chest as he stands. "Why are you so sensitive?"

"Why are you such a pervert?"

"I'm not a pervert. I'm normal. You're the one who needs to loosen up. Relax, dude. Chill. Have some fun. Jesus."

"I can't send an email like that."

"But . . ."

I shift in my seat, uncomfortably. "But . . . nothing."

He stands, swiping at any carpet dust that might have gotten on the knees of his dirty jeans. "If you don't send this one, think of sending a different one. What's the worst thing that could happen? You actually having some goddamn fun? Flirt? Get a hard-on for something other than a spreadsheet?"

Shit.

He's right; one time I did get a hard-on when I saw the company's year-end fiscal spreadsheet. It was gorgeous and sexy.

Sue me; money turns me on, okay?

It's not a crime.

Hunter's bear paw clamps down on my shoulder. Squeezes. "Just think about it."

"Right." My eyes roll because I have nothing else to say.

I'm not writing that woman back.

Whoever she is.

The idea is ludicrous.

When Hunter leaves—finally—he has the good manners to close my door behind him with a click, shutting me in with my thoughts.

No way am I getting any work done right now; I might as well pack up my shit and leave for the day—but it's only mid-morning.

Fuck.

His ridiculous email glows back at me in black and white, a

parody of a love letter. A cheap imitation of flirting. I'd never say any of those things.

What I would say is . . .

What would I say?

I scratch at the stubble on my chin, not having enough time this morning to shave. The whiskers are dark and coarse, covering my strong jaw and under my chin. Bristly.

What would I say?

I delete the bullshit my friend just typed out, eyes fixated on that blinking, beckoning cursor.

Say something . . . it tells me. *Go ahead, you chicken shit.*

Me? Scared?

That's a load of horse crap. I'm not afraid of anything but squirrels, and not a single soul knows about that except me.

Little beady-eyed bastards.

To Whom It May Concern:

As you've probably realized, you've caused quite a stir with your little declaration. It was unprofessional and could be misconstrued as assault, which I'm sure wasn't your intention. I've held off responding, mostly because there is nothing to say; this nonissue will be dealt with by human resources in partnership with IT, and when they find you . . . you'll be fired.

Your boss,

Rome Blackburn.

Postscript: You were obviously inebriated when you composed the email, and it was the result of alcohol.

There.

Professional. To the point. *Authoritative?*

I'm the boss; I'm in control, not some mystery woman who probably works in the damn mailroom.

What the hell am I doing here?

I tell myself it's because I need a firmer grasp on my company.

Not for any other reason.

None.

I don't usually find myself on the lower floors; mostly because I hole up in my office, head down, hands clicking away at my keyboard. Or I'm on the phone, taking important calls.

I have no reason to venture anywhere but my office, bathroom, boardroom, or break room for coffee—and it's Lauren's job to fetch that for me.

But here I am.

And I feel like a tiger, pacing the aisles of the marketing department, slowly stalking up the middle of cubicles, tight-lipped smile and a nod to anyone who glances in my direction.

Anyone scattering like a rat to move out of my way.

"Hello, Mr. Blackburn."

"Oh. Oh, uh, Mr. Blackburn. Uh, Rome. Uh. Mr. . . ."

"I'm just preparing that file for you, sir. I . . . I didn't forget, I . . ."

A few papers go flying.

Loud coughing.

More than one folder rises as a disguise.

What am I dealing with here? A department full of pussies? Christ.

I scan the aisle, thirty-something cubicles—some empty, most of them occupied—one by one, examining every face staring back at me. Staring for . . . anything.

A sign.

A tell.

Glimmer of a guilty expression.

For *her.*

She's here, in this department, I can taste it.

I wet my lips, smiling at George Flanders, my longest in-house ad exec. George might be a floundering old-timer, but his wife makes fucking great pie.

A perverted joke Hunter once told me about "slicing pie" comes to mind and I chuckle, rounding the corner to the break room. Every floor has one; a nice-sized tile room with a fridge, a few booths, sink, counter, microwave, coffeepot, and Keurig. Plenty of snacks and bagels brought in every Friday by a vending distributor.

I shove through the heavy door and pop my head in, then settle my eyes on the young woman in the corner, magazine raised to her face, one hand holding a sandwich. Her oversized dress is a hideous hue of olive-brown, an outdated article I've only seen in old movies. A can of sparkling water is on the table in front of her, and she doesn't hear me enter the room and lean against the counter.

I regard her, my gaze sweeping up her crossed legs, to the puffy fold of her giant dress sleeves circling her elbows. Who the hell is she?

And why is she dressed like that?

I've walked around my company enough to know no one dresses like this.

Not that it really matters . . . but . . . shoulder pads.

She doesn't acknowledge me when I clear my throat.

I push off and make a show of brewing a quick cup of coffee. I don't need one; I've had three already, but it's busy work. To get her attention.

Still.

Nothing.

What the hell do I have to do to get this chick's attention? Detonate a bomb? And why the hell am I even trying?

"Nice weather we're having." Lame.

"Mmm . . ." she mutters.

"I could pitch a tent right here in this room," I groan.

Her magazine rustles as she flips a page. "Yeah . . ."

"Man, Mr. Blackburn sure is a prick."

Snort. Laugh. "*Yeah.*"

Ah. Now we're getting somewhere.

"Did you see that tie he had on yesterday?"

She takes a drink from her water. "He wasn't wearing a tie yesterday." The magazine flutters.

Well. *That's interesting.* "He wasn't?"

She ignores me in a way that only Hunter does.

"What do you think was in the email that got him so fired up?"

Slowly, the pages of her magazine still, and it lowers, her dark eyes boring holes into me as they come into contact with mine. I watch as her cheeks flush, eyes widen in horror, and teeth nibble at her bottom lip.

Peyton?

Peyton in a way I haven't seen her before: messy and rumpled, looking a little worse for wear, makeup slightly smudged—or what makeup she does have on—clothes wrinkled. I don't know what the hell that dress is, or where she would have found it, but it's fucking horrible and should be lit on fire.

I let this awkward moment between us stretch, giving her an opportunity to string a sentence together and salvage the moment.

She doesn't.

She sits there, stunned.

Gawks.

Mouth open wide in disbelief like a carp fish.

I suppress my smirk. "Good morning."

"Morning." Her voice croaks.

"Rough night?"

Her reply is a wane smile that only tips one side of her face. Wobbly?

She's definitely hungover.

She should be drinking coffee to wake herself the fuck up, not water.

"I'd appreciate in the future if you call in and take half a personal rather than come to the office looking like . . ." I let the implication settle, noting with satisfaction that she squirms in her chair. "Then again, you're leaving in . . . what's the countdown at now? Seven days? Six?"

Peyton clears her throat. "Eleven."

I lean against the counter while my coffee brews, arms crossed. "Eleven." I let the number roll off my tongue. "From the hungover look you're sporting this morning, seems like you're regretting your decision of leaving such a powerful company."

That straightens her shoulders . . . her well-padded shoulders.

"I have zero regrets." She folds her magazine, sets down her sandwich, and clasps her hands together. Folds them neatly in front of her. "I'm quite excited for my new endeavor, if you must know."

I shake my head and snag my coffee. "I don't want to know actually. What I do want to know is why you're lounging in the break room, reading a magazine, and eating a sandwich when it's not"—I glance at my gold watch—"even ten in the morning."

Her eyes bounce back and forth. Caught. Red-handed. She bites on the side of her cheek and just when I think she's about to apologize profusely, she straightens her shoulders, brings her sandwich to her mouth, and takes a huge bite from the middle.

Mustard decorates her upper lip, and a piece of turkey dangles past the bread as she speaks. "If you would really like to know, I fancied myself a mid-morning turkey sandwich snack." She stands and folds her magazine under her arm. Picking up her water, she addresses me with a shake of her sandwich. "Now, if you don't mind, I need to down the rest of this delightful turkey yum-yum and make my way to my cubicle. Someone has to do some marketing around here."

Full of confidence, looking prideful as fuck, she brushes past me, water dripping from loose strands of her hair as if she just emerged from a shower.

I watch her retreat, a bit of a hot mess if I'm being brutally honest.

What the hell was she doing this morning, getting dressed in the damn dark?

And why is she *owning* it like she's working the runway?

Ass swivels.

Shoulders sway.

Then there's a hitch in her step, and she stumbles over her own damn feet.

SARA NEY & MEGHAN QUINN

But, she catches herself. Shoulders high again, she disappears behind a wall.

I twist my lips to the side, remembering her words. *Someone has to do the marketing around here.*

Fucking *cocky* woman.

If I wasn't intrigued to find out what she might wear on Monday—another ankle-length trench coat perhaps—I'd fire her ass.

She's not the only one in the marketing department.

Taking a sip of my coffee, I turn out of the break room and head the opposite direction, one thought weighing on my mind: when Peyton leaves, will I be losing an insulting hot mess, or is she actually a vital part of my company?

CHAPTER SEVEN

PEYTON

I can't believe the bastard insulted me.

Okay, fine—yes, I can—I just can't believe he did it to my face. That's another lie. The guy is an asshole; of course he's going to insult me to my face.

I hustle to the desk that's only mine for eleven more days, roll the chair out, and plop down and settle in, hands already poised at the keyboard before sliding my chair in.

A resentful "hmph" leaves my throat as I listen to my computer purr, going through the motions: check the company's social media; add hashtags to a Facebook post; three more to Instagram, and a new photo to the story; add buy links for a sleeping bag to the swipe-up feature.

I make myself a note to have a photo shoot scheduled for the new women's apparel line; they're ridiculously cute layering pieces that leave me disappointed I won't be receiving a discount when the brand offshoot launches.

My lower lip pouts for a few seconds.

I'm going to miss this place—not just my friends and the

SARA NEY & MEGHAN QUINN

people I work with, but the actual job. It's been a great place to work, despite upper management.

Or because of him?

Rome Blackburn might be a dick, but he's created something wonderful here, which means he actually does give a shit, despite the blasé attitude and biting remarks. Roam, Inc. is innovative, modern, and fast-paced. The facility is beautiful; rustic without being over the top. Sleek without being sterile. Break rooms on every floor. Clean. Food delivered every week and stocked in the fridge. My favorite thing to do is sit at a table in the corner break room and graze.

Except this morning; what the hell was Rome doing? He was the last person I expected to see when I set down my magazine, although shame on me for not recognizing his voice. I'm supposed to have a huge crush on him. How did I not know it was him?

Shameful.

He was as stunned as I was to see me sitting there; I could see it in his eyes. Oh, he hid it well enough with a practiced neutral expression, but there was no disguising the flicker of shock when our eyes met.

Rome Blackburn looked . . . interested.

Or maybe that's just the fog from the alcohol that hasn't lifted? *Guh.*

Or maybe he was interested in the little diddy I put on today. I smooth the thick fabric across my legs cringing from polyester blech that is hugging me in all the wrong places.

Yup, pretty sure he was more interested in what the hell I was wearing than in me.

I pound away at my laptop, configuring pixels and tweaking target audiences on a few posts. Yawn. Check the clock, then check my email.

Like I do every morning, I scroll through them, my finger running down the left side of my monitor, fingertip touching on every new message so I don't miss anything important. I go through them one at a time, deleting the ones that are trash, or assigning them to a file folder.

From: Rome Blackburn.

I pause.

Heart immediately kicks into overdrive.

What the hell . . .

Oh shit, Gen added the fake email address to my Outlook profile.

Wait.

Holy shit—he replied.

He freaking replied.

Relax, Peyton, *he's delivering a scolding.*

Don't open it, don't open it, don't open it . . .

No good can come of this.

None.

If he found out the original email came from me, my shit and my ass would be on the front sidewalk.

Going out on your own requires money, and I need these next eleven days. I need this extra paycheck.

I shouldn't open it. Maybe he has a tracking device on the email that will announce who opened it. *Is that a thing?* No, can't be. Gen would have thought about that, right?

My teeth rake over my bottom lip, contemplating.

Should I?

No, you really shouldn't.

But . . .

Fuck it.

I click open the email, face flaming hot red as I read. Neck too. My skin is on fire.

But . . .

My eyes can't read fast enough. A typed-out lashing full of reprimand, the type of email that should scare me.

And yet, I latch on to his very last sentence—the postscript—rereading it with a smirk: *You were obviously inebriated when you composed the email, and it was the result of alcohol.*

How very wrong he is.

I was drunk, but I knew damn well what I was doing when I wrote that email—at least I think I did. The alcohol gave me the courage to do what I've been wanting to do for ages.

What do you say to *that*?

You're drunk, so you didn't mean it . . . is that what he's alluding to?

I was drunk last night—I think everyone on the marketing floor has realized that given my appearance today—but what I said, I meant.

I want to bang him so bad.

Accurate. So freaking accurate. Even in the break room, when insults were rolling off his tongue with ease, I wanted to tear that tie from his neck and lick his collarbone, straight-up gnaw on the damn thing.

I bite down on my bottom lip, taking off half the gloss Gen smeared on my mouth to make me look presentable. My cursor floats above the REPLY button.

I really shouldn't.

Click it.

Ooops. Slippery finger.

Hesitate.

Linger.

Picking up my phone, I dial Genevieve, because what the hell am I doing, flirting with writing him back? It's unprofessional, and he already made his feelings on the subject loud and clear.

Gen answers on the first ring. "Hold on." I hear her chair creaking and then it's quiet, the sound of her door clicking closed in the background. "Okay. Go. Talk to me."

"He answered back." I whisper so no one can hear me in the cubicle next door.

"Read it to me. *Slowly*."

"To Whom It May Concern . . ."

She interrupts with an undignified sputter. "To Whom It May Concern? Who says that?"

"Well, I did, in my first letter."

"And I didn't agree with it then either. It sounds stupid."

I sigh, irritated. "Are you going to keep interrupting? Let's just assume you're going to hate the entire letter, okay?"

Jeez.

"Fine. Continue."

"To Whom It May Concern." I clear my throat. "As you've probably realized, you've caused quite a stir with your little declaration. It was unprofessional and could be misconstrued as assault, which I'm sure wasn't your intention. I've held off responding, mostly because there is nothing to say; this nonissue will be dealt with by human resources in partnership with IT, and when they find you . . . *you'll be fired.* Your boss, Rome Blackburn.

"Postscript: You were obviously inebriated when you composed the email, and it was the result of alcohol."

She's silent for a moment before saying, "Did he actually write the word postscript? Or did you read it as that?"

A small smile tugs at the corner of my mouth. Freaking Rome and his formalities. For some reason, it's endearing that he actually wrote out the word postscript.

"He wrote it out."

"What a tool." She lets out a long sigh.

"He's not a tool." My voice is a harsh whisper. "He's refined."

Looking back at it, there is no *real* content in his email, just a basic HR response, very political, very . . . bossy pants Rome.

I can feel the roll of her eyes from here. "So how are you going to respond?"

"I wasn't going to. Do you think I should?"

"Peyton, he emailed you back, so don't squander the opportunity. Aka, don't be a dipshit."

"Gee, thanks." I laugh.

"He gave you a clear opening with that last sentence—like a total idiot—so take it."

"You think that was on purpose?"

She considers this, and I hear her humming. "Knowing him?

73

Probably not. If it was anyone else, I might say yes." Gen pauses. "Why don't I hear the clicking of your keyboard?"

"Why are you so bossy?"

"Because I'm trying to help you. Now get crack-a-lackin'."

"What should I say?" I bite my thumbnail.

"Call him Mr. Blackburn, he hates that."

I laugh. "Okay . . ."

"Make sure you include a line about wanting to fuck him. Men love that shit—even robot humans like Rome."

"Genevieve."

I imagine her shrugging. "Please, you know it's true. He has a stick up his ass."

"Are you going to insult him or help me?"

"I can't help it."

"I'm hanging up."

"Wait. Wait. Blind copy me on it, would you?"

"You have serious issues; you know that?"

"Yeah, you tell me that all the—shit. Someone is coming. I got to go. Copy me on it."

The line goes dead, and I'm left on my own.

Eyes trained on my monitor, my mouth twists into a line of concentration.

Click.

Click, click, click. My hands fly across the keyboard on their own violation, all caution gone out the window along with my resignation letter now filed with human resources.

I've already broken the damn ethics policy, and who knows how many others . . . why not go for broke?

Screw it.

Let's see if I can make anything happen with this? At least let's see if I can make the powerful Rome Blackburn squirm.

Mr. Blackburn,

I'm sure you think I should be ashamed of myself for sending that email —and perhaps I should feel a little guilt? But I'm not ashamed and unfortunately have zero guilt. Surprise, surprise, it felt great, and there is one thing I won't apologize for: telling you how I feel. Maybe the way I did it was crass, or tacky—it certainly wasn't classy—but at least I finally did it. This is not me apologizing for my behavior, because this is me patting myself on the back for having the lady balls to speak up.

A few more things before I end this message . . .

You're not going to find me, but you can sure try.

Since you're such a fan of postscripts, here is one for you: it wasn't the alcohol that made me write that email. It just gave me the courage I needed to say something.

I still want to bang you. What do you have to say about THAT?

Love, sincerely,

Sober.

~

T o: HandsRomingMyBody@RoamInc.com
From: RomeBlackburn@RoamInc.com

Dear Sober,

This back and forth has to stop. It's extremely unethical, improper, and against the policies. I did not email you to get a reaction; I merely responded in kind to give you a warning and to outline the consequences of such correspondence. This one-sided flirting will end right now.

RMB

~

F rom: HandsRomingMyBody@RoamInc.com
To: RomeBlackburn@RoamInc.com

Maybe you should stop emailing me then if it's "so improper." And while you're at it, stop lying to yourself. If you weren't enjoying this—even just a little bit—you wouldn't have hit REPLY in the first place. Admit it.

LSY (Love, Sincerely, Yours)

Postscript: what do your initials stand for?

~

F rom: RomeBlackburn@RoamInc.com
To: HandsRomingMyBody@RoamInc.com
Your ability to take a simple direction makes me question your ability to make a reliable employee.

~

F rom: HandsRomingMyBody@RoamInc.com
To: RomeBlackburn@RoamInc.com
Your inability to answer a simple question like "what do your initials stand for?" confirms the title you wear around this office is correct: pompous ass.

Postscript: I still want to bang you, pompous ass or not. Or maybe because you're one . . . the jury is still out.

CHAPTER EIGHT

ROME

C lick.
    Unclick.
Click.
Unclick.

I fiddle with the pen pinched between my fingers, eyeing my computer.

Reading her email over and over again.

Pompous ass. I've been called worse, and I've also acted worse. Her words don't faze me. At least *those* words don't faze me.

It's her postscript that's making me question my sanity as my finger hovers over the reply button. This should end, right now. I should trash this email thread and start looking over the mock-ups George brought to my office earlier this morning for our new women's line.

Sighing, I click the red X in the top corner and minimize the email. Get it out of my sight.

Focus.

This foolish behavior is taking up too much of my time.

Mock-ups. I need to look at the mock-ups. Bring the boards close to my eye, observe the colors and type font. Strong and . . .

I still want to bang you.

Fuck.

Type font. Strong and feminine. The picture could be better, it could use . . . what could it use? I study the picture, the pert ass in yoga pants catching my attention.

I still want to bang you.

The words hang over me like a rainy cloud, constantly beating me from above, killing any kind of work ethic I might have.

Jesus Christ.

I drop the mock-ups and push away from my desk, exhaling heavily. I stand and pace, rolling up the sleeves of my black button-up shirt. Didn't go with a navy-blue suit today. *Couldn't.* I didn't want to give the impression that I enjoyed the compliments, or that I was looking for more.

But it was tempting, so goddamn tempting.

Pacing back and forth, I rake my hand through my hair, trying like hell to figure out what to do about this email. The *responsible* CEO would trash it and move the fuck on. The hard-up CEO, who hasn't had an ounce of excitement in his life for years, is curious to find out what other responses he can garner from the mystery woman.

I'm also wracking my brain to figure out who the woman is.

Want to know how pathetic I really am? I spent the entire weekend going through our list of employees, divided them in a spreadsheet by male and female, then marital status, and high-lighted the single women in the database.

Then, I proceeded to look them up on social media, trying to pinpoint those who had boyfriends.

It was a low point in my life, but for fuck's sake, it's driving me crazy. I was able to gather a group of twenty-two women.

Twenty-two single women to sift through.

The list is on my desk, printed and catching my attention every few seconds—it's nothing but a distraction, and the entire reason reason I haven't gotten any actual work accomplished.

Staring at the names on the list and the mock-ups, I scratch my jaw, the rough scruff scraping over my fingers as I devise a plan.

If I can't get any work done because I'm trying to figure out who this mystery girl is, why not try to kill two birds with one stone?

On a mission, I snap the list off my desk and barge through my office doors. I float the paper onto Lauren's desk and say, "Meeting in the executive boardroom in ten minutes. All the women on this list are required to attend. Make sure the mock-ups are on easels."

Startled, Lauren traps the paper under her hands and gives it a quick scan. "What if they're in another meeting?"

As I head back to my office, I say, "Then make them leave."

The door slams behind me. Water, I need some fucking water before this meeting.

~

I watch them, study them closely as they file in one by one, taking seats in the black conference room chairs, filling up the back first. No one wants to sit in the front. I don't blame them.

Arms crossed, a scowl written across my forehead, I stand to the side, my suit jacket left in my office, too heated with frustration to put it on for the meeting.

The room is silent. The soft click of the conference room door sliding shut echoes through the small space. Pushing off the wall, I take them all in. A sea of blondes, brunettes, and black hair—one ginger—sit before me, curious gazes in their eyes, some annoyed, some scared shitless, having never been in one of the meetings before. I don't normally call on accounting to give me input on mock-ups, but like I said, I have ulterior motives.

Silently, hands in my pockets, I walk around the room, taking in all the small things about these women.

Coiffed hair, curled and sprayed to stay in place.

Black mascara speckled under the eyes from an already long day at work.

Turtleneck covering up a still visible hickey. Nice try.

Smeared red lipstick.

Glasses that need to be cleaned.

Peyton.

Sips too loudly on their straw.

Painted fingernails, clacking away on an iPad.

Wait . . . Peyton. I turn my gaze to her once again, seeing how she sits tall in her seat, twirling her pen in her hand, ready to take notes. She isn't brimming with confidence, but she isn't cowering in her seat like some of the other women.

Hmm . . .

When I round the corner of the table, I catch the gaze of another employee from across the table, her eyes cast down but glancing up at my crotch every two seconds. I take her in: red hair, freckles decorating her porcelain skin, and classic green eyes highlighted by dark liner. Pretty.

I don't remember her name, and I don't remember looking her up on social media. Did she hear about the meeting and invite herself?

I make a quick count of the heads in the room. Twenty unfamiliar faces.

How is it possible that I don't know any of their names when they work for me? Well. Except for Payton Lévêque, and she's on her way out of the company.

I make a mental note to look up a redhead when I get back to my office.

A feminine clearing of a throat draws my attention to the back where Peyton is sitting. Her hand is raised like she's in grade school and I'm the teacher.

What the hell does she want?"

Not in the mood for her antics, I say, "What?"

Don't believe for a fucking second that I don't notice how she swallows hard before asking, "Is there a point to this meeting? I have a really important phone call in ten minutes, and I'd like to see this move along."

My jaw clenches, her insubordination hitting me directly in the chest, heightening my irritation to dangerous levels.

Taking the position at the head of the table, I lean both palms on the cool glass and pin her with my stare. "If you have a problem with attending this meeting, Miss Lévêque, then why don't you do us all a favor and pack up your belongings early? We'll be fine getting along without you."

Metaphorically folding her cards, she backs down, melting into her seat. "I'll send them an email telling them I'll be delayed."

I give her a condescending smile and gesture my arm toward the room. "Please, email them while we wait for you."

I don't miss the gasps of shock around the room as we volley off shots back and forth.

All eyes on her, Peyton fumbles with her phone, fingers typing a mile a minute, then shoots off an email. When she's done, she rests her phone on her lap and gives me her full attention.

"Are you ready, Miss Lévêque? Can we proceed?"

Twisting her lips to the side, eyes narrowed, her sassy mouth says, "You may proceed."

Christ. Anyone else I would have fired by now, but after a conversation with George during one the weekly meetings I have with all my department heads, I know he's struggling with Peyton's departure and is trying to soak up as much from her as possible before she leaves.

Apparently, she's a real asset to the company he wishes we could have kept on.

Figures.

Standing tall, I adjust the folds on my sleeves and say, "I brought you all here to test your reactions to the mock-ups of the new women's line we're releasing soon." Semi-true.

From the looks of it, it might be our redhead friend who can't seem to keep her tongue from licking her lips at me every two seconds.

"I want to go around the table and hear your initial reaction to the ads. Starting with . . ." I point to the redhead.

She points to herself, pushing her chest forward, the buttons on her shirt straining. Jesus, what department is this girl from? I can't even take her seriously.

"Yeah, you. Also state your name and department for me."

Smiling wickedly, she says, "I'm Sasha from marketing. I'm interning to take Peyton's job." *Ah, that's why I don't know her—she's a newbie.* I quickly catch a roll of Peyton's eyes when I turn her way.

Looks like Peyton isn't on board with her replacement. That makes me chuckle inwardly.

If Sasha is just starting, the emails couldn't possibly be from her.

I cross her off my mental list.

"My first initial reaction to the ads." She bounces her index finger off her chin. "Super pretty."

Oh, for fuck's sake.

This is the replacement we found for Peyton? She's supposed to show some form of marketing intelligence, and all she has to say is pretty?

I'll be having a conversation with George.

Pressing my tongue against my teeth, trying not to lash out on the new girl, I nod to the next girl, prompting her to introduce herself.

Voice shaky she says, "Hi, I'm Diane fr-from accounting and the ads are nice to look at."

Another winner.

Another employee I cross off my list.

We move around the room in rapid pace.

Margie from archives thinks the ads are nicely placed.

Samantha from marketing likes the font.

Theresa from reception wants her butt to look that nice.

Giggles from around the table

Shoot me fucking now.

Pulling on my hair, we reach Peyton who has her pen perched against her mouth, studying the mock-ups with laser focus.

The weekend must have freshened her up, because instead of soaking-wet hair and a trench-coat dress, her hair is long and curled over her shoulders, and she's wearing a black tunic over a black and white-striped button-up shirt. She looks professional, just like the day she resigned.

Leaning forward, pen poised at the screen, she doesn't say a word.

Yet. . .

"Peyton, you look like you want to say something."

"Do I?" she blurts out, obviously trying to look casual and failing. "I might have a few thoughts."

"Please."

She clears her throat and her pen waves in the air like a pointer. "What would I do? What would I do? I think . . ." She chews on the tip of that pen now, biting down on the black cap, straight, white teeth blinding. "I think they're pandering to our audience. It's overdone. Too many fonts, for starters—there should only be three, that's a design rule of thumb." She casts an apologetic look around the room.

"Go on."

"Three fonts, but here, I'm counting five." Now she taps the pen on the tabletop, giving it a few raps. "It's also very wordy."

"Wordy?"

"You're going to lose people with all this text. Keep it simple. Eight words or less for a header."

My nostrils flare. "Anything else?"

I pay my marketing people good money for this shit—why wasn't Peyton included on the team for the new campaign when it's clear here she has a grasp on what we needed? Better yet, why wasn't she running it?

"Yes. I'm done."

"*Are* you though?" My sarcasm is palpable.

"I mean . . ." Her voice trails off. "You said you wanted this to be a quick meeting and I'm Social Media acquisition."

Peyton shrugs.

My body tenses. Fists clenching at my side, I slide my tongue over my teeth, feeling how tight the pressure in my jaw is.

This meeting was a mistake. I'm getting nothing out of this, especially with Peyton running her mouth like this, trying to be *helpful* in a very public way.

Before the next marketing team member has an opinion, I stalk to the door, fling it open. "You're free to go. Miss Lévêque, a moment please."

Shuffling quietly and at a rapid pace, the women file out, happy to leave the tension-filled room. Eyes trained on Peyton, I watch a few women pat her on the shoulder before leaving. One elbows her in the rib cage.

Must be her friends.

She's going to need the encouragement when I'm done with her.

Once the last of them have exited, I slide the door closed, the frost of the glass blocking us from the peering, prying eyes of the office.

I take a seat in one of the chairs and cross my ankle over my knee, striking a casual pose, pinning Peyton with my *don't fuck with me* look.

We sit in silence, her fidgeting with her hair, me still as a goddamn statue. I can sit here all fucking day, intimidating her with my fixed stare. Unwavering and dead fucking serious, that's me.

No one talks to me like that in my boardroom, let alone in front of other employees.

She's treading on thin ice, even if she was right about the ad campaign.

"What was that?"

"You asked for my thoughts on the ad. And I gave it."

"That was before I knew you were going to rip the whole thing a new asshole."

"Did you want me to lie? I can do that, too." She clears her throat, flattens her lips into a thin line, and smiles. "The ad is wonderful as is. Don't change a thing."

I'm not amused.

"See? I can lie."

"Scale of one to ten, how bad is the ad copy?"

"Seven point five."

Shit.

I spent forty thousand dollars on that mock-up no one is wild about.

"Was there anything else you needed, sir?"

My head rears at the word Sir; she used it on purpose.

"There's nothing more I need." At least, not right now. "You're free to go."

Yes, I know I'm being a stubborn jackass right now; Peyton has a good eye, and it sounds like she has fantastic idea. But I cannot bring myself to seek her advice, because all I want to do right now is stick my tongue down her throat.

Fuck. Me.

CHAPTER NINE

PEYTON

"What did lover boy want?"

My head whips around, glancing every which way as Genevieve's voice carries, embarrassingly loud. "Would you keep your voice down?"

"Sorry. We've been dying. Does he finally want to bang you?"

I wish. "No, Gen. He wanted to talk about the new ad campaign. You know—'cause we're at work?"

"Oh." I swear, her shoulders sag. "That's it?"

"That's it." My eyes roll. "You don't have to look so damn put out about it."

"Yes, I do. I have a lot riding on this."

"Huh?"

"Nothing. Just a small, personal bet with Kim and Viv."

I hold a palm up to shush her. "Please. Don't tell me. I don't want to know."

Genevieve laughs. "So what else did he say?"

"Not a whole lot." I shrug it off, trying to act as cool as possible, not like I just got ripped a new one by the man I'm crushing on. "It was no big deal."

And yet, it was. It was a huge deal, because while he was giving me a classic Rome Blackburn tongue-lashing, I couldn't stop myself from ogling him.

Sleeves rolled up, showing off his ripped forearms, the black of his shirt highlighting the pale silver of his eyes. The scruff on his jaw, sinister and sexy. The pinch in his brow and sharp line of his eyebrows, intimidating and hot as hell.

And the way his deep voice rolled over me, igniting a wave of butterflies in my stomach.

I was so desperate to tell him the email was from me, that I want nothing more than to accompany him back to his office. But instead, my face turned bright red, I shivered in my seat, and when he excused me, I tucked my tail between my legs and scampered away.

Gen leans back into my cubicle wall and sighs. "Well, I guess it could have been worse, he could have fired you."

"He can't fire me, because I've already resigned." I bite the side of my cheek. "I am actually surprised he didn't pack up my shit, though. I really thought that was going to happen."

"Did he say why he didn't?"

A sly smile passes over my lips. "George."

Gen claps her hands and laughs. "Oh, freaking incompetent George. He's going to be so lost without you."

I do feel bad for George. Such a nice man, but he is going to struggle, big time.

"He might be slightly incompetent, but at least he knows when he has something good, unlike Rome." I flick my hair over my shoulder causing Gen to laugh, just as my email dings with a message.

My eyes fall to my emails and on a message from Rome.

THE message.

I swivel my chair around, giving my computer my full attention. Whispering, I say, "Gen, it's him."

Making a gleeful noise, she scoots forward and quietly claps her hands together. "What does it say?"

Taking a deep breath, a ridiculous smile on my face, I open the email.

Gen and I both read at the same time.

From: RomeBlackburn@RoamInc.com
To: HandsRomingMyBody@RoamInc.com

Do you realize you called the CEO of this company a pompous ass in your last email? Keep slinging the insults. I can't wait to watch your face fall flat when I catch you, because my pompous ass will be kicking your sorry ass out on the curb.

Enjoy your little emails now. They're only getting you into more trouble.

RMB

I bite on the tip of my finger, getting a little nervous. "Uh, Gen?"

"Yeah?"

"You don't think he can do more than fire me? Like, sue me or anything, right?" I nibble a nail.

Gen chuckles and shakes her head. "No way. He wouldn't do that—it would be bad press. You have to read past his threats and look further into the meaning of this email. He's testing you. He's trying to scare you. He wants to see how serious you are. If he was serious about doing anything to truly end this, he would have a task force put together by IT to figure out where the email came from. There has been nothing. Believe me, he's interested."

"You think so?"

Gen nods her head and maneuvers my gaze back to the computer. "I know so. Message the bastard back."

I think about it for a second. Should I really continue? I don't want to start a new company with Rome Blackburn pissed off at me. I mean, he's already furious, and if he found out I'm sending the emails, I think he might lose it, especially after what happened today.

He has the power to tarnish my reputation in this business. Is that something I'm willing to risk?

I think back to the intensity in his eyes, the way he vibrated with anger. But what I remember more is the small smirk I caught on his face as I left the boardroom.

I hold on to that image as I type back.

Feeling way too frisky for a Monday, I stand and hand Gen my phone. "Take a picture of my ass."

"What?" Brow pinch together.

"Just do it. I have a plan."

"Uh . . . okay." She holds the phone up to my butt, and I turn sideways, showing its curve, and pop it out just a bit.

"Don't get much background, just the butt."

Thinking I'm mental, she takes the picture. I send it to myself through email. I have plans, big plans.

~

ROME

It's been seventeen hours.

SEVENTEEN HOURS with that godforsaken email burning a hole in my inbox. I told myself I wouldn't open it.

It wasn't worth my time. And the little clip on the far right side, indicating an attachment, yeah, I don't care about it either. It's probably some weird picture of a glittering rose or something. A rose from my secret admirer. Some stupid girly shit like that.

I don't need a fucking rose. I need to get my head out of my ass and work.

I sip my coffee, drum my fingers on the desk, flip my pen in my hand.

Stare at the email.

Sip my coffee.

Finger hovers over the email.

What if it isn't some stupid glittering GIF? What if it's a picture of her? Would she do that? Better yet, maybe it's something more.

I grind my teeth together, weighing my options.

Goddammit.

Squeezing my eyes shut, I click on the email and plead for a rose.

Please, be a rose; please, be a rose. For the love of God, be a fuckin' rose.

I peek my left eye open getting ready to be bedazzled by a GIF when at the bottom of the email, I see a preview of a picture.

A picture of a perfectly curvy and covered ass.

Shit.

Dragging my hand over my face, I let out a sharp breath and read her email.

Dear Pompous Ass,

Since we're speaking of asses, thought I would send you a picture of mine. Don't bother looking too hard. I can answer your question now; no, I'm not wearing underwear.

I'm so cheeky, aren't I? < - - Pun intended.

Okay, your turn, send me a picture of your ass.

Postscript: I like when you roll your sleeves up on your dress shirt. Just makes me want to bang you even more.

Fuck.

Sitting back in my chair, I drag my hands over my face and then lean forward again, opening up the picture at the bottom.

Coming to full screen is a picture of the nicest fucking ass I've ever seen. Wrapped in tight black pants, her ass arches from her back, a slope I want to run my hand over, I want to cup, I want to fucking spank.

I adjust myself in my seat, studying the curve of her ass, the background behind her. It looks like she's in a cubicle, so that means it could be ANYONE. Great.

And black pants? That gives away nothing.

I lean forward a little more, trying to see if I recognize—

The door to my office flies open and Hunter comes strolling in, a lollipop in his mouth and a smirk on his face.

Frantically, I try to hit the exit button, but it's too late. Hunter notices my panic, his smirk turning into a full-on grin as he rounds my desk and takes in the ass on my screen.

"Well, well, well, what have we here?" One hand on my desk, the other gripping the back of my chair, he leans forward to examine the picture. "Damn, whose ass is that?" I don't answer him, and it takes him all but two seconds to figure it out. "Is that mystery girl? Fuck, she has a nice butt, man."

He claps me on the back.

Shaking him off, I say, "It is."

"Has she revealed herself?"

"No." I pick my pen back up and start fiddling with it. "She's relentless. My threats have no effect on her."

"Why would they? If your stupid memo didn't stop her, why do you think your emails will? Plus, why do you want it to stop?"

"Need I remind you of the company's policies?"

He waves a hand at me and sucks on his lollipop. Suck. Pop. "Lighten the fuck up and send her a dick pic."

"You're psychotic. I'm not sending her a dick pic."

"Why not? Talk about a way to fucking shock her. Just stick the camera down your pants, take a quick snapshot, and send it on its way." *This man is my best friend. Has he met me?*

In a million years I would never send a dick pic.

I cross my arms over my chest and study my asinine friend. "Is there a reason you're here?"

From his back pocket, he pulls out a crumpled set of papers stapled together in the corner and tosses them to me. "Got you those reports you were looking for."

I eye the folded papers on my desk and then look at my friend. "You know how to send emails, so what the hell are you doing giving me a hard copy?"

He shrugs. "I just like seeing your angry face. It makes me happy."

Why the hell are we friends again?

"You need to leave before I lose my shit."

"Whoa, whoa, whoa. Dude, you need to calm down. Look at how tense you are. Jesus, take a breather." He sucks on his lollipop again, smacking his lips. "We've been friends for a long time and believe me when I say, I admire your work ethic. Kind of wish I had some of that in me." *Me too.* "You've become a hermit over the last year, and I'm starting to get worried. You're my best friend, and I don't want to see you croak at thirty-five because you refused to have any sort of fun." Lick and suck. "For once, let loose. Who knows, if you actually give in to these emails, you might find yourself less tense, less of a raving bitch around the office, and more satisfied when you get home." He shrugs his shoulders and stands from his chair. "You don't know who she is, so what do you have to lose? Nothing. But you have a whole lot to gain."

Walking away, he shimmies his shoulders and says, "Loosen up, dude. It'll be good for you."

My office door slams behind him. *Why does he always do that? Why can't he ever shut the door quietly?* I turn my head back to the computer screen when the door cracks open again, Hunter sticking his head through. "By the way, want to print that picture for me? I can go around and compare and contrast and report back. That's the kind of work I don't mind doing."

"Get the fuck out of here."

His laugh echoes through the door as it slams again.

Fucking imbecile.

I run my hand through my hair and stare at the picture one more time, her words ringing through my head.

I like it when you roll your sleeves up.

It makes me want to bang you even more.

Hell . . .

Is Hunter right? Do I need to loosen up more?

I do spend a ridiculous amount of my time at the office, but I justify it because I don't have a girlfriend or a family—so what else am I supposed to do with my damn time? Sit at home twiddling my thumbs? No. I pour that time into my company.

I used to be fun. Sort of.

Used to go out more, but that was before the company blew up and I had employees to take care of. Jobs to create and a brand to build. A brand I freaking love.

Love.

Something I haven't thought much of—until now.

Until those damn emails have me up at night, and now I'm thinking about stupid shit like loosening up and having some fun. Which is so unlike me.

My laser like focus is for shit. Lately, I've been spending more time at a little coffee shop by my house, watching people. Hell, I've even thought about getting a dog.

Jesus, Hell really has begun freezing over.

Giving in, I lean forward in my seat and decide to take Hunter's advice and send a reply—a scary decision I know—but at this point, he's right, what *do* I really have to lose?

~

From: **RomeBlackburn@RoamInc.com**
To: HandsRomingMyBody@RoamInc.com

Miss WhatEverYourNameIs,

I regret to inform you that there will be no butt shots coming your direction. Being the CEO of this company, I like to keep all my body parts private, including pictures of my ass. I suspect you were expecting such a response from me, but I will tell you this: that ass of yours is officially the wallpaper on my desktop. Thanks for that.

Postscript: Still trying to find out who you are while I stare at your inappropriate ass cheeks.

~

From: HandsRomingMyBody@RoamInc.com
To: RomeBlackburn@RoamInc.com

Did you hear that? That was my mouth hitting the floor from your response. Allow me to do a quick recap here:

1. *You think my ass is sexy (Thanks, I do lunges.)*
2. *If my ass is your wallpaper, I'd love to see the proof.*
3. *You're warming up to me.*

Admit it, you look forward to these emails. If you didn't, my ass wouldn't be parked on your laptop screen.

Postscript: What does your middle initial stand for? Humor me. I'm a details kind of girl . . .

~

From: RomeBlackburn@RoamInc.com
To: HandsRomingMyBody@RoamInc.com

Miss—

You realize, in addition to dealing with this situation with you, I also have to keep this pesky little Fortune 500 company afloat? Flirting and evading your prying questions should be the last of my worries.

For your edification: see attached picture of my desktop. I will admit your ass isn't all that bad to look at.

Postscript: RMB – Rome Michael Blackburn

~

From: HandsRomingMyBody@RoamInc.com
To: RomeBlackburn@RoamInc.com

You know, Rome, the more details you share with me, the more I want to . . . you know. Bang you. Sorry for putting it that way, but I was drunk and impulsive and the word stuck. The more details you share, the more I want to cuddle you. *Thoughts on snuggling on the freshly cleaned copy machines? Or a freshly cleaned set of white cotton sheets?*

Postscript: Your middle name makes you human. I like to know the middle names of people I want to yell at. **shrugs**

≈

F rom: RomeBlackburn@RoamInc.com
To: HandsRomingMyBody@RoamInc.com

First of all, the word "bang" doesn't bother me—I'm a man, I can handle words like bang, screw, and fuck. Make love? No. Cuddling? Hell no. I haven't done that since my . . . never mind. I don't like cuddling. Cuddling is for sissies. Real men DO NOT CUDDLE.

Confession time: were you one of the people who had sex on the copy machine in the supply closet? I'll be sending the cleaning bill your way.

≈

F rom: HandsRomingMyBody@RoamInc.com
To: RomeBlackburn@RoamInc.com

No. I'm not the one who "got it on" (cue Marvin Gaye) on top of the copy machines, but I know who did. Send me the cleaning bill, and I'll pass it on to the guilty parties. Yes, plural. It happens more regularly than you'd probably like. Maybe you should tighten up that no fraternizing policy you're so fond of?

And for the record: if I were to screw in the office, it sure as hell wouldn't be in the copy room. That's so tacky. Gross. It would be in your office, pressed against one of your big windows. Better yet . . . bent over that massive . . . desk of yours.

Postscript: I probably shouldn't tell you this, but what the hell? I've had daydreams of office sex with you in each and every board meeting.

CHAPTER TEN

PEYTON

A man is standing next to my table at the coffee shop near my apartment, casting a shadow over my paperwork and blocking my light.

I cast my eyes up.

And up.

And there he is.

Rome Blackburn, in the flesh, in my little neck of the woods, looking just as surprised to see me as I am him.

His mouth parts.

Mine does too.

He stands at the edge of my table, hands in his pockets, looking down at me, almost like a dark, angry storm cloud. His expression is moody.

"Miss Lévêque." His greeting is stuffy and formal, so like him.

"Mr. Blackburn," I volley back, smiling sweetly, dragging out both syllables of his name.

Black.

Burn.

The way I murmur his name has the desired effect, and he scowls, just like I knew he would. So predictable. So moody and stubborn.

So good-looking.

God, I'm so ridiculously easy . . .

I shift on the wooden bench I've been perched on for the better half of two hours, left hand finding the cardboard coffee cup. Cuffing it, I give my hand something to do other than fidget.

"Were you . . . meeting someone here?" This café can't be anywhere near his place; the area isn't fashionable enough. I picture my boss in a sleek high-rise, not a neighborhood full of families and struggling artists.

"No. I'm here for coffee." As if that explains why he is in my part of town and not his.

I hum from the center of my chest. "Let me guess. Black. No cream. No sugar."

His lips twitch. "Wrong."

"Espresso shot."

"So wrong." He crosses his arms. "Iced latte. Soy. Three sugars."

"What! *Sugar?*" I tease, lips smiling wider. "Sugar, but not to make *you* sweeter."

Tone it down, Peyton. Stop flirting with your boss.

He doesn't bite. "Do you always come here?"

"Me? When I'm not working for you, yes." Which isn't that often, to be honest—but when I have freelance, this is where I love to work. Little bit chaotic, just enough hustle and bustle with the right amount of noise.

A notebook is in the center of my table and Rome's hawk-like gaze lands on it.

"No laptop today?"

"I'm a purist."

"Odd for someone paid to be online all day long."

This makes me laugh, partly because it's true, and partly because the look on his face is a mixture of horrified, disgusted, and admirable. I can't decide which one.

"What's in the notebook?"

"None yo bizness."

His brows shoot up, surprised. And if I had a nickel for every time this man's nostrils flared, I wouldn't have to start my own business. I'd be independently wealthy.

"Is that a notebook full of ideas that are going to transform Roam, Inc's new women's line?"

I laugh. "No talking about business. I'm not on company time as of"—I check the invisible watch on my wrist—"six PM. Sorry."

"You still owe me nine more days."

I sip from my cup. "Seven."

"Seven days, then."

I cradle the coffee cup, blowing over the brim. "You pay me for social media—not to come up with marketing strategies." I am all too delighted to point this out.

"But you do those."

"Indeed I do." Another sip. "Which you casually rejected at my resignation."

"Because you were quitting."

Resigning.

Huge difference.

"Did you even look at my portfolio?"

Rome hesitates so long he doesn't have to answer.

I smirk, knowingly. "Ah, so you did."

I lean back, gloating, an arrogant arch to my brows. "I'm good, aren't I?"

His lips form into a thin line.

I set my cup down and throw my hands up, exasperated. "Oh my God, why won't you just admit it? What on earth is wrong with you?"

More silence stretches, only the sounds from the café filling the gap between us.

"You're good."

Two words. Coming from him—the man who compliments no one—his words carry weight.

"Thank you."

"I'm going to need you to refocus your energy in the next seven days on marketing."

Say what?

My tongue makes a clucking sound.

"Not in my job description."

"Miss Lévêque, might I remind you—"

"Might I remind *you*, Mr. Blackburn, that it's after working hours, and a Friday, and I'm done with Roam, Inc. for the day." His mouth drops open. "You love meetings. Schedule one on Monday with my secretary. I should have a block of time on Wednesday."

"You have a secretary?" Oh God. The look on his face. I have studied his gorgeous face for years. *Years.* I've seen him angry, disinterested, frustrated, and very occasionally . . . mildly happy. But I haven't seen this face. He's *shocked.* God, it is so hard to hold back the laughter in my throat. *He's so fucking adorable.*

"No. I'm just messing with you." I swear, the look on his face . . .

Silver eyes narrow in my direction. "You're enjoying this, aren't you?"

"Mmm. So, so much." Immeasurably.

"By next week you'll be four days out from your end date."

"Yeah." I flip my hair. "Not much time, is there?"

I can almost hear his ass cheeks clenching from irritation. My heart is racing, knowing where this whole conversation is heading.

"You're going to force my hand in this, aren't you?"

"Whatever do you mean?"

"I'm not going to sub-contract you after you leave. You will not force me into it."

Tsk-tsk.

Man, he is so stubborn.

"Force you? Me? I'm a little pussycat." I'm practically purring— and at the word pussy, Rome Blackburn's face turns a pinkish hue I've only seen on myself in the mirror.

Rome Blackburn, blushing.

Interesting.

I flip open my notebook and pull out a glossy, square business card, tucked away in a side pocket. Set it on the table and slide it forward with the tip of my index finger.

"You know where to find me when you need me."

And he does need me.

Rome snorts, the card staying in its spot on the edge of the wood.

"Take it. Don't be shy," I prod. "It won't bite."

His hands remain in his pockets, where they've been this entire time.

"Don't be so stubborn. We both know you're going to come crawling to me in seven days when I leave the company." Preferably on his hands and knees.

"I never crawl."

"Ugh, don't be so literal."

"I won't beg you to come work for me."

"I already work for you."

"You know what I mean." The man is practically rolling his cold, platinum eyes. "It's not going to happen."

"Okay. If you say so." Sip.

Sip.

Slurp.

I smile.

"You . . ." he starts, clamping his mouth shut.

"Me . . ." I sass him back.

One hand comes out of the pocket of his dark jeans, and it points at me, accusing. His mouth is gaping, ready to shoot me a retort.

My gaze flickers toward the cash wrap.

"Line's getting really long. You should put down your finger and get in it."

"Are you handling me now?" *I wish I was.*

"Handling you? No." Maybe just a little. Testing my boundaries? *Absolutely.* "I'm just suggesting you get in line before the wait is too long."

"I'm going to."

Another patronizing smile. "Then go."

His feet remain rooted to the concrete floor, liquid gaze narrowing. "Stop doing that."

"Doing what?" My lashes flutter.

"Whatever it is you're doing."

"Drinking coffee and outlining my business?" My smile is saccharine; innocent as can be as I mentally pat myself on the back and thank God I'm sitting down—I don't know if my knees could withstand the look he's shooting me right now.

Confused.

Like he's trying desperately to figure me out.

A perplexed Rome Blackburn is a sight to behold.

Irritated, obviously, because the man is always pissed off about something, the big baby.

"I can grab your drink if you want? They know me here, maybe—"

"I don't need you *buying* my drink."

My chuckle is low, hidden by the white insulated cup in my hands.

I shrug at him, slender shoulders moving up and down slowly. "Suit yourself."

"I will, thanks."

God, it's taking every ounce of self-control I have not to bust out laughing—he takes himself way too seriously.

"Well . . ." My sentence trails off. Eyes flicker to my business card on the table. "Are you going to take that?"

"No." He is so rude. "I have one already."

It was in the packet I gave him. Which he looked at and read.

Which makes me want to jump up and do hip thrusts into the air—a victory dance.

"What's that look on your face for?"

"What look?"

101

"You look like a cat that just ate a plate full of cream."

The tang of victory is so strong I want to lap it up.

"Do I? Mmm, tastes amazing."

Rome Blackburn is going to give me a chance, whether he knows it yet or not.

Like a total brat, I lick my lips.

"Don't do that."

"Don't lick my lips?"

"It's unprofessional."

"But it's Friday . . ." As if that explains everything away. My flirting. My behavior.

But then something else occurs to me at the exact same time: if Rome hires me, he's going to *be my client*.

My. Client.

I won't be working for him. He'll be contracting my company, and I'll have to handle myself with the professionalism he demands
. . .

A pit forms in the hollow of my stomach.

Which means . . .

The emails to him have to stop.

The flirting.

The inappropriate banter I throw in when I message him.

"Sorry. I . . . I had some foam on the corner of my mouth."

His steely eyes slowly move to my lips. Land there, hesitating a few heartbeats before those giant hands of his get stuffed back inside his pockets. "I should get going."

"Right. Well. Have a good weekend."

Instead of going to the counter, like I expect him to, Rome Blackburn walks back out the door.

Completely empty-handed.

And it almost reflects how I feel. After flirting and practically throwing myself at Rome, I'm beginning to see it might be a complete waste of my time. He won't give in. He won't give me my one night of passion. In fact, he probably won't even consider me for future work. All our interactions of late have been . . . rough.

Not once has he taken me seriously as a viable resource in marketing. And if I truly want his business, which I know I do, that needs to change. He expects professionalism at all times. *And really? He actually deserves it.*

So, that's that I guess. Time to . . . time to what?

Move on?

How the hell do I do that?

CHAPTER ELEVEN

PEYTON

To: HandsRomingMyBody@RoamInc.com
I stare at the notification in my inbox, confused at what I'm seeing—an email from Rome. From him first, not a reply to something I've sent him. I stare, shocked that he's messaged me.

It would be thrilling if I hadn't just decided I couldn't keep this little game up; it could hurt me professionally.

I have to stop.

End whatever this is that I've started.

If only it wasn't so difficult . . . and fun.

Bantering with him is fun, and it turns me on, and I've never wanted anyone more in my life than I want him, even when he's being an asshole.

Curious, I click open my emails, scrolling to the only email I give a shit about. Rome's.

T o: HandsRomingMyBody@RoamInc.com
From: RomeBlackburn@RoamInc.com

I must be bored as hell if I'm sending you a note, or maybe because I have an employee driving me nuts, and I need to expel some energy. You, of all people, whose identity I do not know—and who has caused havoc in the office--tell me that isn't the most fucked-up thing you've heard all week. Why do I keep messaging you? I don't know you. I don't know if I can trust you—you're probably gossiping about this shit and showing all your work friends. Is that what you're doing? Be honest; I'm the only one here with something to lose.

RMB

S *hit.*
Shit. Shit. Shit.

I bite my bottom lip and sit back in my chair. I shouldn't engage.

Do NOT engage, Peyton.

You need to be professional with this man. You need to keep him on your good side, because you never know when you might need him.

And yet, I'm almost ninety-five percent positive I'm the unruly employee he's talking about. There is no doubt in my mind he left the coffee shop Friday only to go back to his fancy apartment and stew over our interaction.

Rome is a sharp and shrewd businessman with an amazing ability to find what's working and what's not, but lately, it seems like he's been having trouble, and me sticking my nose into his new campaign hasn't helped.

To be fair, he did ask my opinion.

I can see the uncertainty in his eyes and he's never uncertain. Even though I don't want to gloat about it, I know he's finally figured out my departure is having an impact on the campaign, and I almost feel bad. I was mostly joking around Friday night, but now I've put all these little clues together: the uneasiness in his demeanor; how he already looked through my profile; the weird random meeting about the campaign; and the initiation of an email.

Let's face it. The powerful Rome Blackburn has been knocked down a peg.

And I feel bad.

Gah, why do I feel bad?

Maybe because I can see the vulnerability in his eyes and in his words.

You're probably gossiping about this shit and showing all your work friends. Is that what you're doing?

I'm sure he doesn't have many people to talk to other than Hunter. He's reaching. And damn it, I can't sit back and not respond. Maybe it's my kind heart or my inability to let go of this crazy and fun journey, but even though I know I shouldn't, I write him back.

T o: RomeBlackburn@RoamInc.com
From: HandsRomingMyBody@RoamInc.com

No. I promise you, I am not gossiping about you with my friends. They had no idea that I even harbored a crush on you, if that's what we're going to call it. Crush. Lust. I let it slip that night I was drinking—and honestly, they tried to talk me out of it. You're not the most popular guy in the office, even if you are the boss.

What did you do this past weekend? Anything interesting?

LSY

A nnnd . . . send.
There. I did it.

It's out there in the Interweb now, and I can't take it back.

What's really strange is that I've pretty much confessed to this man about everything I wish I could do to him in his office, from bending over on his desk to getting fucked against his office window and yet, the one thing that is making my stomach break out in a flutter of butterflies is my last question.

What did you do this past weekend?

Seems stupid to be so worried about a simple question, but it's more personal. It brings these emails to a more intimate level rather than just flirty talk.

That's terrifying to me because what if he doesn't answer? What if he thinks—

Ding.

Quickly I look over my back to make sure no one is watching me and open the email.

It's from Rome and my heart-rate accelerates.

To: HandsRomingMyBody@RoamInc.com
From: RomeBlackburn@RoamInc.com

Anything interesting? No. I lay low. For once, I didn't work this weekend. Bumped into someone from work at the coffee shop where I hang out, which was kind of weird. What about you?

Never in my entire life have I been high. I'm a good girl who has never smoked a thing or even tested out any recreational substances, but this feeling shooting my veins, this feeling of Rome having an ACTUAL conversation with me rather than threats and lectures? This has to be what a high feels like.

TO: RomeBlackburn@RoamInc.com
From: HandsRomingMyBody@RoamInc.com

Why was it weird that you bumped into someone from work?

A nd he's totally talking about me. I knew there was an off chance I made a lasting weekend impression on him. I just need to make sure it was a good one and not a bad one.

T o: HandsRomingMyBody@RoamInc.com
From: RomeBlackburn@RoamInc.com

Did I say weird? I meant fucking awkward. This woman is someone I clash with on a regular basis, so it was a shock to see her in "my spot" sitting at "my" table, in my damn neighborhood.

E h, okay.
There goes that good impression.
Awkward? I didn't think it was awkward, more . . . entertaining. Well, it was entertaining for me, maybe not for him as much since I was the one pressuring him when he was looking for help . . .

No! I will not feel bad about that. If he wants my expertise, then he can hire me for what he wants. *There.*

And what was he doing at MY coffee place to begin with? I'm practically married to the damn shop. Our invites are on backorder right now, so there is no way he's been there before.

T O: RomeBlackburn@RoamInc.com
From: HandsRomingMyBody@RoamInc.com

And you've never seen her there before? How is that possible?

I cross my arms over my chest and rock in my chair. Yes, how is that possible?

To: HandsRomingMyBody@RoamInc.com
From: RomeBlackburn@RoamInc.com

Yeah, I was thinking about that too. In all honesty, I haven't been there much lately. Too busy working. Thought I'd go and sit and enjoy the evening —but that didn't happen. She was sitting there, working, and the whole thing threw me off. I walked out without getting my coffee—felt like such a fucking idiot. But whatever. Think I should find a new coffee shop?

Felt like an idiot?
Don't feel bad for him, Peyton. DON'T YOU DARE feel bad for him.

Okay.

I might feel a little bad for him.

I threw him off, made him feel awkward, and then sent him on his way when he just wanted to enjoy a nice cup of Joe.

I giggle to myself, recounting our interaction. I was in rare form. Confidence oozed from me, and I shouldn't be ashamed of that.

The only thing I should be ashamed of is letting my coffee get lukewarm while talking to him.

To: RomeBlackburn@RoamInc.com
From: HandsRomingMyBody@RoamInc.com

You LIVE in that area where she was hanging out? What neighborhood was it?

Time to get a little more personal. Not that I'm going to stalk him or anything . . .

T o: **HandsRomingMyBody@RoamInc.com**
    From: **RomeBlackburn@Roam.com**
I'd rather not say. I live in the same building I lived in when I graduated from college. Granted, I own the building now, but still. Where did you think I lived? No—don't tell me. Some snotty complex in Manhattan or Tribeca? Maybe a brownstone in Gramercy? Are you stereotyping me? Because I own my own company and I'm young? Tsk, tsk, shame on you.
    RMB
    P.S.: Your email handle makes me fucking laugh every time I type it in. Hands roming my body. So fucking ridiculous.

I take a deep breath as another wave of butterflies erupt in the hollow of my stomach.

He's joking with me.

He's interacting *with me.*

He's opening up to me.

This might be too much to take in one day. In the matter of half an hour, Rome has morphed into an entirely different man behind the screen. He's no longer the angry tyrant.

No, he's become the hot guy with a sensitive heart. I am totally screwed. It was one thing to fantasize about fucking him, and another completely to consider emailing him back and forth with ridiculous banter. And chemistry. Don't get me started on the idea of having to continue working with him. But now, the idea of being more? Of possibly being his friend? It's scaring me shitless. Would Rome actually let someone like me in? Could he consider me a friend, or am I setting myself up for an even bigger drop when this is over?

CHAPTER TWELVE

ROME

I have a goddamn smile on my face.

It's spread from ear to ear, and for the life of me, I can't wipe it away. I try to relax my cheeks, I try to pinch my eyes together, I even try to pout my lip like a child, but I can't get rid of this smile.

I have clearly lost it.

Fucking lost my mind.

This is what happens when you work too hard, when you spend hours upon hours hovering over the blue screen of your computer trying to make your company the best in the world. There is a breaking point.

There is always a breaking point, and I think this is mine.

I'm smiling about a goddamn email chain that I shouldn't be partaking in.

I should have deleted this ridiculousness the minute it started.

But I didn't.

I only added to the problem by responding and making this girl's ass the center of my computer screen.

Fuck, it's such a nice ass.

I sit back in my chair, cross my ankle over my knee, and click on the email's that are somehow lighting up my entire damn day, and this dreary and cold office.

TO: RomeBlackburn@Roam.com
From: HandsRomingMyBody@Roam.com

I'm not stereotyping you. Well, not exactly—maybe just a little. **holds fingers an inch apart to display the teeniest, tiniest bit of judgment** I mean, do you blame me? You stalk into the office and sit behind a huge desk, behind a glass wall. It's . . . intimidating. So yes, I would have assumed you'd live somewhere posh. Posh, LOL, what a very British thing to say. Fun Fact: I spent a semester in London when I was in college, and it's my favorite city in the whole wide world, not including NYC.

Can I ask you a question? If you own an outdoor adventure company . . . why are you based in New York, and not somewhere like Colorado? I've always wondered that.

LSY

~

To: HandsRomingMyBody@RoamInc.com
From: RomeBlackburn@RoamInc.com

Why am I in New York? Well, I went to school here, and my parents are in Buffalo, so it made sense. I don't see them often, but we are close. Plus, my grandmother is at an assisted living facility about half an hour out of the city and WHY AM I TELLING YOU THIS? It's none of your business. LOL. But since we're on the subject—yeah, I wouldn't stay if it weren't for them. Maybe someday I'll pull the plug and move the company to a city that makes more sense. But for now, I'd like to remain close to family.

And as far as my neighborhood—I fucking love it. I love that everyone minds their own business and no one puts on pretenses. That's the bullshit I can't stand and why I'm so close to my best friend.

I adjust the sleeves of my navy-blue flannel shirt and twist my lips to the side. Maybe it's time to grab some coffee, peruse the cubicles . . .

That's a good fucking idea, procrastination at its finest. I should be going over Hunter's numbers, but I'm too distracted to even consider going through his jungle of numbers typed and put together in the worst way possible.

I stand from my desk, shuck the jacket, loosen my tie over my head, and undo a few buttons of my white dress shirt. Carefully, I roll up the sleeves and run my fingers through my hair for good measure—and not because somewhere out there is a woman who likes to see my hair tussled.

Nope. It's just a hot day, that's all. I don't even need a jacket.

Time to get some coffee.

The glass doors to my office close behind me just as Lauren's head picks up from the eReader in her lap. She thinks she's so clever, but I know what she's doing.

"Mr. Blackburn, can I get you anything?"

"I'm good. Just make sure you have those accounting reports on my desk by the end of the day." I press the down button to the elevator, and I'm pleased when the doors open right away.

"Yes, of course," she answers as the elevator doors close.

Hands in pockets, I make my way around the marketing and advertising floor once the elevator doors open. Everyone seems to be hard at work . . . for the most part. There are a few people sitting in each other's cubicles, talking and laughing, but the minute they lay eyes on me, they duck their heads and walk away.

I smirk to myself.

Looks like LSY is right. I am known as a tyrant. I haven't even said anything to anyone, but the floor quickly silences, the sounds of keyboards clacking lifts into the air.

I walk past George, who is eating a muffin, napkin stuffed in the V of his shirt, and licking his fingers. When he looks up from his pastry, he waves frantically, so excited to see me on the floor. I nod back and continue to walk to the break room where I find Peyton pouring herself a cup of coffee.

Sneaking up, I say, "Do you plan on making another cup?"

She startles, spilling coffee on the floor, her bottom half backed away from her hands to avoid any coffee burns.

"Christ." She sets down the coffeepot and shakes her hand, ridding it of the brown liquid. "You can't just walk up on people like that."

From above the sink, I rip off a rectangle of paper towel for her and hand it over. "Here."

Giving me a look, she snags the paper towel from me and starts cleaning up. "What brings you down here?"

I lean against the countertop, arms folded, eyes trained on Peyton, who is wearing a tight-fitting red dress that wraps around her waist and ties around the side. Her tits look fucking fantastic on prominent display like that.

Shit, I shouldn't be looking at her tits.

But hell, could her dress be any more low-cut?

I clear my throat and look at my feet. "Thought I would spend a little more time walking around, seeing if anyone needs anything from me."

She's mid-wipe of her hands when she looks at me from the side, her head tilted, her eyes pinched together in confusion.

"You decided to walk around to see if anyone needs anything from you?"

"Yeah." I shrug nonchalantly while snagging an apple from a bowl behind me and taking a bite out of it.

Bite. Chew. Chew.

Her eyes narrow in on my mouth, watching intently as I work the apple around.

Chew. Chew. Bite.

Her eyes stay fixed on my lips, longer than they should, longer than what's appropriate for a workplace. I count the seconds that go by.

One.

Two.

Three.

Blinking rapidly, she pulls her eyes away and crumples the wet paper towel in her hand only to toss it in the trash in front of her.

Clearing her throat, she rests her hands on the counter and looks around frantically as she says, "Uh, do you want coffee?"

Chew. Bite. Chew. "This apple is actually working for me." I tilt my head and say, "Are you okay, Peyton? You're looking a little flushed."

She pats her cheeks, eyes widening. "Do I? Oh, must be the temperature in here. It's called air conditioning, Rome. Try turning it on."

"It's a constant, cool sixty-eight degrees in the office at all times. Maybe . . . it's *you*."

Bite. Chew.

Nervously, she laughs and flips her hair over her shoulder. "Oh no, I put my deodorant on this morning, so I'm good." Eyes widening, a horrified look crosses her features as she bites down on her bottom lip, shaking her head as if trying to shake the last few seconds form her memory. "I mean, I'm not going through menopause. Still a young caterpillar over here."

"Caterpillar?" I lift my brow in her direction.

"Did I say caterpillar? That's weird, I don't know why I said that." Another nervous giggle. She picks up the coffee mug and examines its contents. "You know, I think it's the coffee. A little too much caffeine on an empty stomach."

"Oh . . . do you want some of my apple?" I lend my half-eaten apple to her that she eyes only to be followed by her gaze landing on my mouth again.

"No." She shakes her head. "I'm good. Going to grab a Pop-Tart from the vending machine. Screw the diet today, you know." She nods and then rests her hands on her hips, looking around. Fuck, she's flustered . . . and I love it. She had me out of sorts on Friday night, as if I had disrupted her little domain. And now, she's on the back foot. Not so sassy and confident now. *Interesting.* "Guess I'll go do some more social media posts. Can't like comments enough."

"If you're just liking comments, why don't you come up with some marketing ideas for the women's campaign?"

She pauses and then whips toward me, the fire I saw the other day in her eyes returning as she's snapped out of her stupor. And I smile. I can't help it. Turns out I like Peyton both sassy and contrite. "Care to pay me more to do that?"

"Does it look like I'm about to cut you another check?"

"It would be*hoove* you to do so."

"Don't say be*hoove*; you're not seventy."

"And you're my boss for only two more days, so unless you plan on paying me extra, I'm going to sit in my comfy spinny chair, answer emails, and like all the comments I want." She leans forward. "On your dime."

With a wink, she walks away, a sway to her nice, dress-covered ass.

∼

To: RomeBlackburn@RoamInc.com
From: HandsRomingMyBody@RoamInc.com

I bet by now you want to know what floor I am on at the office, don't you? **flips hair** Ha ha. You can't see me and have no idea what I look like. Is it driving you nuts? Trust me—you'd think I'm cute. Maybe. Possibly? Ugh, I don't know—what's your type? You tell me yours and I'll tell you mine. Deal?
LSY

To: HandsRomingMyBody@RoamInc.com
From: RomeBlackburn@RoamInc.com

My type. Physically? I'm going to assume that's what you mean, but I'll dive a little deeper, if only for my own edification. Taller women. Smart, obviously—someone educated. Someone professional who understands that I do not have time for anything other than a quick lay or a one-night stand. She doesn't want a relationship. I'm attracted to dark features—dark hair and eyes. Quiet.

Can't stand a woman who has a smart mouth. Know any like that?

RMB

To: **RomeBlackburn@RoamInc.com**
From: **HandsRomingMyBody@RoamInc.com**

Do I know any women with smart mouths? **coughs** I might know one or two, ha ha. Won't admit to whether or not I have one myself.

taps chin My type . . . my type. What's my type . . . I have a few of them. Tall and athletic. Fit. Um . . . Oh! I love tattoos, although I've never dated anyone with any. And piercings, which is totally random. Beards get me hot. I follow this amazing account on Instagram of hot dudes with beards and tats, ha ha. But anyway, I digress. My type is handsome and smart and funny. Someone who can make me laugh. But not in a cheesy way, because I can't stand predictable jokes.

To: **HandsRomingMyBody@RoamInc.com**
From: **RomeBlackburn@RoamInc.com**

I'm not funny.

To: **RomeBlackburn@RoamInc.com**
From: **HandsRomingMyBody@RoamInc.com**

No, you're not. Not even a little.

But . . .

There is something about you . . .

T o: HandsRomingMyBody@RoamInc.com
   From: RomeBlackburn@RoamInc.com

Something about me . . .

Like what?

T o: RomeBlackburn@RoamInc.com
   From: HandsRomingMyBody@RoamInc.com

Well, let me see if I can put my finger on it; paint you a picture, if you will. When I see you, there's something about you that makes me stop and watch you. You have this way about you—I don't even mind your cold glares. They mean something. And you don't blow smoke up anyone's ass or sugarcoat anything. Which I know a lot of people resent or take personally, but I know why you do it. I know you work hard and take it seriously and that you care. We can all see it, and I respect you for it. You're handsome. You're smart. You're . . . yes. You're intimidating, but what man in your position isn't? And your friendship with Hunter O'Rourke is too damn adorable —yeah, I said it. ADORABLE. I've seen you get pissed at him for joking around, and I die every time.

LSY

T o: HandsRomingMyBody@RoamInc.com
   From: RomeBlackburn@RoamInc.com

There is nothing adorable about Hunter O'Rourke. He's a pain in the fucking ass. MY ass. You'd think that as my business partner he'd act like a goddamn professional and why the hell am I telling you this?

Keep in mind that since we're using the company server, any correspondence between us is private and confidential, and I could sue you for sharing the content of these emails.

RMB

To: RomeBlackburn@RoamInc.com
From: HandsRomingMyBody@RoamInc.com

Wow, you and your non-disclosures and legal mumbo-jumbo, always wanting to sue people. You seriously need to relax, boss. It hadn't occurred to me to share these emails until YOU MENTIONED IT. Bring it down a notch, Rome. I'm not going to tell anyone your secrets. So feel free to start sharing a few of them . . . ha ha. I'm a very good listener.
LSY

To: HandsRomingMyBody@RoamInc.com
From: RomeBlackburn@RoamInc.com

What kind of boss would I be if I didn't point out the obvious? Before we get carried away with . . . whatever this is.

To: RomeBlackburn@RoamInc.com
From: HandsRomingMyBody@RoamInc.com

"Whatever this is." Did you just admit, in your own weird way, that you're actually enjoying this back and forth? Do tell . . . bring it to my good ear. **leans in close** Whisper it to me like a confession.

To: HandsRomingMyBody@RoamInc.com
From: RomeBlackburn@RoamInc.com

I'll admit, I'm entertained and curious. Have you noticed I've been walking around the office more? It's not because I'm trying to be a dutiful boss, it's because I'm trying to find out who the hell you are. I'm hoping one day I catch you writing back to me. Guard your screen. I'm looking.

To: RomeBlackburn@RoamInc.com
From: HandsRomingMyBody@RoamInc.com

You've resulted to creeping on your employees? Come on, Rome, you're better than that. Instead of hovering behind people trying to read their inboxes, why don't you conduct a little sleuthing instead?

Ask me some questions, any questions besides the obvious. Let's see if you're really smart enough to figure this mystery out.

CHAPTER THIRTEEN

PEYTON

"What? Why are you not coming?" Kimberly asks in her whiny tone that grates on my nerves.

"I'm not in the mood to drink, plus you guys have this whole party planned for Friday, so I might as well save all of my liquor tolerance for then."

"But we're going to get chicken fingers," Viv interjects.

I pat her on the shoulder. "And as lovely as that sounds, I think I'm going to enjoy myself a nice little quiche from the corner bakery and head to my apartment where I can lounge in a long T-shirt and that's it."

"No bra?" Gen asks.

I shake my head. "No bra."

She sighs and puts her arms around Viv and Kimberly. "Give it up, ladies, we can't compete with no bra. We had a chance with quiche as her dinner, but with the extraction of underwire, we're doomed."

Knowing Gen's right, they bow their heads and turn away

toward the bar. "You slay us," Viv says over her shoulder. "Hope your boobs enjoy themselves."

I take the subway home, getting bumped and bruised by every other New Yorker trying to make the busy commute. Not in the mood for reading or listening to any podcasts, I hang on to the metal bar next to the door and stare out the window, the tunnels passing by me at a rapid speed.

I hate to admit it, but I'm going to miss this commute. A little. There's something about stopping by the corner bodega to pick up your favorite bagel and coffee on the way into work, scanning your key card to make it through the doors, and then making your way into an overcrowded elevator to join the hustle and bustle of the city.

But on the other hand, there's nothing like working in your underwear, on your couch, in your home.

Thankfully my favorite bakery isn't too busy, so I'm in and out in minutes, warm quiche in hand. I waste no time in slinking out of my dress, slipping off my bra—yes, that feels good—and throwing on my Whitney Houston T-shirt that falls to mid-thigh.

I hop on my couch, pop open a La Croix I got from the bakery, and break open my quiche.

Ahh, this is life.

Did I mention I'm a sucker for playing cribbage? I have an app on my phone, and there is nothing I want more than to kick my legs back and play a few games.

I open the app just as an email sounds off on my phone. An email from Rome.

An email for LSY.

Oooo, someone is working late.

Snuggling in close, quiche plate resting on my knee, I open up the email.

To: HandsRomingMyBody@RoamInc.com
From: RomeBlackburn@RoamInc.com

Flexes Fingers I would be nervous if I were you, LSY. Do you know why? Because I'm relentless and the moment you open the floodgate for questions is the moment I figure out who you are, and I'm still partial to firing your sexy little ass.

Are you sure you want to tempt me?

I bite on my finger, reading his message over and over. He's so playful, that it makes my heart skip a beat and my common sense fly out the window.

I open the company messenger app on my phone and scroll through the executive names, knowing full well I'm about to break a policy. It's the company's phone, and the company's app, and I'm about to use it for personal use. To flirt.

With my boss.

I close my eyes, find his name—next to it is a little, green dot, which means. . .

He's on the app.

I've never talked to him live before so this is a huge step, but then again, it might be more fun to get his initial reactions to my comments.

Debating it for all but two seconds, I type out a message to him, making sure I'm signed on under my LSY persona.

HandsRomingMyBody: *Hey you.*

My text turns into a new message on the app and I wait on bated breath to see if he will respond. Nerves prickle up my spine, my fingers feeling numb, my mind playing mutiny with my heart just as little dots appear letting me know he's typing.

Oh God, I don't think I've been more excited.

I stuff a giant bite of quiche in my mouth as his message comes across the screen.

God, I am so giddy seeing his name pop up, it does all kinds of things to my body.

RomeBlackburn: *Christ, messenger box pop-up scared the shit out of me when it dinged.*

I laugh out loud and hunker down to message him back.

HandsRomingMyBody: *Concentrating a little too hard?*

RomeBlackburn: *Hunter O'Rourke's fucking reports (pardon my French) are going to be the death of me. Why are you still working late? If I go to each floor, will I find you hunkered down in your cubicle?*

HandsRomingMyBody: *Don't get too excited. I'm home. Just checking my work emails like a good employee would. **pats self on the back***

RomeBlackburn: *Yeah? And what kind of work emails are you answering?*

HandsRomingMyBody: *Yours. If you want a break, I'm free to answer any questions you might have.*

RomeBlackburn: *Why don't you call me? That will be more fun.*

There is no way in hell I'm going to let him call me—he would totally recognize my voice.

HandsRomingMyBody: *Nice try. It's either questions here or no questions at all.*

RomeBlackburn: *It's almost like you want to get caught.*

HandsRomingMyBody: *Maybe I do . . .*

RomeBlackburn: *Fine. What's your name?*

HandsRomingMyBody: *Don't be dense. You know I'm not answering that. Come on, be creative, Rome. I know you have it in you. Drop the CEO title for a second and be a guy who's just talking to a pretty girl.*

RomeBlackburn: *Way to hit me in a soft spot.*

HandsRomingMyBody: *Well . . .*

RomeBlackburn: *What are you wearing?*

HandsRomingMyBody: *Typical guy question. **rolls eyes** But if you must know, a vintage Whitney Houston shirt that touches me mid-thigh and panties. It may or not have a few holes.*

RomeBlackburn: *I'm going to need proof.*

I inwardly roll my eyes and think about it for a long, hard second. Should I send him a picture?

If I lay back a little bit more, I probably could get a good shot of my legs barely covered by my shirt.

Just enough to drive Rome Blackburn *crazy*.

I mean—who doesn't love vintage Whitney? This shirt is a classic.

Setting my dinner to the side, I lean back on my couch, position my legs to make them look as sexy as possible, and point my toes in the air, giving them a wiggle even though he's not getting a video. Blue, sparkly polish. Cute dainty toes.

I'm adorable. And braless.

Who could resist this?

I snap a few pictures, pick the sexiest before hitting send, a secretive smile tugging at my lips the entire time.

HandsRomingMyBody: *There is your "proof."*

He takes a second to answer, but when he does, pure female satisfaction courses through me.

RomeBlackburn: *Fuck. Don't send me any more pictures.*

HandsRomingMyBody: *Are you going to make that your wallpaper now?*

RomeBlackburn: *Maybe.*

HandsRomingMyBody: *It's the legs, isn't it?*

I have really great legs; they're my favorite body part.

RomeBlackburn: *It's the legs. And the toes. And the legs. God, it's making me hungry . . .*

HandsRomingMyBody: *I'm nibbling on the best quiche; should really try it. It's from this little shop around the corner from where I live— Edith's Treats. You'd never know how fantastic everything was until you step foot inside. It's so freaking good.*

RomeBlackburn: *I know where that place is. What's in this magical quiche you're panting over?*

HandsRomingMyBody: *Spinach, roasted peppers, and broccoli. **Kisses fingers** magnifique.*

RomeBlackburn: *I have a package of Saltine crackers in my desk. That's my dinner, so I guess your quiche is better than what I'm having.*

HandsRomingMyBody: *Saltine crackers? Those are for sick people. Are you sick? Why the hell aren't you getting some food delivered like a normal person?*

RomeBlackburn: *No time to call in anything.*

HandsRomingMyBody: *But you have apps. And time to talk to me? But you didn't get food . . .*

As he's typing, I quickly pull up a blank text message and text my friend Tony, who works at the pizza place across from the office. They deliver to the office for me *all* the time and have access to the building. I order up a pepperoni calzone, have it sent to Rome's office ASAP, and charge it to me. The delivery guy responds back with a simple text: *Give it fifteen minutes.*

I love those guys.

I love any guy that feeds me.

RomeBlackburn: *Priorities. I'm trying to figure out who you are; that takes precedence over my stomach.*

HandsRomingMyBody: *Okay, wanna play a game? You ask me anything and I'll answer honestly?*

RomeBlackburn: *Sure, we can do that: What do you like most about working for Roam, Inc.?*

HandsRomingMyBody: *That is NOT the kind of question I was going for, but okay—I'll answer. Despite the tyrant of a boss I work for (ha ha) I really like the image the company portrays, supporting the active life-style, and honestly . . . the free stuff too.*

RomeBlackburn: *Your favorite part of working here is the FREE stuff? Not the hot guy who sits on the top floor and signs your paycheck?*

HandsRomingMyBody: *Maybe. We'll call "him" an added bonus. Can I ask you something?*

RomeBlackburn: *Fire away.*

HandsRomingMyBody: *Ever flirt with an employee before?*

RomeBlackburn: *I don't shit where I eat—it's not my style and it shouldn't be anyone else's either. So, no. I haven't ever flirted with an employee before.*

HandsRomingMyBody: *Yet here you are, talking to me.*

RomeBlackburn: *Because apparently I've lost my fucking mind. How do you take your coffee?*

HandsRomingMyBody: *At work? With loads of that Irish creamer, because the coffee at work is disgusting—no offense. When I'm not at work, I prefer lattes. I float back and forth to what I order that day.*

RomeBlackburn: *So it isn't just me? I'm going to have Lauren switch up the coffee, because drinking that basically amounts to "roasted grounds and a heavy dose of shit" and that's not on the top of my list.*

HandsRomingMyBody: *Roasted shit? As in . . . poo? Yeah, I won't be able to get that out of my head for the rest of the night.*

RomeBlackburn: *Hold up. Why is there a guy in my office holding a bag of food? Did you just have food delivered? Are you FEEDING me?*

HandsRomingMyBody: *Can't have Sexy McBossyPants going hungry. **wink** Enjoy, the calzones are among my faves and TO DIE FOR.*

RomeBlackburn: *Taking care of me. I'm actually in shock. And thankful. And to be honest? A little stunned . . .*

CHAPTER FOURTEEN

ROME

W here the hell is everyone?

One glance out my office window and I see no one.

I don't have time to lift my ass out of this seat to know there isn't any noise coming from the common area outside my door where most of the cubicles on this floor are. The place is a dead-zone and I have no goddamn idea why.

And instead of caring enough to find out, I find myself rooted in my chair, staring at my computer.

Last night, I learned a little detail, a little nugget of information that could help me figure out who LSY is.

And I don't think she even realized . . .

She slipped up.

Even though I was smiling like a damn fool the entire time talking to her when I should have been looking through Hunter's reports, I smiled even wider when I realized she gave me the golden ticket I was looking for.

My cursor drags along my computer screen, lands on the icon

for a search engine, my fingers deftly typing out the words, "Edith's Treats." Enter.

She was so excited about her damn quiche that she didn't realize she gave me a radius of where she lives.

Fucking sleuthing it up this morning.

An image appears of a small bakery on a corner about three short blocks from my apartment building—and just one over from the spot where Peyton in the marketing department was having coffee.

Interesting.

Peyton.

I stare off into the distance, my mind wandering; today would be her last day if I'm doing the math correctly—wouldn't it? I pull up her file, noting the photograph attached.

She's pretty.

Sexy, if I'm being honest.

Smiling at the camera for a picture taken for the website of our staff. Navy blouse. Hair down. Red lipstick.

Jesus, Peyton is . . .

Hot.

Why did I wait so damn long to pay serious attention? Do I really have a stick so far up my ass that I haven't noticed her? Or is that why every time I've interacted with her in the last week or so, I've found it hard to pull away and leave her?

My eyes scan the details provided by human resources: Age, twenty-seven. Position, President of Social Media Marketing and Acquisition. Address looks vaguely familiar, and curiosity has me googling the area.

My area. My neighborhood.

My coffee shop.

My head starts to spin. Every interaction I've had with her running on repeat as I lean forward and stare intently at the computer as if it's supposed to verbally confirm exactly what I'm thinking.

Edith's Treats is right on the corner, perfectly spaced between

SARA NEY & MEGHAN QUINN

her place and mine. *"It's from this little shop around the corner from where I live . . ."*

Jesus Christ.

I lean back in my chair, drag my hand over my face, and blink a few times.

No. There is no way.

I lean forward again, match her address with the bakery and the coffee shop.

Fuck.

FUCK!

Peyton is HandsRomingMyBody.

Peyton is the employee who wants to bang me.

Peyton has been fucking around with me this entire time, lowering my defenses, making me talk about personal shit, sending me goddamn food.

I glare at the desktop, anger billowing in the pit of my stomach, the heat in my body skyrocketing to inferno levels.

She's been lying to me this whole time. She's been right under my damn nose, playing with me . . . tricking me. Probably laughing behind my back with those friends of hers I always catch her with. *Look at me, fooling the boss.*

Not okay.

I rise, slamming my chair back into the windows, skirt around my desk and yank open the door.

Silence.

Well. Except for the low buzzing sound of modems and computers humming in tandem. The fluorescent lights flicker. A printer scanner at the far side of the room beeps.

No sign of life.

"Where the fuck is everyone?" Seriously, it's in the middle of the goddamn workday, not a Saturday—and as far as I know, it's not a national holiday.

I don't think.

Asses should be in those seats.

Heads should be down, fingers flying across the thirty or so computers wired into these desks. Papers should be flying out of the printers, and the phones should be ringing.

Something.

But not this.

I pace around the long corridor, glancing into offices, one by one, checking for signs of life. Any stragglers that can tell me what the ever-loving fuck is going on around here.

Make my way toward Lauren's desk, float around the granite counter to look for any clues. If anyone would know what's happening, it will be here.

One sheet of paper, lying limply across her keyboard, with a message printed in black, bold letters: WISH PEYTON FAREWELL ON HER LAST DAY! Cake and ice cream, break room on the third floor. Ten o'clock.

I glance at my watch.

Ten thirteen.

I punch at the elevator button—like one of those assholes who hits it ten times hoping to make it come quicker—stuff my hands inside the pocket of my gray dress pants (no fancy meetings today, so I'm casual, sans tie), button-up shirt brushing my chest as I stab one more time at the illuminated button. Bounce back on the balls of my feet, agitated.

They threw Peyton a going-away party when she quit? *What the actual fuck?*

Throwing a party for someone who has been deceiving their boss, all for a laugh? I don't fucking think so. Not at my office, not during business hours.

Not happening.

My jaw ticks when the elevator doors finally slide open and once I'm inside, I stab at those buttons, too, with my knuckle. Hit the third floor.

My jaw is clenched, because the noise level when I arrive is as loud as it should be upstairs, only there are people congregated around the entrance to the break room, spilling out and standing around, holding cups and plates of cake, and laughing.

Peyton isn't even a power player here. *What the hell is everyone doing celebrating?* It's not like she's retiring. She fucking quit. She created a new job, and she's leaving, and that is that.

End of the fucking story.

As soon as I'm spotted, a few hushed whispers fill the air; I take in a nudge. A few coughs. My employees moving aside to create a narrow path in front of the door for me to enter through.

And I do.

I stalk toward the break room like a man on a mission, plowing through like a dump truck, eyes scanning for one person: Peyton Lévêque. It takes me a few seconds to settle on her—there are shit tons of people crammed into this room, which is probably a fire hazard or health code violation.

Then.

There she is.

Like a goddamn ray of sunshine, light streaming behind her from the window, a halo shining above her pretty head.

Her lying, beautiful head.

Dark hair, wavy and glossy, down around her shoulders, the rich color picking up red from the sun.

She's holding a glass—it's poised at her lips and she's about to take a sip—when our eyes meet. She lowers it, her mouth parts, and her smile spreads.

Until I scowl. Then, her face morphs from happy to concerned in a second. *Damn right she should be concerned.*

I nod.

She nods.

My eyes trail down the front of her and I note her dress—it's baby blue, wrapped and tied at the waist, and shows off her curves while highlighting her legs in those sexy-as-shit heels.

Stop thinking about her curves and legs. You're not here to admire her.

The pile of gifts in the corner pisses me off, bringing me back into the present, back to my rage, and has me lifting my arm; crooking my finger.

Peyton's brows go up at the same time her head cocks and she pokes a finger into her own chest. "Me?"

"Yeah. You." I know she can't hear me, but I say it anyway—and if she's any good at reading lips, she'll haul her ass over here right quick.

Her cup is passed. Skirt gets smoothed out. Chin tilts high. She heads over.

Good girl.

"Follow me," I order her when we're on the outskirts of the room. When we're clear across the office common area, I pivot to face her.

She's shorter, even in heels, so I have to dip my head to glare at her. "Want to tell me exactly what the *fuck* is going on in there?"

A shrug. "They threw me a party."

"I can *see* that." I'm so annoyed. "I'm asking why?"

Peyton is unperturbed. "'Cause I'm leaving?"

"You quit. Parties should be reserved for employees who are celebrating birthdays or monumental occasions—not young women who leave for greener pastures."

Or better yet, parties should not happen at all.

She wilts under my bark, her eyes shifting back and forth over mine.

"Sir, I'm not using this as an excuse, but I had no idea they were planning anything."

Sir.

That gives me pause, and I want to fucking laugh.

Wow, she's good at pretending—not giving away any hints of her being *HandsRomingMyBody* anywhere. Not fidgeting. No signs of distress on her face. Not a flinch or a blush.

I cross my arms, shirt stretching across my chest. "How long is this party supposed to last?"

"I'm not sure. Lauren was in charge. They haven't done games yet."

"Games," I deadpan, because—*are you fucking kidding me?*

"Just a few fun ones, like, *What's in your desk drawer?*"

Paper. Staples. Post-it Notes. Tape.

Yellow notepad. That's it—that's what's in my desk drawer—and I mentally facepalm myself for playing along in my head.

My lips stay sealed closed.

Peyton prattles on. "And then Donna in accounting made Pin the tail on the Bo—" Her lips clamped shut.

Obviously my brows shoot up when she fails to finish her sentence. "Pin the tail on what?"

"The . . . um. Beaver."

She's so full of shit. "Is that so? You're playing pin the tail on the beaver."

"Yup. Mm-hmm."

"Are you sure it's not something else?"

Her lashes flutter innocently. "Like what?"

"Oh, God—I don't know. Pin the tail on the boss?"

When her face flushes, I know I've nailed it. "I fucking knew it." I get even closer, a sneer on my lip. "And you know what else I know, Peyton?"

She backs against the wall, pressing her spine to the gray, textured partician. "What else do you know?"

She gulps. Licks her lips. Holds her breath.

I lean in—get in good and close. I sniff her hair . . . because it's impossible not to. Lower my voice. "I know you sent *that* email."

Her eyes widen uncharacteristically large. Wide. "What email?"

"Don't be coy. You're HandsRomingMy . . ." I actually choke on the damn words. Embarrassed. "Body."

I give her credit though; she presents a stiff upper lip and doesn't immediately cave. Lifts her chin a notch. "I don't know what you're talking about."

"And I'm sure you do."

One of her shoulders rises in a shrug. "Sir, the only emails I've sent you were regarding—"

"Wanting to bang me."

Peyton chokes on her surprise. "Sir, I assure you—"

"Stop calling me 'sir' and cut the bullshit, would you? It's not doing you any favors." All it's doing is pissing me off even more. "Did you or did you not send me that email?" I press a hand against the wall behind her, getting in even closer, letting her feel my palpable anger, letting it smother her.

At first, I'm not sure she'll admit it and assume she's going to do one of three things:

1. Cry because she's embarrassed and humiliated, although now I'm looking at her, it doesn't seem like she's either.
2. Lie and say it was a joke.
3. Continue denying it.

Her mouth puckers before it opens, no sound coming out as she gathers her words, thinks them through, and strings them together.

"Rome. I . . ." Peyton looks at the carpet, then back at my face. Blows out an exasperated puff of air. "Fine. You're right. It was me."

Was. Not. Expecting. That.

"Are you happy now? You figured it out. And I'm leaving, so you can live in peace. I'll never bother you again. You won't have to even look at me. Not that you did anyway," she mumbles, crossing her arms.

"You don't even realize how unprofessional sending me those emails were, do you?"

The snort that comes out of Peyton's nose is anything but lady-like. "Please. Of course I realize it. Why do you think it was anonymous? I'm not an idiot. You and your propriety are the only things you give a shit about." My eyes widen. "Oh. Look. Big guy doesn't like it when I swear. Well, too damn bad."

"You watch your mouth when you're talking to me. I'm your boss." I sound like a real dipshit, but I have no idea how to handle this woman. Not a single clue.

She's confident, she's not confident. She's so up and down, and I can't pinpoint exactly what to say to make an impact.

Peyton's laugh is loud. And when she tips her head back and lets it hit the wall behind her, the smooth column of her throat contracts with the motion. Her smile would rival that of the Cheshire cat.

"You're not my boss. I'm done. I can say or do whatever I want."

"Not if you want to use me for your portfolio."

She flips her hair. "My portfolio speaks for it*self*. I don't need your company in it."

My body inches closer. "Is that so?"

"Yeah." Her body is so close to mine. "That's *so*."

"And you expect to get my business? You're the most unprofessional woman I've ever met in my entire life."

This does not faze her. "Is that so?" She mimics my tone of voice and condescending attitude.

"Yeah." I mimic her stance and tone of voice. "That's so."

"I disagree." Her eyes rake down my body, and I feel it from the center of my chest where she's staring, down my stomach and to the tips of my damn toes. *Shit.* "You've never complained about my job performance before."

"That's because I had no idea what you were like to work with."

"And what am I like to work with? I've never been written up." She gestures toward the break room at all the people. "Clearly my coworkers like me."

I can't stop the snort from leaving my nose. "They just like free food."

A diminutive shrug, and Peyton chuckles at me.

Her smug attitude infuriates me. "That's all you have to say?" I ask, my teeth grinding together.

"I haven't technically *said* anything."

"Don't get smart."

"You're not the boss of me."

My mouth curves into a smirk. "That's right, I'm not."

"Nope." Her mouth pops the P. "Not even a little. Not anymore."

The space between us couldn't be any smaller, and the only thing stopping me from shoving my greedy tongue down her throat is the flash of movement in my peripheral vision.

Everyone is watching.

It's like we're a bad accident on the side of the goddamn road, and no one can take their eyes off it, instead going slower to inspect the damage.

No one moves.

No one speaks.

No one but Peyton. "Go ahead and do it."

Her voice is small, but it carries just enough to reach my ears.

"Do what?" I spit out almost sarcastically.

"Kiss me." She's daring me, but I'm not an idiot.

I rear back like she's kicked me in the nuts, putting space between us, hissing, "Are you fucking insane?"

Another laugh. "That's what I thought. McBossypants and his proper, Mr. Goody-Two-Shoes manners."

"We. Are. At. Work," I bite out, words halted.

"I'm not at work—I only came in to clear out my desk. You're the only one at work here."

So glad she can be nonchalant. "You just cannot help needling me, can you?"

"Needling you? What are you, seventy?" She's laughing at me. "No, I'm not needling you—obviously not." She taps her chin. "You're adorable when you get yourself worked up into a snit."

A snit.

What the fuck.

No. I do not get myself worked up into snits; I'm commanding and in control of my impulses—unlike some people, apparently.

"I like it," Peyton adds, crossing her arms.

"You need to stop."

"Does it make you uncomfortable when I'm honest?"

"No. I prefer when people lie." I haven't rolled my eyes this hard since I was thirteen years old.

"Well, if it's opposite day, I love that I'm not working for you anymore, and I'm glad I never get to see your grumpy face again."

Wait. Huh?

I have no idea what to fucking say; but she's in my face, staring expectantly—and so is everyone else.

Through my clenched teeth, I say, "People are watching."

She tilts her head. Smiles. "They are."

"You should probably go back to your party."

I've said nothing that I came down to this floor to say—that she quit and doesn't deserve a fucking farewell party. That she's unprofessional—well, okay. *That* part I did say—that her blue dress makes her look smoking hot to the point of distraction.

And I think about her way more often than I should, even before I realized RoamingHands was her.

And I think about her way more often than I should.

And that I'm so goddamn mad at her for putting me through the wringer, for making me feel more than is appropriate for an employee, and that because I'm equal parts furious and turned on —because she's fucking hot—I'm tempted to cause a scene. And I never cause scenes.

How has she made me behave like someone I'm not? I barely know myself anymore.

And why is it that not only am I flustered, but I want to bend her over a chair and spank her to teach her a lesson?

CHAPTER FIFTEEN

PEYTON

"You should probably go back to your party." Rome's voice is clipped and commanding, hell-bent on being a hard-ass. Hell-bent on being in charge.

But I don't want to go back to the party.

Not even a little. I'd rather stay rooted to this spot and volley insults back and forth with him. With Rome. Who's staring me down like I'm the last person on earth he wants to be seen standing with.

The fire in his eyes gives him away.

He can't take his eyes off me.

Good.

I fold my arms over my chest and say, "Or maybe I stand here and argue with you some more."

Leaning even closer, he whispers, practically hissing, "My office in fifteen minutes, Miss Lévêque."

With a turn on his heel, he heads toward the elevator, his well-tailored jeans showcasing his firm and yummy backside as he walks away. They look expensive—as if he had them custom-made for his body.

Ten bucks says he irons them.

Shoulders tense, he sifts his tan fingers through his thick hair, stretching the back of his shirt, while he stands impatiently waiting for the elevator, not giving me a second look.

It takes two seconds for the vultures to attack.

"Holy hell, what was that all about?" Gen asks, scaring the crap out of me, a cup in hand.

"Yeah," another voice intones, this one deep and definitely male. "What was that all about?"

Startled, I turn to find Hunter O'Rourke staring at me, plate full of cake and ice cream hovering balanced close to his mouth, forking a chunk as his gaze flicks back and forth between the bank of elevators and me.

Chews. Swallows, one fork after another into his mouth.

He's watching me expectantly, brows raised. "What crawled up his ass and died?"

I almost laugh. Almost. But Hunter is technically my boss, too, and I don't want to embarrass myself.

"Uh, we needed to tie up some loose strings."

"What kind of loose ends?" Hunter looks me up and down as he shovels another chocolate chunk onto his tongue. He licks it before raising his fork and pointing the tines in my direction. "He looked a little too agitated for loose ends. Did you piss in his Cheerios?"

Oh jeez.

"I might have pushed his buttons just a little."

"On your last day. Imagine that." He shakes his head. "I guess that's one way to make a dramatic exit." Hunter takes yet another big bite of his bottomless piece of cake. "Thanks for the slice. Good luck with life. If there are any leftovers, let me know. This is so fucking moist and delicious."

Hunter bumps me with his hip as a friendly goodbye, then saunters toward the elevators, most likely headed to Rome's office.

With the way those two bicker and carry on, there's no doubt in my mind he's heading up to give him a little shit.

Once he's out of earshot, Gen—who's been waiting patiently for Hunter to leave—can't hold it in any longer. "Okay, spill. What the hell was that thing with Rome Blackburn all about?"

No one is paying us the least bit of attention, so I pull Gen to the side, around the corner, and out of earshot. Gripping her shoulders, I look her in the eye, telepathically trying to send her a message without saying the words.

"Why are you staring at me like that, you weirdo. Did he hypnotize you?"

I roll my eyes.

"For real though. If I say 'whiskey tango foxtrot' are you going to start jumping up and down on one foot."

"Gen. He *knows*."

"He *knows* knows?" Her brows pinch together, momentarily confused. I nod, slowly, lips thinned, waiting for her to comprehend. And when she does, her eyes widen.

"Stop it right now."

"I'm being serious."

"Are you being serious?"

Honestly, why do I bother with her?

But Genevieve carries on caterwauling without me. "Oh my God, Peyton. He knows. Holy crap-ola."

"I know." I'm freaking out, too. *Somehow*, I managed to hold it together when Rome was right in front of me—in my face—when I could smell his delicious cologne, and see every fleck in his gorgeous grey eyes. *God, I wanted him to lean in and kiss me so bad.* Yet, held it strong . . . even when I told him it was me. Now? Now, I'm freaking the hell out. He. Knows. It. Was. Me.

My friend grabs my shoulders, giving me a little shake. "This is nuts. He knows and he didn't make a scene. Wow. This is . . . wow."

"I mean . . . he did have smoke coming out of his ears, just a little."

"How the hell did he find out?"

"I have no idea. All I know is that he busted in on the party to call me out on it. Now he expects me to run up to his office in fifteen minutes, probably for another tongue lashing."

Gen smirks. "A tongue lashing." Wiggles her brows. "One can dream."

I smack her. "Shut up."

"Maybe he's going to give you the kind of going-away present that will rock your world."

My nose scrunches. "What are you talking about?"

Gen sighs and flicks my forehead—actually flicks it. And it's so freaking rude I'm about to protest, but she cuts me off.

"Dude, he's totally going to take you up on your offer to bang him."

There is no way. Not Rome. "Do you think he wants to have sex?"

Impossible. He's so pissed at me.

"Uh, yee-ah," Gen whisper-shouts. "Why else would he call you up to his office on your last day? You're done. There is nothing left for him to say. You did your exit interview with HR, and your access has been revoked."

That's true.

I bite my thumbnail.

"Baby, you could have cut the sexual tension between you two with that cake knife; I could *taste* the sex from here."

"Ew, don't say shit like that. What is wrong with you?"

"I'm serious." She taps my cheek and I swat her hand away. "Fifty bucks says you're about to get bent over a desk by Rome Blackburn. Your dreams are about to come true."

"Stop that." But what if she's right? My face is flaming hot, and I press my palms against my cheeks to cool them off. "You're making me nervous and sweaty. He's not about to bend me over a desk." Although I wouldn't hate it. "I'm sure there's something else he wants to talk about."

Gen crosses her arms and taps her toe on the carpet. "Yeah, like what? You don't work here anymore."

I pause, needing to give the question some thought. All my notes and day-to-day schedules have been turned in to George in marketing. I sent my notes to the temporary solution from another department, having typed out my daily task lists and giving her a copy. Brief rundown and overview.

The ins and outs of managing social media. Passed over the "Social Media for Dummies" that I found on Amazon for my replacement as a joke.

Gen is right; there is nothing left for me to do here but find the front door.

"My office in fifteen minutes, Miss Lévêque." His words ring in my ears.

"Oh my God," I gasp. "I'm totally going to get bent over."

"You sound dreamy—like you can taste it now, too." She shakes her fists in the air, excitement pouring out of her. "As God as my witness you, my friend, are about to get banged." Her gaze trails down my torso critically. "I hope you shaved your legs."

"I always do." I bite my bottom lip and say, "Wait. What if having sex with Rome is a bad idea?"

Genevieve makes a buzzer sound with her throat. "Merp! Wrong question. No second-guessing yourself."

"I know, but—"

"But what?" Her perfectly shaped brows pinch together, ala Frieda. "How on earth is this a bad idea? This is all you wanted, your birthday wish. All you need to do is get up there and flash him that smile. Oh, and unbutton your dress."

"Genevieve."

She shrugs and takes a sip of whatever's in her cup.

My sigh is loud, filling the hallway where we're hiding.

"I have a *business* to think about now, Gen. I can't just do whatever I want without thinking. I'm trying to contract Roam, Inc."

Like a temporary high, the excitement of heading to Rome's office begins to wear off as soon as I realize this is all coming to an end.

I quit.

I won't be here tomorrow.

I won't see my friends, and I won't see Rome.

No more exciting emails, no more late-night chats with the boss, no more flirting and sending him food. I'm going to miss this.

I'm going to miss working for Rome.

The only way I can work with him ever again is by keeping things professional between us—just like he prefers it.

Her brow is skeptically raised. "No offense, babe. You know I love you and totally believe in you. But do you really think you can get Rome Blackburn—the most stubborn man *on the freaking planet* —to hire you to do outside marketing? You *know* he doesn't do outside hires. He does everything in-house. That's how he's able to pay us so well."

She's so right, he does hire within and self-performs most things company related. Marketing. Design. Quality control. Advertising and new product development. Everything within reason, except the actual manufacturing of what we sell.

Gen might be right; he probably won't hire me.

He's already told me no twice.

Fortunately for him, I'm tenacious. I might hear the word no, but I'm always plotting—I want this job, and I'm willing to do whatever it takes to get it.

I mean. Almost anything.

I cough, shooting Gen a smile.

Straighten my skirt, because . . . I am heading up to Rome Blackburn's office.

My former boss.

The man I have a schoolgirl crush on.

He needs me—he wants me.

I can see it in his eyes. All I have to do is force him to recognize it . . .

~

"Would you get the hell out of here? I have a meeting." I hear my former boss grind out between clenched teeth as I approach his office, the floor completely devoid of any humans besides him and Hunter. Lauren is still at the party along with the rest of the company.

"What meeting?" Hunter sounds amused. "Come on, be honest. The meeting is with your right hand, isn't it?"

"Sod off, for fuck's sake."

"Sod off? Are you British and didn't tell me? What else don't I know?"

I swear, I can hear Rome fuming and he isn't saying a single word in reply. I imagine that his lips are drawn into a thin line and he's biting back his temper.

"Secrets, secrets, everyone has them." It sounds like he's rising. "You wound me, you know that? We're blood brothers, and if you know who your little pen pal is, you should tell me. It's only fair."

"I'm not telling you who it is."

"Aha! So you admit that you know who it is. I fucking knew it. Is it Peyton, whose moist cake I just devoured?"

"Jesus Christ."

"So you're not denying it."

"She's on her way up, so can you get the fuck out of here?"

"Blink once if she's the one who wants to bang you."

Silence.

"Are you blinking once or having a seizure? What is that shit you're doing with your face?"

I can't help the laugh that escapes my lips, hand flying to my mouth.

"Tell me to get the fuck out if it's Peyton Lé—"

"Get the fuck out! And shut the door."

Suddenly, Hunter O'Rourke backs out of the office, doing a weird little dance—it's more of a jig, actually—red plaid shirt bold and bright against the dreary gray the walls are painted. His arms are above his head and he's pumping his fist in the air when his eyes land on me, standing square in the middle of the corridor, eyes wide.

I can actually feel how wide my eyes are.

He stops dancing, giant smile spreading like the Cheshire cat across his face. "Well, well, well, if it isn't Rome's resident pen pa—"

"O'Rourke! Leave. Now." Rome fills his doorway, a deep edge creeping into his voice and an even deeper crinkle in his brow.

Our eyes lock.

My stomach drops.

Uh-oh, he's not happy—not even a little bit, and I curse Hunter O'Rourke for giving him shit. The last thing I needed was for him to be in a bad mood when I wanted to pitch to him one last time before I left.

Dammit, dammit, dammit.

I square my shoulders and clear my throat.

"All right, all right. I'm gone." Hunter's hands go up in mock surrender. "Hey, Peyton—thanks for igniting the beast and then leaving us all high and dry."

The bastard actually winks like he's funny, does a small skip, and salutes, walking briskly down the hallway.

Whistling.

Incredulously, I stare off after him. What the . . .

"Lévêque, get in here. Now." His head nods toward the interior of his office.

I stand my ground, nervously. "Say please."

Rome glares. Flares his nostrils. "*Please.*"

I scurry through the door like a rat, feeling phony—all false bravado and twisted nerves.

My heart has never beat so erratically, and my nipples never been this puckered. I'm scared, I'm nervous. I have no clue what to expect.

The door slams and Rome stomps to the front of his desk, leaning against the wooden top. Hands behind him, I notice that his knuckles are white from the firm grip on his desk.

"Why? Why did you do it?" His head is tilted down, but his eyes are blazing a hole right through my chest. "Tell me. I have a right to know."

Wow. He's not wasting any time.

My hands tangle together as tight as the knotted nerves in my tummy. This Rome in front of me? I'm not used to him. I'm used to pissed-off-boss Rome, who's demanding and insistent because he's a perfectionist. Wants everything done right the first time. Demands respect and commands a room.

This Rome is different. He's vulnerable and unsure and guarded because he looks . . . a little bit hurt, actually. Which is weird.

Like he took the whole thing personally.

Because it was personal.

But I never meant to hurt him or humiliate him.

I owe him an explanation—it's just having a hard time forming on my lips.

"I . . ." I clear my throat. "It was at my birthday and . . . I was drunk. Really drunk, like I wrote in the email—more drunk than I've been in a while."

I'm a lightweight; ask anyone.

"So you decided to prey on me while intoxicated?"

"Prey on you?" I'm surprised. That's what he thinks? "No. I wasn't preying on you—not at all. It's just . . ."

I let out a long, ragged breath and take a step forward, farther into his dungeon of his office. Its walls are a darker gray than the common area behind me, dark desk and silver finishing. Masculine and hard. Like him.

"It was my birthday. We actually saw you at the bar that night, and the whole thing was a blur, but there you were."

"I don't go to bars." He doesn't roll his eyes, but it's close.

"Yeah, you did. The night of my birthday, we saw you. You were alone, but it looked like you were waiting for someone who never showed up. You had one drink and then got up to leave."

I exhale, unclenching my fingers. "You never even looked in my direction—just like every other day here in the office—and it was so disappointing. And I would have come over, but it really did look like you were meeting someone, and I didn't want to interrupt. Then my ridiculous friends hid from you, ducking down in the booth, and it was too much for me to handle with all the alcohol I'd had." I can't believe I'm admitting this out loud. "All I wanted was a little bit of your attention."

My voice is unexpectedly small, and I hate it.

Rome seizes the calm as an opportunity to study me, strong jaw moving back and forth as he considers my confession.

I can't stand the fact that he's not saying anything—I never could, and crack within seconds.

"You never looked over at me. And when you left, in a drunken stupor, I admitted to my friends that I had a secret crush on you." My hands are now gesturing, animated while I tell my story. Spill my guts. "Gen got this *crazy* idea to create a fake email address and had her tablet in her purse because she's always—"

Rome cuts me off. "Genevieve Porter in IT?"

Like an idiot, I nod.

He pushes off his desk and rounds the corner. "She's fired."

His long arm extends, fingers reaching for the phone cradled on his desk.

Holy shit.

"Rome! Please, no." *Oh my God,* he cannot fire my best friend.

Tears are already welling in my eyes, panic racing in circles around the middle of my gut. Gen cannot be fired. Why did I just say her name? Why? I'm so, so stupid.

"Please, Rome. Please don't fire her," I beg again, voice strangled from the tears. My hand holds his down as it grasps the telephone.

He is unflinching as he begins ticking off Gen's offenses. "She created a company email account for personal use, on company property. Used that same company property for personal gain. Created an email address to anonymously harass the boss and lied about it." He's leaning against this desk, arms crossed. "Shall I continue?"

"She needs this job . . ." More than I do.

My hand is still pressed over his, holding it down, preventing him from picking up his office phone and calling human resources. Or security.

"Give me one good reason why I shouldn't toss her ass to the curb with yours right this second."

Reasons why Gen shouldn't be fired. Reasons why Gen shouldn't be fired—there are a ton, but my freaking brain can't come up with a single one.

I swallow hard, wracking my brain for something that might stop this relentless man from firing my best friend.

"She felt bad for me," I muster, feeling foolish. "I was so hung up on you, wanting you to see me as more than one of the employees that sit in the cubicles of this office building that she tried to help me. This is on me, not her, please, Rome, *please* don't punish her. I know you're upset, but be upset with me. Genevieve needs this job."

"She should have thought about that before she broke company policies."

"Please." I'm whispering.

He doesn't move. He doesn't even flinch.

Holds his ground, stone like a statue.

I can't help bristling at his unrelenting attitude.

It's breaking my heart.

"Is that how this is going to be, Rome? You can't fire me so you're going to fire Genevieve? That's low, even for you."

Oh God, did I just say that? I try to keep my eyes from widening, but honestly, I've shocked myself, too.

"Excuse me?" He pulls his hand away from mine and rounds his desk, coming up short a few inches from me.

My chin tips up. "You heard me."

"Do you really think I grew this business by sweeping shit like this under the rug? No. I've had to be ruthless from the beginning, weeding out the toxic, making sure this company is a fine-tuned machine. Little word of business advice, Peyton—you're going to have to toughen up, or the sharks are going to eat you alive, and you'll be out of business within six months."

How dare he.

"You're too nice."

Too nice?

"Screw you." I poke him in the chest as I shoot back at him, my voice stern and unwavering. "You can be a ruthless CEO by having a little compassion and without being an ass, and that's what you're being right now. An asshole. You have a problem with me emailing you, and since you can't punish me directly, you're going after Gen. I get it. But it's no wonder people call you a tyrant."

"Do you honestly think I give a shit what everyone says?"

"You should," I spit back. "Maybe if you had half the respect *I've earned* from your employees, they would work twice as hard, work smarter, and you wouldn't have the issues you have right now."

His nostrils flare.

His jaw ticks.

"What issues?"

"Well. Take marketing for example. The department is a mess. George isn't creative—this place has sucked the artist flow right out of him."

"Is that all?"

I huff. "No." Pause. "The entire accounting department is so boring, I do a death march when I have to walk past."

"They're *accountants*."

He has a really good point, there.

"A brighter shade of gray on that floor would certainly make it less dull."

His eyes blaze with heat and anger as he takes a step forward, trapping me against the wall. His cologne is the first thing to invade my space—spicy and masculine—then it's his chest, broad and rapidly falling up and down.

His hands find the wall behind me, straddling my body and

closing in around me. The pale grey of his eyes turns ice cold as they stare me down, his breath heavy as he speaks to me.

Every last hair on my body stands to attention, awakening my nerves on an entirely different level. How long have I wanted to be this close to him, to have his face inches from mine, to have the opportunity to closely take in the ridges and sharp lines of his handsome face?

So long.

And yet, I wish it wasn't under these circumstances.

I wish instead of the anger that's coming off him, it was passion for me. Lust.

An unstoppable yearning.

"You think it's easy running this company? Do you think it's been easy trying to do my job when I have you writing me every day telling me you want to bang me?"

Bang me.

When he says it, it sounds so dirty.

Rome's eyes leave mine and travel down my body, fixating on the cleavage heaving beneath my dress, because I can barely catch my breath.

Finally, our eyes meet.

He speaks. "Do you think it's easy for me to get any goddamn work done when I have you strutting around in a dress like this, enticing me with your smart mouth and sassy attitude?"

"Excuse me? *Strutting?*" I don't *strut.*

I gulp—*hard*—trying to catch my breath as every nerve in my body begins to pulse, my body feeling more alive than ever with him this close.

He bows his head forward, his cheek brushing against mine, the stubble scraping along my sensitive flesh. What would it feel like to have that scruff scrape against my inner thighs? To have that sharp-witted tongue pleasuring me? To have those lips pressing wet kisses against my skin?

What would it feel like to have *this* man's mouth on mine for just one kiss?

Just one . . .

. . . kiss.

My mind drifts; wanders.

What does he taste like?

What would it feel like to be owned by Rome Blackburn, for just one sex-filled night?

I shift against the wall, my legs rubbing together to ease the friction, a low throb inside my center launching a crusade against my traitorous heart.

It wants more, damn her. It wants *him*.

Rome leans in.

Bends at the neck.

Breath nicking the bare column of my neck and finally, lips gently move across my skin, setting off a wave of goose bumps up and down my arms, collarbone, and legs.

His hot whisper is in my ear now, low. "Something is bound to slip, Peyton." Long, dramatic pause as he runs his nose up the column of my neck. "Something is bound to break."

"W-what's bound to break?" I whisper back, unable to keep my gaze steady. That beautiful nose of his leaves my neck and grazes my cheek.

Gently.

Lips inches away, Rome's forehead rests against mine, and he takes a break to compose himself, deft fingers millimeters from tangling themselves in my hair.

I want to reach out and touch him the way he's touching me.

I want to run my hand up his chest; explore the soft fabric of his cotton shirt. Fiddle with the waist and pull it up; expose the tan and muscled chest I know is hidden under the thick fabric of his designer t-shirt.

Desperately, I want nothing more than to loosen his belt, undo his pants, and shove them down his hips until they're falling to the floor. I want to caress him, hold the weight of his arousal in my hand, stroke him, lick him, and suck him.

Pleasure him until he can't take it anymore—right here, in his office—until his tightly wound control slips and he has no choice but to take me over his desk and make every fantasy of mine come true.

He moves his mouth to the other side of my head where his nose leads the way down my cheek to my ear.

"How long have you wanted me, Peyton, hmm?" His voice is deep—so sinister I feel light-headed with every sentence. It leaves me breathless just hearing my name fall from his lips.

"How long have I wanted you?"

Years. *I've wanted you for years.*

He breathes in and nods. "Yes, how long?"

My palms press against the wall, my chest rising and falling, my nipples so incredibly hard.

"I can't re-remember," I stutter. *Lie.*

"Ballpark it for me. Humor me."

"Maybe, um . . ." I lean forward, catching a whiff of him. God, he smells so freaking good. "Uh, a couple years."

"How many? Be specific."

"Do details turn you on?"

"Yes."

"Three years."

He sharply lifts his head from its bent position, brows shooting into his hairline. "Three years?"

"Give or take." My lip gets caught between my teeth.

He makes a humming sound and moves one of his hands to my hip, his thumb pressing into my hipbone, anchoring me against the wall.

"And during those three years, how many times have you envisioned me pressing you against this wall, spreading your legs, and fucking you while you bite down on my tie to keep quiet?"

My eyes squeeze shut as I try to catch my breath, the erratic beat of my heart making it difficult. I try to wiggle under his grasp but his hand pinned to my hip doesn't let me move. The need for him between my legs grows stronger and stronger.

I swallow hard. "Almost every damn day," I answer honestly. "Given a few different positions."

He takes a moment, letting my words sink into the silence. When he speaks, it's rough and ragged. "Then what are you waiting for? If this is what you want, take it."

Take it.

He makes it sound so easy.

As if my entire career doesn't fall on this one little decision. To him, it's nothing, probably just another random fuck, but this random fuck is built on a truckload of sexual tension.

For me, there is so much riding on this.

If I give in, if I take what I've wanted for so damn long, it might be one of the most passionate moments of my life but with huge consequences awaiting me post orgasm.

As much as I would like to say I trust him, I don't. Like he said, he's ruthless, and even though I'm desperate to know what it feels like to have his lips all over my body while he's buried deep inside me, I can't take that chance.

Do I trust him not to fuck me over after? *Or to fuck over Gen?*

He's angry. Probably embarrassed, and even though it would be good at the time, I can't give in to this all-consuming passion in the off-chance that he could ruin my reputation after.

Pulling back, meeting my gaze with his, he searches my eyes and for a brief moment, I see it, that vulnerability, the uncertainty he carries deep within his soul that he doesn't dare show anyone. But I see it.

"Take me," he repeats, this time, his thumb rubs across my hipbone, the gentle touch erasing all thoughts I had of him betraying me.

No, there is no way he would do that to me.

But that doesn't mean I can allow for this to happen. I want his business, I want to work with him professionally, as a partnership, and for that to work, there is no way I can give in to my feelings even though I want nothing more than to throw caution to the wind in this moment and finally feel his lips pressed against mine.

Hating what I'm about to do, I let out a long breath and say, "I can't."

"You can't?" His brow creases, confusion written all over his face.

I shake my head. "I can't."

With my second dismissal, his face hardens. Confusion vanishes with anger quickly replacing it. He pushes off the wall and turns his back toward me, his hand tightly gripping the back of his neck.

Needing to explain, I take a step forward and say, "Rome—"

"Leave." He walks to his desk, not sparing me another glance.

"Rome, please."

Snapping, he spins on his heel and points to his door. "Fucking leave. You've fucked around with my head enough to last a lifetime."

"It's not like that."

He sits in his chair and moves his mouse, the telltale sound of his computer coming to life filling the silence.

"Please let me explain."

He scratches the side of his jaw, his movements jagged, harsh. "Either leave in the next three seconds, or your friend is fired. Don't fuck with me again, Peyton."

"Rome—"

He reaches for his phone and before I can say one more word, I quickly sprint out of his office, tears welling in my eyes.

I can't believe how horribly I screwed this entire thing up. I wish I never sent that stupid email, because not only do I think he's never going to work with me, but I have a strong feeling I hurt him, and *that* realization just about kills me.

CHAPTER SIXTEEN

ROME

"Sir, everyone is waiting for you in the conference room." Lauren peeks her head through my office door.

"I'm well aware that everyone is waiting, Lauren." I just don't give a shit at the moment.

My secretary hesitates outside the door, unsure. Not wanting to poke the bear. "Uh, are you going to *join* them?"

"Not right away. I need a few minutes to myself."

"Okay . . ." Her voice drags out the word, concerned. "Should I tell them you're in the bathroom or something?"

Why is she asking so many damn questions? She's not my babysitter; she's my assistant, for fuck's sake.

"No, Lauren. Don't tell them I'm in the bathroom, they'll think I'm taking a shit—just let them sweat it out."

"Okay." She lingers. "Do you need anything? Lunch? Water? A *chill* pill?"

Jaw ticking, I make eye contact with her, unable to muster anything but a scowl. "Want to keep your job, Lauren?"

I'm only half joking and she knows it.

She nods.

"Then leave. Now."

She scurries away, slipping out the door so fast it slams on its own, leaving me in peace.

Once she's out of sight, I lean back in my chair and pull on the collar of my dress shirt that's choking my neck. I hate it; I hate the rat race and having to find partners.

And I hate that I still look for Peyton in the damn break rooms.

Three weeks.

It's been three weeks since Peyton left. Three blasted weeks of piss-poor marketing pitches. Three weeks of no erotic and funny emails. Three weeks of zero excitement in my life. Three weeks of me acting like a goddamn moody bastard.

I don't know if it's because I miss the interaction with Peyton, if it's because I'm at a total loss with this women's line the company is launching, or if it's because I'm so goddamn hard up and itching to bury my dick inside Peyton that I'm being a "hormonal bitch" as Hunter so kindly put it.

"I can't, Rome."

I can't.

Fuck. I can still hear Peyton's words on a loop in my head. She can't. She wouldn't. How the fuck is that possible? Were her emails just a way to break me down, to show my vulnerability, to try to learn about me on a separate level so she could take me down when she was ready?

Well, it fucking worked, because I feel like I'm losing my damn mind.

She's all I think about.

I find myself rereading our messages and emails over and over again at night. I stare at her company picture, at the Whitney Houston shirt picture, at the ass picture. I'm a pathetic mess of a man who is supposed to be running a Fortune 500 company and yet, here I am, staring at a company picture of a former employee.

Pathetic.

And yet, I'm angry as fuck too. I feel betrayed, like she chipped away at all my defenses so I would share personal information with her, and then she . . . she left.

Had she planned to tell me who she was before she no longer had access to her emails? Or was she just going to finish that day and never contact me again? Why list all the things she liked about me if she was never going to talk to me again?

Why tell me she wanted to bang me if it was all a lie?

Even though it felt so very real. Raw. Honest.

She exposed me, made me want to find her . . . and then she just left. After all her talk of wanting me, she left.

I shake my head and push my hand through my hair. Shit, my emotions are running more erratic than a teenage girl's at this point.

Pushing from my desk, I straighten my tie and try to be the professional that I am.

Adjust my pants, tighten my tie, check my cufflinks, put on my jacket.

Take a deep breath.

I got this.

I make my way to my door just as Hunter comes through, wearing a red flannel shirt, jeans, and boots. "Dude, everyone is waiting for you in the conference room."

I grind down on my teeth. "I'm aware."

"Laughlin and Associates is ready to leave."

"Then let them. They need my business. I don't need them."

Hunter scoffs. "After last week's lackluster ad copy ideas, I'm going to guess you need them more than they need us."

I hate that he's right even though I won't admit that. My marketing department is lacking in creativity. If they're not copying Nike, they're coming up with grade school-type ideas that make me want to pull out every last strand of my hair.

"Well, I'm on my way now." I push past him but not before he can take me by the arm and stop me.

"You have to let it go," he whispers.

"Drop it."

"Rome. It's over. She's done with. Let it the fuck go and move on because this brooding, it's not doing anything for you or the company. She fucked with you, I get that, but you can't keep harping on it. She's not worth it."

"I'm not harping on it."

"You're sulking."

"Fuck you, Hunter." I try to pull away, but he keeps me in place.

"Prove me wrong then. Get your head out of your ass and be the Rome Blackburn I know."

Why does this motherfucker always have to be right? Drives me crazy.

Freeing my arm from his grasp, I straighten my suit and say, "Are you coming? I want you in this meeting."

He eyes me up and down, trying to gauge my mood. I put on my mask and put Peyton on the back-burner. I can't bring her into this meeting.

"Right behind you, boss."

∼

I hate that I want to know what Peyton thinks about these campaigns. I hate that with every presentation, I try to imagine what Peyton would be saying, how she would pick them apart like George said she's done with previous campaigns we've done in-house. *Yet I never knew who she was.* Not that I want to admit it, but she has an eye for this stuff and that drives me crazy because that means she was right, and the last thing I want is to admit she was right.

Although, I know she would hate all of these, just like I hate them.

There is nothing special about them. They don't highlight the line or make them stand out. They don't even touch upon the hiking, kayaking, or rock climbing portions of the clothing line, only focusing on the running aspect. Running is a drop in the pool when it comes to my company. We are outdoors adventure, not a goddamn running company.

What is so hard to understand about that?

"And that just about wraps it up," the bald man from Maxwell Agency says. "What do you think?"

It's shit.

It's all shit.

You lack creativity and basically you should retire because you have nothing special to offer to our field of work.

But I don't say that.

I take a sip of my water, swallow slowly and then cap my bottle. "Thank you for your time." I stand from my chair and button my suit jacket. Hunter follows behind me. "Thank you all for your time. We have a lot to discuss. We will get back to you shortly."

I give them all a curt nod and make a beeline for my office, Hunter hot on my heels.

The minute the glass door shuts behind us, we both let out a long, pent-up breath. Staring each other down, we both break out in a laugh at the same time, not something I partake in very often. But fuck, I can't help it.

"That was a nightmare." Hunter goes to my mini fridge and pulls out cheese sticks, hands me one and takes one for himself. "Like a living nightmare. Did those people even review their campaigns before presenting?"

I unfold the cheese stick and knock it against Hunter's —*Cheers!*—before biting off half of it. "I don't think anyone knew what the hell we were looking for in that meeting." I think back to the ideas thrown at us. "You have to admit though, the idea of matching what dog you are according to your interests in the clothing line . . . that had real potential."

"I think an intern from Buzzfeed came up with that shittastic idea. But I couldn't help but wonder—"

"What dog you would be?" I finish for him.

"I keep leaning toward huskie. Is that weird?"

"Nah, I see it." I shove the rest of my cheese stick in my mouth.

"You're totally the chihuahua."

Both my eyebrows shoot to my hairline. "You're kidding, right? No way in hell I'm the chihuahua. Pit bull, that's me."

"Yeah, keep telling yourself that." Hunter sits in one of my chairs and asks, "What are you going to do?"

I take my seat across from him. "No fucking clue. Those were the top agencies in New York City, and the best idea was a dog test." I run both my hands over my face. "Christ, are we in trouble. I blame kids show—like Paw Patrol—they're corrupting our society."

"How do you even know what that show is?"

"Farrah is obsessed. It's all she talks about when we FaceTime." Naturally, I never miss FaceTime chats with my sister Bailey, or niece Farrah. She is far too adorable.

Hunter nods. Farrah also has Hunter wrapped around her five-year-old, pint-sized fingers.

Hunter nods. "How is Bailey doing? Still have the hottest legs in town?"

"Talk about my sister like that again, see where it gets you."

He chuckles and presses both his hands behind his head, leaning back. "Well, looks like we might have to put the launch on hold, unless . . ." His voice trails off.

"Unless what?"

Why do I know where this is going?

Reaching into the pocket of his flannel shirt, he pulls out a business card and tosses it on my desk.

Without even looking, I know what it is. Through my teeth, I say, "Over my dead body am I calling her."

"Because you're a stubborn ass wipe? Great, our women's line is going to tank because you're too prideful to give her a call."

"We can do better than her."

"Really? Because I'm pretty sure I hear George cry in his office every day over the loss of Peyton. She was a huge asset to the team. We need her on this."

"She left us."

"To pursue her dreams, just like you did so many years ago, so you can't fault her on that, man." He raps his knuckles on my desk when he leans forward. "If anything, call her so we don't have to use the dog test people. That's company suicide right there."

CHAPTER SEVENTEEN

PEYTON

Thirty-six.

That's how many emails I've sent today to prospective clients, the list on my notepad glaring at me because I have thirty-two more contacts to message.

I wanted every one to be personal, tailored to each client's needs, and I've been at this table all damn day long. Pounding the pavement, as one would say.

I'm my own boss.

I work for myself.

I have my own office . . .

That's a lie—I'm at my favorite coffee shop, and thank God they haven't kicked me out for loitering, because all I've bought from them was a medium ice tea, and that was at ten o'clock this morning.

I shoot the barista another awkward smile and wave, certain she's been judging me for being cheap. But I'm self-employed. Every penny counts, and I've been counting mine all weekend.

Technically, I could afford to quit working for Roam, Inc.— but the numbers staring back at me from my bank account scare the absolute shit out of me, and I'm desperate for them to grow, not deplete.

If I don't get a contract soon, I don't know what I'll do.

No way can I go back to Roam, Inc. if this venture fails. He would never in a million years hire me back—he made that clear enough when he kicked me out of his office, and essentially out of his life.

I have to make *Fresh Minted Designs* succeed if it kills me.

I raise my water glass, the ice having melted hours ago, ring of condensation dripping onto the corner of my laptop.

"Shit." I scrub at the keyboard with the sleeve of my long-sleeved shirt, trying not to hit a key and send my entire document out of whack.

I've done that before and it's horrible. Once, I wiped down my computer monitor with Windex, turned it a sick shade of green, and had to get the entire monitor replaced.

My luck with technology is clearly abysmal.

Ugh, where is a damn napkin when I need one?

I twist my torso, elbow inadvertently taking up too much space, skimming across the surface of the tiny table, knocking into my cup, and tipping it. Water spills in one quick fall over the side, and thank God I got a medium cup and not the large one I'd wanted.

Plus, it was half empty so there's not much on the floor.

Your cup is half full, Peyton. *Half full.* Positive thoughts only.

Nonetheless, when I stand to clean it, and my foot slips, yanking the cord out of the side of my computer and earbuds from my ears, I curse.

"Goddammit!" I spin, grabbing for cords and my laptop so that doesn't come careening down, too.

Fuck my life.

I swipe a few napkins from the neighboring table, giving the girl seated there an apologetic, awkward cringe, and bend to mop up my mess. Back and forth I run the brown napkins across the tile, sopping up the puddle.

Left with only a handful of soggy napkins, an expensive pair of black tennis shoes steps into the space I'd just painstakingly dried so no one would slip if they treaded past. Tennis shoes attached to a hairy set of tan legs; masculine and long, my gaze trains on muscular calves. Knees.

Up, up, my eyes trail.

Blue mesh shorts.

Crotch. Ahem . . . a nice crotch.

"Take a picture, it'll last longer," a deep, familiar voice mocks, big hand extending.

I take it, climbing to my feet, embarrassed.

Rome.

Of course he'd see me making a mess.

God, I hate myself right now.

"Thanks." I brush the hair out of my eyes, swiping it away, face flaming red. When and if I bumped into him again, this was not the impression I would have wanted to make.

"Busy being productive, I see? That six-month clock is ticking." He's referencing to the amount of time he thinks it will take me to fail; go out of business.

Ugh, what an unsupportive *asshole*. I have tried, tried and tried, to wipe his unfair assessment to myself. If there was anyone I wanted to be in my corner, it was this man who built his own business from the ground up incredibly well. But alas . . . asshole.

Rome hands me another napkin from another table, just as I'm wiping my palms on the leg of my yoga pants. Awesome, I'm a mess today.

Our fingers touch when I take the linen from his hands, our eyes meeting briefly.

"Thanks."

He has no reply, damn him, so I sit back down, rearranging my little corner of the coffee shop, folders on the verge of falling off the table, too. I know he's probably watching me with one of his unreadable expressions, as I fumble around, spine straight, determined to ignore him.

But also win his business.

"Just come from working out?" He's decked out in athletic apparel; the man is seriously a walking advertisement for what looks hot in athletic apparel. *Just like he is in jeans. And in his gorgeous navy-blue suit.*

"Heading there after this pit stop."

"Caffeine before a workout? Isn't that frowned upon?"

What is he up to?

He's not holding a coffee, and he's making no move to head toward the cash register. Plus, him standing here, looking so damn delicious and ready to get sweaty is getting me all hot and bothered.

"Would you like to sit down?" There is one empty chair at this teeny table, and I give it a little nudge with the toe of my shoe as an offering.

Surprisingly, he takes it, pulling it the rest of the way out and parking his firm ass opposite me.

Huh. Imagine that.

His platinum eyes survey the coffee shop before settling on me, his irises steely and unnervingly astute. I have a feeling he's noticing everything about his surroundings, including me.

"Other than you dropping shit all over the floor, how's it been going?" Rome crosses his arms and leans back in the chair; not far enough to tip it, but more casual than I've ever seen him before.

I like this side of him.

He seems . . . at ease. And he's asking me questions about myself—which is so unlike him.

"It's been good." I sound way too chipper and have to tone it down a notch or he'll know I'm full of shit. "I mean, it's a little slow to start, but I'm just starting to reach out to people."

Sixty—give or take—with zero replies, because I had no leads going into this "self-employed" gig. Just a leap of faith and some money in the bank to get me started.

Obviously I don't mention this.

Rome nods. "Economy might be on an upswing, but starting from the ground up always is a disadvantage."

Now I nod—like I know what the hell he's talking about. "That's true."

"It'll get better. Just don't take the first no at face value."

"Is that so? Because you were my first no." And second no, and third. Probably my fourth no, too, if I put him on the spot right now and ask him for a chance at his marketing department.

I'm not a sadist, so I don't bother to ask.

Not yet.

We sit in silence and Rome's attention turns toward the window, out toward the street he just came from and together we watch the people outside on the busy street.

I adjust myself in my seat, waiting for him to say something.

"You're not even going to ask, are you?"

"Ask what?"

He directs his steely gaze in my direction. "About the job."

"What job?"

"The marketing consulting position."

I repeat those four words in my head, drawing a blank. "I have no idea what you're talking about. Is someone hiring? Because I'm done working in an office, you know that."

"The marketing position at Roam, Inc."

They've never had a consulting position. Of course they create one once I'm freaking gone.

"Oh."

"That's all you have to say?"

"What am I *supposed* to say?"

"You're supposed to ask if you can have it."

"But I don't know what *it* is."

"It's the new women's campaign. It needs direction and a fresh set of eyes."

Is he saying what I think he's saying? "What is it you're saying, Rome? Be specific."

In typical Rome Blackburn fashion, he's tight-lipped again, choosing his words slowly, one at a time before spitting them out like most people do.

Then. He rolls his eyes. "Just ask."

I want to. But I'm afraid to.

It's been a really long, shitty day, and I just spilled water all over my damn self, and the floor, and sent out a jillion emails that are sure to be rejected, and I don't know if I can handle him rejecting me, too.

Nonetheless, a sliver of hope springs up in my chest. It leaps when he raises his brows expectantly.

"Rome. Are you willing to give me a chance at designing a campaign for your new women's line?"

He pretends to think about it, mulling over an answer. "Maybe. I'll think about it."

Eyes widen in annoyance.

"You jerk." The words fly out of my mouth before I can stop them because—what the hell? He did that on purpose.

But the room seems to still because Rome Blackburn does something I've never seen him do in the five years I worked for him.

He laughs.

A belly laugh so deep and throaty . . . holy shit, does it sound incredible, I mean—wow.

Just. Wow.

He laughs—at me, no less—shoulders shaking a little, white teeth flashing. Perfect lips tipped into an actual smile that has me staring rudely at his mouth.

I don't know what to even say; he's that good-looking when he laughs. And the sound . . .

"The look on your face right now." He chuckles. "It's priceless."

That's because you're so damn hot, I want to say. It has nothing to do with the job he's clearly going to offer me.

"Is that why you're here? Did you come looking for me?"

His head tilts. "Possibly."

My chin notches up a bit. "Don't waste my valuable time by playing games or I'll say no based on principle."

His smile fades back into the impassive mask I'm used to seeing. "Fine. You're right. I'm here to offer you the contract."

Holy shit.

Holy shit.

Breathe, Peyton, breathe.

Why am I so uncool? Why can't I hide my emotions and feelings better, because right now I want to leap out of my chair and do fist pumps in the middle of the coffee shop—and I have no idea how much the contract is even worth.

I want it.

I need it.

The job I mean—not sex.

Did I say sex? Why would I be thinking about that? This is a business meeting, *clearly.*

"So, let me get this straight; you're here to offer me the contract. You came here, hoping to reel me in." I'm baiting him to see what he'll say.

Rome scoffs. "Let's not get ahead of ourselves."

"Then why are you here?"

His lips purse. "You need a job."

"Oh, you're a philanthropist now, helping the newly unemployed and gainfully climbing their way to the top from the ground up? How magnanimous of you. No thanks, I'll pass."

"Suit yourself." His mouth says the words, but his ass doesn't leave the chair.

My eyes narrow. "Why are you doing this? Why can't you just suck up your pride and admit that you need me, and that's why you're here?" I take a deep breath and collect myself. "You've got a lot of pride, but I do, too. And it's not going to allow me to take a job that you couldn't even bring yourself to offer me. I refuse to force your hand—so if you need me—like I suspect you do, then now is the time to say it."

I give my head a little tip. *Go on*, I encourage him as if he's a child. *Say it, don't be shy.*

Mr. Grumpypants is slow on the uptake, but he considers my words. I can see them spinning in his brain, his jaw ticking and moving as he thinks. Maybe he's even grinding his teeth a little. It's so hard to tell.

"Peyton." Just my name.

One word.

"Yes, Mr. Blackburn. Sir." I give him my sweetest smile, knowing he hates being addressed as either.

He moves his jaw back and forth, and then it hits me hard in the chest. "You need me more."

Shit.

Can he see the desperation in my eyes, the nerves shaking my hands? Does he know I've contacted company after company looking for business without a response?

Either way, I'm pulling an Elizabeth Bennet and putting on my *too-proud* pantaloons.

"Maybe"—I tilt my chin in the air—"but I'm willing to turn you down just to prove a point. You're not willing to sacrifice your new line. That's why you're here."

I hold my breath, my boldness getting the best of me.

Boldness or stubborn personality?

Maybe a little bit of both.

His lips thin into a contemplative line as he lets out a long, irritated breath. "You really know how to push my buttons, do you know that?"

"I do." I do indeed. Don't smile. *Don't you dare smile.*

Rome's nostrils flare. "I'd like to offer you the marketing position for the women's outdoor collection."

"Me?" I demure.

"Jesus Christ, could you—"

"I'm joking. Relax. Man, you're wound up so tight."

He's not amused, and pushes himself up out of the wooden

chair across from me, rising to his full height. "I'll have Lauren email you the details."

I stand too, thinking it would be a good idea to end our impromptu meeting with a handshake.

I stick my hand out.

He stares at it.

I wiggle my fingers until he takes the hint, and slides his palm against mine. Pumps my hand once and releases it, stepping back to leave—but not before a thousand bolts of electricity shoot through my entire body.

Whoa.

He shivers.

"Uh, just one more thing before you go."

He turns toward me. "What's that?"

"I . . . work remotely, so I wouldn't be coming into the office unless it was for meeting with the entire marketing staff. I think creative juices flow better in a creative environment."

"Places like"—he gestures around—"this?"

I grin. He's such an ass. "Exactly."

"So you'll be taking meetings here, with whom exactly?"

Whom. He's so adorably stiff.

"Why . . . I'll be taking my meetings with *you.*"

CHAPTER EIGHTEEN

ROME

"How'd the meeting go? Did you lure her in?"

"I didn't need to lure her in; she was happy to have the opportunity."

Hunter laughs—he knows I'm full of complete crap. "Bullshit. She probably told you to fuck off."

Not in those exact words, but yeah. Basically. "It did take some convincing."

"Well, what the hell happened?" Hunter pops a salsa-coated chip in his mouth.

With my tequila pinched between my fingers, I lean back in my chair and think back to my conversation with Peyton.

She was a hot mess, knocking drinks over, pulling out her cords while tripping everywhere—but fuck if her ass framed in those black yoga pants didn't do something to me.

I was reminded just how much I want to *bang* her.

How much I want to shut that sassy mouth of hers with my lips.

How much I want to pin her against the wall and pop open one of her godforsaken blouses just to finally see what's underneath.

I might have been pissed about the emails; I might have been pissed that I succumbed to admitting that Roam, Inc. needs her help, and I might hate that I still want her just as badly as I did before—but what's making all of this tolerable is the knowledge that she needs me, too.

She needs *me*.

It's a heady aphrodisiac. I wish I could bottle it up and sell that shit along with my tents, gear, and travel products.

Peyton needs me. I could see it in her eyes as she studied me warily; the concern, the disillusionment, the overcompensation. I saw past the smoke she was trying to throw at me—she could try and sell the fact that her life is *so much* better after she's left Roam, Inc., but I fucking know better.

Her business is already tanking and needs me.

A small part of me wanted to teach her a lesson by getting up from the table and walking away—not offering her the job at all. *"I'm willing to turn you down just to prove a point. You're not willing to sacrifice your new line. That's why you're here."*

I hate that she's right.

Annoys the absolute shit out of me.

"I'm waiting," Hunter singsongs, taking a sip of his giant frozen margarita, rimmed with sugar rather than salt. It's a good thing the guy tests out adventure equipment for a living.

"What?"

"You were about to tell me how Peyton told you to fly a kite, and how you had to beg."

"When was the last time I begged for something?"

Hunter pauses, giving it some serious thought. Snaps his fingers. "Eighth grade—you begged me to call Savannah Goodrich and pretend to be you, so she'd leave you alone at the dance."

"Savannah Goodrich was a clingy bitch."

"Dude, speaking of bitchy; you were so whiny."

"Whatever—we were thirteen, let it go. I don't remember you calling anyone pretending to be me."

Which is a crock full of shit; I remember it like it was yesterday—me, being afraid of a teenage girl that had a huge crush on me, and not wanting her to follow me around the middle school dance. I begged Hunter to call her and tell her I had a wart on my lip that was highly contagious and didn't want her to see it. Spent the entire rest of the dance hiding in the shadows like a pussy, because I was too chickenshit to dance with her.

Hunter and I were always doing crap like that—swapping places when we could and causing mischief. It's a good thing we were neighbors and best friends, and *not* identical twins, because, Jesus, we'd have gotten into so much trouble.

I fiddle with a corn chip, breaking off one end and popping it in my mouth, chewing to buy myself some time.

"You're being really weird about this," Hunter grumbles. "I have a right to know. It's my company, too."

God, I hate when he's right.

"Fine. I found her at a coffee shop. She needed a job, I offered her one, end of story."

Hunter scoffs mid-sip, shooting strawberry margarita into the air. "Stop acting so blasé about it. We both know you had to convince her."

"Not true." Nope. She forced my hand by being a hard-ass, because that is the sassy, strong-willed woman she is. And with every fucking unrelenting word from her mouth, I wanted to kiss her. Devour her. *And I am not telling Hunter that.* "Technically I could have figured a marketing plan out without her help." Eventually.

I casually take a sip of my drink while Hunter shoves his mouth full of chips.

"God, do you actually believe your own bullshit? You know we can't do it without her." A smile plays at his lips as he chews. "When is our first meeting with her?"

I cock a brow. "What do you mean, *our*?"

"I have skin in this game, too. I want to make sure we're on the right track, keep you in line."

The last thing I want is him meddling. "I can handle it."

What is Hunter up to?

He's never interested in the marketing campaigns—I can't recall one damn meeting he's attended. What he is interested in is tents; he has some weird obsession with the innovation of new tent designs, and whenever we come out with a new style, he wants to be a part of every aspect of it.

He's the one that tests them all out. He has no hand in how they're advertised, produced, or sold.

That's my area of expertise.

Hunter shakes his head and brushes his hands off into the black napkin resting on his lap. "From here, it doesn't seem like you have a handle on anything. It actually seems like you're drowning." He makes a fish face. "Blub. Blub. Blub."

"I'm not drowning. My marketing department is incompetent."

"*Our* marketing department."

I roll my eyes.

He points his rigid finger at me. "This is all on you, boss, I'm out in the field pitching tents." He pops another chip loaded with salsa in his mouth. "I have her info, I'll set up a meeting."

"Please don't."

"But I'm gonna." He rubs his hands together. "I've been bored, and this is gonna be so fun."

Why do I get the feeling this is going to be more than a meeting about a women's line?

"Nice place," Hunter says, looking around and pulling out a wooden chair in the back of the coffee house, away from everyone else. "Very modern with the urban country décor. Oh look." He points behind me with a giant smile. "Shiplap."

Jesus H Christ.

I drag my hand over my face; this is not going to end well.

Sliding into the booth next to Hunter, he scowls down at the seat.

"What the hell are you doing?" he asks, eyeing me up and down.

What is his problem? "Taking a seat, what the hell does it look like?"

"If you sit there, it's going to look like we're one of those weird couples who sit next to each other rather than across."

"The fact that you think we'd even make a decent couple repulses me. You're not my type."

He's nonplused. "I'm just saying; I hate those people. They make me sick."

"We have to sit next to each other; this is a meeting. When she gets here, she'll sit there." I point to the seat across from us. "And we can talk easier."

"Well, she's not here, and we both look like idiots." He motions to the other side of the table. "Sit over there for fuck's sake."

"Now it just looks like we're having a lover's squabble." I laugh as he nudges me with his hip, trying to edge me off the booth bench.

"You think I want a woman to see me jammed in a booth with you? I'll lose all credibility."

Whatever. I'm not in the mood to argue with him, so I scoot out, taking the seat in the corner, placing my iPad on the table in time to see Peyton rounding the corner from the small entry of the coffee house.

Her dark, shoulder-length hair is wavy and mussed today—as if she spent the morning on the beach, soaking up the salty air. Long, summery skirt in a neutral shade of gray, it hugs her swaying hips. Her tight tank top is gray; necklace, silver and hanging between her breasts.

I bet those tits are perfect.

Goddammit, she's so hot.

And those lips? They're glossy and natural, shimmering in the sunlight streaming through the window, begging me to do naughty things with them, or maybe I'm just a horndog knowing she wanted to sleep with me.

Christ.

Scanning the coffee house, Peyton spots Hunter and me in the back, a slow smile curving her lips when we make eye contact. Then her gaze flickers to Hunter.

She gives us a curt wave before making her way toward us.

It isn't until she's seated beside me, and the waft of her citrus perfume hits me. I should have stayed on Hunter's side of this tiny table.

I'm a fucking moron.

Hunter—that dickhead—stretches one of his jean-covered legs over the spare chair, forcing Peyton to fill the space next to me. As she slides in, her firm little rear end doing a shimmy to get comfortable, I shoot my best friend a look that only garners a perverted wiggle of his eyebrows.

Asshole.

God, I hate him sometimes.

"Well hello, boys." Peyton's greeting is flirty and cute, and her slim shoulder brushes mine as she situates herself. Squirms her ass. The last time I'd been this close to her was four weeks ago. Christ. Just thinking about how soft her skin had been as I'd grazed my nose and lips over her neck and cheeks. How much I'd wanted her to turn her head a fraction so I could taste her lips. Every part of me—and I mean *every* part of me—was tuned into her body. The softness. Her scent. *And yet she hadn't taken the chance I'd thrown at her.* Get it together, Blackburn. Business. Meeting. "Hunter, I'm so glad you could make it. I would love to get your perspective on the line."

He drapes his arm over the empty chair. "Mr. Tightpants here threw a mighty stink about it, too. Went on and on about how he wanted to spend time with you alone, didn't you, grumpkins?"

What?

"No, I didn't." I sound like a freaking child and clear my throat. Starting over, I use a more even tone. "I did *not* say that."

"Well, maybe not those words exactly, but you did insist I stay home." He takes a slow sip of the ice water in front of him. "I think he has a crush on you, Peyton."

"Hunter," I snap, because *Jesus Christ, why is he like this? Why is he talking?* "Be a goddamn professional."

The bastard shrugs. "When have I ever been professional?" If he had gum in his mouth, he would have snapped it just to piss me off.

We stare each other down, silently communicating:

I'm going to kill you.

No, you're not. I'm your best friend.

I don't care if you're my best friend. You're a dead man.

You like her. Admit it.

Never.

Peyton taps her pen on the table like a judge bangs his grovel. "Sorry to disrupt this stare down, or pissing match, or whatever it is you two are doing—but I think we should get to work. It's seven, and this place closes at nine . . ."

From the corner of my eye, I catch a blush on her cheek when she pushes her silky hair behind her delicate ear.

Huh, have I ever noticed that she wears earrings?

And from this angle, her lips are fuller than I expected, her eyelashes long, fluttering open and closed as she sifts through her papers.

My eyes travel down the column of her neck, smooth and long, the perfect length for me to explore. Her collarbones are prominent, guiding my eyes to the tops of her breasts.

I shift in my seat.

From where I'm sitting, the neckline of her shirt is low enough for me to ogle the lace of her white bra supporting her perfectly sized tits. A handful. That's all I need.

I bet her nipples—

"Yo, lover boy. Her eyes are up here, and the ad campaign is on the table," Hunter says, a nod to the table, a giant smile on his smug face as I'm caught red-handed.

I adjust in my seat, sit farther from Peyton, and take in the ad copy she's spread across the table.

Fuck, they're good.

They're so much better than what we've received from every other agency, including our in-house team.

The colors are vivid and strong, yet feminine. The typeface bold and inspiring, and the photographs she chose from the photo shoot really show off the angle we're going for; active wear for *all* types of women.

"So I was hoping to set Roam, Inc. apart from all the other outdoor companies by highlighting its best attributes." She turns to me and wiggles her eyebrows. Fuck, she's cute. "Meaning, look at all these gorgeous women." She lays down picture after picture. "What do all these women have in common?"

"They're real," I answer, noticing every shape and size.

"Exactly. They're real. It was one of the things I loved about this line at first. How you showcased women from every walk of life: old, young, short, tall, curvy, petite. You covered all your bases and put them in all different outdoor gear highlighting their best features. When I saw the pictures for this photo shoot, I kept thinking, this was a social media campaign I was excited to work on because the possibilities of promoting were endless, but along the way, I feel like you lost the vision. You put it on hold, lost momentum, and now that it's time, you're at a loss."

Nailed it. That's exactly what happened.

"But," she continues. "Not only can I bring this ad campaign back to life from the dead, we can have one hell of a launch."

Turning away from me, bent over enough on the bench that her pert little ass is directed right in my line of sight, Peyton digs through her bag on the floor.

I take that moment to observe her backside—the same backside that is still the wallpaper on my computer. Firm and heart-shaped, begging for my fingers to press into it. Squeeze.

From the other side of the table, Hunter coughs loudly, covering his mouth and kicking me under the table like he did when we were in middle school.

Busted again.

He shakes his head at me, disgusted. "You really do need a babysitter," he hisses just as she's sitting back up.

For the next half hour, Peyton presents us with multiple campaign ideas—all varying slightly, but centering around the main focus: outdoor adventures for *every* woman.

Novice. Intermediate. Expert.

Stay-at-home moms and cross-trainers. Hikers, backpackers, and someone wanting to walk in their neighborhood.

I don't know how she managed it, but the whole thing is fucking *brilliant* and it chaps my ass that I didn't think of any of this myself.

Or that no one else on my payroll did either.

Smacking his hands together, Hunter stands—makes a giant production out of stretching his hands over his head—yawns, and makes an audible sound. Why is he so damn dramatic all the time?

"Damn, this is some good stuff, Peyton." Another fake yawn." I'm sure the boss already has which one he wants to choose in his head. I approve all of them."

Not that it matters.

His approval means jack shit to me right now, especially after the half-assed performance reports he recently turned in. He can have an opinion when he gets *his* work done properly.

He checks his watch—a Roam, Inc. brand with thick, water-proof leather wristband that can be submerged up to one hundred feet—and declares, "Well, kids, playtime is over for Uncle Hunter. I have to get going. I have a dinner date that I don't want to miss, but first I should take a nap." He wiggles his eyebrows and taps the tabletop. "Nice work, Peyton. Should have hired you for market-ing, not all that social media bullshit. Now we have to outsource you and really pay you the big bucks."

He gives us a two-finger salute, clicks his heels, and takes off.

Smug bastard.

And because he left early, Peyton and I are stuck sitting awkwardly next to each other, on the same side of the table. We look like *that* couple—if we were a couple.

Avoiding my eyes, Peyton takes a dainty sip of water. Caps the bottle. Sets it down.

Clears her throat.

Fingers a few pictures that have been laid out on the table in neat little rows, and finally says, "Can you say something please? I'm kind of dying over here."

I scratch the side of my jaw, my stubble coarsely scraping my fingertips. "Are you looking for more compliments?"

She turns toward me, vulnerability in her eyes, my approval important to her. She is beautiful, extremely talented, witty, and dynamic, yet *my* approval is important to her.

"I'm looking to see if I did a satisfactory job. Did I present you with something you would feel confident using? Did I give you any kind of idea that you could be ex*cited* about?"

Excited. Just the way she says it . . .

Hell, I'm *excited* about the tank top she's wearing, how I've seen the cup of her lacy bra five times in half an hour. Yeah, I counted. And yeah, I'm excited.

That she's here and that she brought me a proposal we can definitely work with.

The campaign is going to be amazing.

Still, I cannot help giving her a hard time. "I'm going to have to think about it."

She blinks a few times, shock registering across her face.

"Oh." More blinking. "Yes, of course."

She slowly and methodically begins gathering the materials laid out on the table, gently placing each photograph in a folder labeled "visuals." Takes a few hand-drawn commercial boards and slides them into a leather portfolio. The papers go in yet another folder, along with a few articles from our competitors and their ad campaigns geared toward women.

When she's done collecting her materials, Peyton rises from the table, too, slinging her bag over her shoulder and hands me a blue folder.

My fingers take it, keeping my gaze fixed on her down-turned head, all confidence washed away in seconds.

I desperately want to tip her chin up, force her to look at me, to see that I'm just playing hardball, but I don't. This is business, and even though I'm going to easily hire her and take her on, she needs to learn not everything comes so easily. If she wants to succeed, then she needs to see this side of the business, the desperation.

We scoot out of the tight corner and make our way out of the coffee house where we both pause to say goodbye.

Like the professional she's trying to portray, she holds out her hand to me. "Thank you for letting me present to you today, Mr. Blackburn."

Her formality makes me smile. At least she hasn't *sir*'d me tonight.

I take her hand in mine, the feeling of her palm soft and slender, the perfect fit against my large hand. "Thank you for taking the time to come up with these ideas. I'll get back to you soon."

She nods and swallows hard. I can see she wants to say something else, but she holds back, tamping down that wild tongue. *That's my girl.* Shit. No. Not my girl. Professional.

Instead, she puts a few feet of distance between us. "I look forward to hearing from you, Mr. Blackburn."

Taking a step forward, cutting down the distance, I pinch her chin between my fingers and force her to look at me head-on. "Call me, Rome. I like the way it sounds coming from your mouth." *More than I should.*

With one last look in her eyes, I spin on my heel and make my way toward my brownstone. I'm turned on and fucking horny as hell. I have some business to take care of, and it doesn't have to deal with Roam, Inc.

CHAPTER NINETEEN

PEYTON

I can't breathe.

Even three hours later, tucked under my sheets, the meeting long over with, I still can't breathe.

Why weren't they sitting next to each other? Why did I have to sit next to Rome?

When I walked into the coffee house and saw the open chair next to Rome, I knew I was going to have one hell of a time getting through my presentations being that close to him.

And I was right.

I could feel his gaze blazing up and down my body, those steady, sure eyes focused in on the way my chest rose and fell with every strangled breath I took. I could feel his body language angled in my direction, and when he took the pictures from me, the light graze of his fingers across mine, innocent and yet so sinful, I felt it to my bones.

Professionalism? *What's that?* I can barely remember if I gave a good presentation or not, because I was so wired over being that damn close to Rome that I couldn't concentrate. I fumbled over my words, I dropped papers on the floor, and every time Hunter chuckled, I became more and more frantic.

It's probably why Rome didn't jump at my ideas. I was a hot mess. *So. Professional.* Not.

Sighing, I throw my head back on my pillow. God, I stayed up late every night for the past three nights practicing my pitch, making sure everything was perfect, and then I go and screw it up because Rome's cologne frazzled my mind.

He has to think about it.

I don't blame him. If I sat through my presentation, I'm pretty sure I would be just as contemplative as he was.

And here I thought the job was in the bag.

I bite my bottom lip as tears start to prickle at the corner of my eyes. This is stupid. I shouldn't be crying. I gave him one hell of a presentation, yes, I might have been nervous, but my ideas were solid and that's all that should matter.

Feeling a little more confident, I pick up my phone from my nightstand and open my email, hoping to see an email from Rome telling me how amazing I am.

But when there are ZERO new messages in my inbox, I once again become self-conscious.

Well that confidence was short-lived.

If I wasn't so set in stone on staying in my bed and never getting out of it again due to a vast amount of humiliation I had to endure today, I would walk over to my freezer and pull out a pint of ice cream.

Maybe there is something good on TV to take my mind off things. But the remote . . . it's so far away, on the other side of my bed.

Succumbing to my laziness, I pick up my phone again just as I receive a text.

From Rome.

Butterflies take flight in my stomach, sending my body into a nervous frenzy. Sitting up and positioning myself against the head-board of my bed, I read his text.

Rome: *Question about your presentation tonight.*

Oh God, okay, be on point. Quick with your response but smart.

Peyton: *Hopefully I have an answer for you.*

I wait as the little dots dance right away.

Rome: *Were you nervous?*

That's the question he wanted to ask about my presentation tonight?

Leave it to Rome to call me out on my nerves. He could never let anything go. He observes, assesses, and then lets it be known what he sees, never sugarcoating. It's one of the reasons I respect him so much as a CEO but also one of the reasons why I want to smack that handsome face of his, especially when his assessment is pointed in my direction.

It's not like I can lie to him, because he already knows the answer so I decide to be real. Maybe he'll respect that, an honest-to-God answer.

Peyton: *Yes, beyond nervous.*

Rome: *Why?*

Why? Is he serious?

Well, besides the fact that I not only made it known many times that I wanted to bang him, or how he is the most gorgeous man I've ever seen, I want to earn his respect. I want to impress him. I want him to see the worth in me.

Peyton: *Despite the obvious?*

Rome: *What's the obvious?*

Ugh, he's going to make me say it, isn't he? Knowing Rome, he is. He's making me work for this job. I know he is, so I might as well give him all the truth.

Peyton: *The obvious: the way I so blatantly confessed my attraction toward you far beyond a professional level.*

Rome: *Ahhh, that.*

Peyton: *Yeah, that. It's kind of hard to be taken seriously when I not so eloquently asked you multiple times to bend me over your desk.*

Rome: *It was flattering . . . and entertaining.*

Peyton: *Moving on.*

Rome: *Why else were you nervous?*

I nibble on the inside of my cheek and type out a response before I can chicken out.

Peyton: *Because I respect you, your work ethic, what you've been able to create with Roam, Inc. I value your opinion, and since I'm out on my own now, I don't know . . . I hate to say it, but I'm kind of seeking your validation.*

I squeeze my eyes shut when I send the message, a little embarrassed but also slightly relieved from my confession. If there is one thing that was helpful with our almost-daily emails, it helped me to be honest with Rome. And I think that's a good thing. I actually think he prefers complete honesty rather than sniveling and pandering to his every quip and mood.

Rome: *Seeking validation from someone else? That's how you get yourself into trouble with your business, Peyton. Never seek validation from someone else, only yourself.*

Rome: *Be confident in your work, in your business model, in the product you've created. Your confidence will extend to your clients, and they will hire you because of it.*

Who is this man right now? Is this really Rome Blackburn giving me sound advice about my business? I know it has to be, but it's doing funny things to my stomach, flipping it upside down and inside out.

And that's when it hits me.

He cares.

He might put on a steely, impenetrable mask, but past his fortress of a façade, there is a beautifully kind man beneath it all. Just as I suspected, but I never thought I would truly see it in person or be on the receiving end of this side of him.

Peyton: *That's some really sweet advice, Rome.*

Rome: *Don't let it get around. I need my employees to fear me.*

Peyton: *Your secret is safe with me.*

I pause, wondering if it's appropriate to ask him about my

presentation. We're being pretty honest with each other right now, the usual wall erected between us on a temporary hiatus.

Before he can text back, I send him a second text.

Peyton: *Be honest with me, did any of my ideas tickle your fancy?*

Rome: *Tickle my fancy? Not sure about that, but yeah, I was . . . impressed.*

Oh.

My.

God.

My heart rate picks up, galloping inside of my chest at a relentless pace as his words sink in.

He was impressed. I, Peyton Marie Lévêque, impressed Rome Blackburn. It's almost as if all the cosmic forces lined up and shined down upon me, giving me this small moment, this small victory.

I impressed him, and I know I shouldn't care what he has to say, but I can't help but care a little. He's a talented titan in the CEO world and to be able to impress someone of his caliber, well, it feels freaking good.

Rome: *Let me guess, you're doing a happy dance right about now.*

I laugh out loud and shake my head while I type.

Peyton: *No, I'm actually trying to pick up my jaw off the floor.*

Rome: *Are you really that shocked?*

Peyton: *Uh, yeah. You're . . . wait, should we be having this conversation through text?*

Rome: *Probably not.*

Peyton: So . . .

Rome: *Have dinner with me tomorrow night. We can discuss everything.*

Why does the word "everything" feel like it carries so much weight?

Peyton: *Dinner as in business partners?*

Rome: *Yes, what else kind of dinner would it be?*

I don't know, one where you pull my pants down and show me

the good stuff, right there in the middle of the busy dining room, waitstaff passing water glasses over our writhing bodies.

Peyton: *Just making sure.*

Rome: *Do you like Italian?*

Peyton: *Oui, oui monsieur!*

Rome: *That's French.*

Peyton: *Eh, close enough. Send me the details tomorrow morning?*

Rome: *I'll have Lauren send you everything.*

My smile falls for a brief second hearing about Lauren's involvement, but then again, this is business, and that's it. No need to make this into anything other than that.

Peyton: *Sounds great. I look forward to it.*

Rome: *Okay. I have some more reports to go over. I'll see you tomorrow.*

Peyton: *Don't work too hard, Rome. And thank you . . . for the chance, the opportunity to talk to you and Hunter—for everything.*

Rome: *No need to thank me. You did your job. That's more than enough. Good night, Peyton.*

I can't wipe the smile off my face as I scoot down in my bed, phone to chest, a new opportunity on the horizon.

Not to mention, I get to have dinner with Rome tomorrow night. It might be all business, but that doesn't mean I can't look drop-dead gorgeous for the meeting.

After all, the saying goes: dress to impress. What they don't tell you is *who* to impress.

CHAPTER TWENTY

ROME

"...So you see this image here? She's tired, but she's determined, right? And you know just by looking at her she's going to . . . Rome? Are you paying attention?"

I'm not.

Not at all.

In fact, I haven't heard a damn word Peyton has said since she walked into the restaurant tonight, shiny, black leather portfolio tucked under her arm. All legs and tan skin, the red dress draped on her body isn't normal business meeting attire for several reasons:

1. It's blood-red. Sexy.
2. It's tight.
3. It shows off way too much cleavage to be professional.

She looks smoking hot, and it's distracting as hell.

And now her brows are raised, and she's eyeballing me expectantly like I'm supposed to spout off some profound bullshit about the picture she's holding between two fingers.

Her nails are dark gray.

I peel my eyes away and stare at the photograph.

Some lady at a sink, wearing our workout gear and staring determined out the kitchen window, like she's going to conquer the mountain in the distance once she's finished her errands.

"Yeah, I'm paying attention."

Not.

Peyton smiles, a dimple I'd never noticed popping up in her cheek. "You liar. Prove it."

I think fast on my feet. "Something blah blah that mountain looks high? That woman is obviously going to need hiking equipment."

For a brief moment, Peyton doesn't say anything—just stares at me, the wineglass in her hand poised halfway to her parted lips. But then, she laughs.

Tips back her head and laughs. "You're funny when you want to be, do you know that?"

I am? Since *when*? "No one thinks I'm funny."

"I do." She takes a sip of wine and studies me over the rim of the glass.

"You're obviously drunk."

"Not at all."

"Easily amused?"

"Nope. I'm a tough crowd."

She is not—this woman laughs at everything. "Well, you should be tested, because you obviously have a concussion."

Peyton laughs again, the wine bubbling in her throat, her red, pouty lips smiling. White teeth. Dimple. Dark hair.

She's the poster girl for a classy, sexy, girl-next-door, all rolled into one.

I fiddle with my knife. "Do you want to take a break from discussing this and order an appetizer or something?"

She looks surprised by my suggestion. "Sure. It's not like you were paying attention anyway." Her eyes don't roll, but they're close. "And can I remind you, this dinner meeting was your idea —not mine."

"I like to eat real food, not nibble on coffee shop rabbit bait in the middle of the day." Scones and croissants and shit. "We weren't getting anything done at that place, either."

Peyton's laughter is louder this time, and she covers her mouth with her linen napkin, remembering herself. And her manners.

We're at a really nice fucking place—my favorite steak restaurant for surf and turf; she confessed to loving lobster to Lauren when my assistant called to confirm the date and time. So Italian was thrown out the window. The atmosphere is darker, all the tables lit with small lamps, the house lights dim. Hunter green leather booths and mahogany wood, this place is classy and sophisticated and *not at all* suitable for the meeting Peyton and I are pretending through the motions of having.

"We accomplished so much at that first meeting. What are you even talking about?" Her pert little nose is wrinkled and confused and I want to tap it with my finger.

Jesus Christ. What the hell is happening to me?

I don't flirt—I'm terrible at it.

I don't laugh or crack jokes.

I work and work then sleep and eat. Then get up and work some more, occasionally getting out of the city to do what I originally set out to do: enjoy nature. The outdoors. Which I rarely see anymore, locked inside my office, in the concrete jungle of a city where I made my home.

Peyton is studying me thoughtfully, head tilted. "Wanna tell me what's on your mind? You look lost in your own thoughts right now."

If she could get out of my headspace, that would be fanfucking-tastic, thanks.

I pick a slice of bread out of the basket on the table, and pull it in half, setting one piece on the bread plate. The other half I take a bite of. Chew.

"I'm in a very weird place right now, both personally and professionally, I guess." I cannot believe I'm admitting this to anyone, least of all her. "It just occurred to me now that I haven't done anything active outside in . . . Christ. I don't even know."

"What would you do first if you could?"

"Hike a mountain." I used to do that a lot back home, though nothing on a grand scale.

"Which one?"

"I don't know—nothing like Everest if that's what you're thinking."

We both laugh, the sounds mingling.

"Wasn't exactly thinking Everest, more on the lines of maybe something in the Adirondacks."

I ponder that, twisting my water glass on the table. "I love it up there."

"Let me guess, you have a cabin there."

A smile tugs at my lips. "Maybe." And I wish I could take you there, someday. You and me. Mountains. My cabin. Solitude.

Nudity.

She rolls her eyes but then scoots forward as if she's about to tell a secret. "Do you let contracted employees stay in the cabin for free?" She wiggles her eyebrows, looking adorably cute.

A belly laugh bubbles out of me as my head tilts back, humor hitting me square in the chest. "Only if they do a good job for me."

She rubs her hands together. "Then I'll start planning my little jaunt now, because I know I'm going to blow your socks off with this campaign."

Blow.

Wish she would blow something other than my socks off right about now.

I shift in my seat, my eyes glancing at her cleavage again as she takes a drink. So goddamn full. What I wouldn't give to pull her across this table, unzip the back of her dress, and take her nipples in my mouth, right here in the dining room of this fancy-ass restaurant. I wouldn't care about indecent exposure. I would only care about how she tastes, how her hardened nipples feel in my mouth.

I clear my throat. "Have you always had an eye for graphic design?" I ask her, stuffing the other piece of bread in my mouth and chewing slowly, giving her time to answer.

"Yes. Well, yes and no. It wasn't my major or anything in college, but I did like glitter and design growing up." She smiles at the table for a brief moment, biting her lip before raising her head again. "I thought I'd be an architect, but I wasn't great at math. So I had to change my major, ended up with a business degree. Draw in my free time, photography and all that jazz."

"So. The creative type."

"Sure, I guess."

"Is your apartment all bright and colorful?"

"Is that how you picture it?"

I study her. She's not the flighty type, just . . . happy. "No."

"What do you picture?"

I quiet, thinking. I picture her naked, standing in the middle of an all-white room, her tits full and aching for my touch, her long legs ready and willing to wrap around my body.

But I don't say that. "I imagine your place to be like the Pottery Barn threw up inside your entire living space. Just trendy vomit everywhere."

"What." Peyton chokes. "Okay fine. It's true. That is what my place looks like, so sue me. Sue me for liking trendy, beige things." She shoots me a sidelong glance, finger trailing the rim of her wineglass. "What about you? What does your place look like?"

"Not like Pottery Barn barfed inside of it."

"Want me to venture a guess?"

I lean back in my seat. "Sure. Have at it."

"Well . . ." She begins. "I see lots of black—to match your mood. Lots of cold spaces. Concrete floors. High ceilings—and stainless steel. You bought it that way and haven't decorated any of it yourself. Someone came and did it for you, and you hate it, but it was too expensive to change, so you left it."

What. The. Fuck.

Her brow goes up. "I'm right, aren't I?"

I cannot help but laugh—a loud, booming laugh that goes along with the hand I whack onto the table. That's how fucking surprised I am that she has me pegged.

"Yeah. You're totally right."

"How right am I?"

"That's my place, down to the concrete floors." Which I hate because the entire damn apartment is always freezing. And if I'd had known, I would have put in carpet. "I have to wear slippers every damn day no matter how warm it is outside."

"You. Wear slippers?"

"I do."

"What do they look like?"

"Guess."

"Um . . . black leather with Sherpa insoles?"

"Pfft," I scoff. "Hardly. They're grizzly bear slippers. Hunter gave them to me and they're badass." Every time I take a step, the bear opens his mouth and looks like he's snarling.

"Is that some joke? Or do you seriously have teddy bear slippers?"

"I did not say teddy bear—I said grizzly."

"Same thing, kind of."

"No, they are not the same thing."

Peyton holds her thumb and forefinger together with one hand, squeezes one eye shut. "Lil' bit."

I can't tell if she's teasing me, or flirting with me. Either way, I like it.

She takes a sip of wine and looks away, biting her bottom lip.

Definitely flirting.

Red, sexy dress. Red lips. High heels.

Flirting.

There are papers still on the table, and I motion to them. "Maybe we should clear these out of the way so nothing gets spilled on them."

"Oh. Good idea."

We make quick work of cleaning them up, sliding everything into Peyton's black leather portfolio. It's smart and expensive, and looks great with her entire look tonight. Classy, sexy, and professional.

"I'm curious. Why New York? Why not somewhere else for the company, like . . . Colorado or even Chicago, where they have kettles and moraines? I know you initially said it was because of your parents living in Buffalo, but you could have changed your mind by now."

It's a good question, one almost everyone asks. Especially the journalists who've done stories on me in the past. Yet, coming from Peyton, I'm more relaxed to talk about it. She actually wants to know . . . me. That was something so surprising about the emails we sent each other. She seems to want to know more. Even now that I know who LSY is. It's no longer a mysterious game, but it's . . . friendship? "It's New York City. This is where Wall Street is, and big business—and that's what I always wanted my business to be. Big. Publicly traded. I didn't think I could do that anywhere else."

"I see. And now?"

"Now I *know* I could have." But now it's too late.

I'm here. The business is here.

The only thing I can do is open more branches in more rural locations—like Colorado Springs, or Vermont. Or Washington State.

Someday it will happen—just not right now.

And right now, I don't want to talk about it anymore. I want to talk about her.

"What made you decide to start your own brand?"

She sits back in her seat mimicking my pose. "Oh. Brand . . . I like the sound of that. A lot." A drink of her water hits her lips. "Don't get me wrong, I loved working for you—probably a little too much. But I was great at what I did, and honestly, no one wanted to promote me because of that. If that makes sense."

Yeah, it makes sense. You get someone good and you want to keep them right where they are.

Sucks that she quit though, when I could have used her somewhere else.

"I do miss seeing you around the office." Her words surprise me, and I try not to show it.

"What are you talking about? We barely saw each other."

"Oh, I saw you plenty." Peyton chuckles knowingly. "You just didn't notice."

"When?" I hardly went down to the lower floors.

"I don't know if you noticed, but I'm friends with Lauren. She and I did lunch a lot, and I'd grab her, and see you. Always so serious." She pulls a grumpy face. "Always at your desk."

"I never saw you." How is that even possible when she's all I can think about now? When she's all I seem to see?

"No. Your head was always down."

It's not down right now. It's up, and my eyes are staring straight at her. And under the glowing lights of this dim restaurant, she's really fucking pretty.

If I'm being honest with myself, I'm really fucking disappointed she won't be in the office on Monday, because the first thing I would do is raise my head and stare at her when she came to collect my assistant for lunch.

Maybe even throw her a flirty wink.

Would I?

"You're doing it again," she teases.

"Doing what?"

"You're lost in thought."

Why the hell do I keep doing that? It's so unlike me. It's unnerving and rattling me just a little. I like being in control of my thoughts and actions, and Peyton is making me . . .

"Shit, sorry."

"When was the last time you got laid?" Her question is random, and out of the blue, inappropriate, and has me almost choking on my own saliva. Peyton is being fucking serious and looks like she really wants to know.

When I part my lips, I almost say something asinine, like *Pardon me?* or *I beg your pardon?* but I bite my tongue and manage not to blush.

"I'm not sure."

She doesn't believe me; it's written all over her pretty face. "You're not sure? How can you not be sure? I thought men knew all the little details about sex."

It's not a *little* detail, it's an embarrassing fact, and I'm not about to share it with her.

I deflect.

"Why do you even care?"

One of those expertly manicured brows rises. "Oh, you *know* why I care."

I do.

She wants to bang me.

And I haven't had sex with anyone in . . . months. How many months, I have no idea—Hunter would probably know if I asked him. That fucker knows all my personal business, and remembers most of it, too. He's the most annoying factotum I've ever met in my damn life.

"Six months," I blurt out, just to see the look on her face, choosing a random number and guessing it's close enough to being accurate to appease her.

"Nuh-uh, I don't believe you."

"You don't have to believe me. It's a fact."

"Six months? Stop it. Right now."

"Okay." I clamp my lips shut to be annoying, the same way I used to do to my mom as a kid when she'd tell me to stop doing something.

"For real? How can that be?"

"Work, work, sleep, eating . . ." I list all the reasons I haven't felt motivated to have sex with anyone. "Stress." I finally look her in the eye. "What about you?"

Peyton pushes the fork around with her finger. "I dunno, maybe . . . two years?"

I almost fall off the chair. "Two years?"

"Give or take."

And now that I know this, there will be no un-knowing it. Peyton Lévêque hasn't been laid in seven hundred and thirty days, and she wants to bang me, and now I have to wonder . . .

What the hell am I going to do about it? Because the *no fraternizing policy* no longer exists between us. But, I still think about the look on her face when I had her right before me in my office. *I can't.* Two words that have haunted me ever since.

CHAPTER TWENTY-ONE

PEYTON

I 'm not playing fair. I'm well aware of this.

I'm also not listening to my inner business-self telling me in a rather dramatic fashion to NOT STEP FOOT ON THIS ELEVATOR.

Go back to the coffee house.

Stick your head in your work.

Don't even think about the man you had dinner with last night.

Or the fact that he hasn't had sex in six months.

Or the way he raked his eyes over you multiple times, nibbling on his bottom lip when he blatantly stared at your cleavage.

Walk away right now, Peyton. Walk. Away.

I've never been good at listening to that inner voice, so here I am, stepping into the elevator and pressing the button to his floor knowing the *real* reason I'm dressed to kill and heading to Rome's office.

Lunch with Lauren, of course.

Because why else would I be here?

I chuckle to no one as the elevator doors slide closed on me, shutting out the lobby, elevator car begging to climb, floor after floor higher up the skyscraper I've become very familiar with.

Taking a deep breath, I adjust the white blouse I've got tucked into a tightly fitted royal-blue skirt. Shift in my nude heels. Flip my loose, wavy hair over one shoulder. Pucker my glossy lips.

Just having lunch with a friend—that's it.

An old friend.

A friend I would visit on occasion just to sneak peeks at her good-looking boss, Rome. Visit just to see him diligently working on his enterprise. Catch glimpses of him, hoping maybe someday I'd catch his eye, too.

Watching him work is inspiring and sexy as hell.

The elevator dings and the doors part, revealing Lauren at her desk, expertly listening to Rome as he hovers above her, catching snippets of their conversation.

"I need that file typed out and back on my desk within the hour. Will that be a problem?"

"No, sir."

He sighs. *"Would you stop calling me that?"*

"No can do, sir." She's such a brat.

"Lauren, I swear to God . . ."

Lauren is full-out laughing when I approach, although my focus is on ogling Rome's backside as he leans across her counter. Navy-blue pants, white shirt tucked in tightly and cinched by a brown leather belt.

Our clothes match, which is such a girl thing to notice.

His shoulders are tense, sleeves rolled up to his elbows, and his hair is disheveled as if he's been raking his fingers through it relentlessly today. Which he no doubt has, the way he gets stressed out so easily.

"Oh, relax, boss. You're so keyed up this morning, what's your jive?"

This makes me laugh.

Which makes Lauren look up in my direction and cringe.

Busted lipping off to the boss.

Her pretty blonde brows dip into a frown, then up, head cocking in Rome's direction. Eyes widening.

Crap—she's going to cancel on me. I can see it in her eyes; regret.

I've been spotted by Rome, so I stand taller when his head rears at the sound of my heels clicking against the marble floor, his eyes raking me in from head to toe.

His eyes widen, surprised I'm standing here—but then narrow on the front of my blouse. Skirt. I can see his pupils dilate from here, eyebrows sharpening as his steely gaze rakes its way up from my exposed legs. Up to my less-than-proper button-up job on my shirt, cleavage prominently on display. *He likes what he sees.*

"Peyton." Gruff and pained, he continues, "What are you doing here?"

I saddle up next to Lauren's desk and rest my hand on the high countertop. "Came to have lunch with my friend." I eye her. "But from the looks of it, we're going to have to reschedule."

"Lauren is busy," he snaps. "She doesn't have time to eat lunch."

I hiss between my teeth and tap my finger on the marble slab of her desk. "Tsk, tsk. That's an HR violation, Rome. She has to have some sort of break."

"She can eat and work at her desk like everyone else does." He turns his gaze back to Lauren and says, "I'll pay you extra. Bounce these files for me and get them back ASAP."

Spinning on his heel, he doesn't say another word as he makes his way back to his office, fingers of his right hand pulling on the brown strands of his dark hair.

A little shocked, I turn to Lauren and ask, "What the hell was that about?"

She sighs and leans back in her chair, looking deflated and tired. "Shit hit the fan this morning."

"I can see that. What happened?"

"Project Mountain announced a new women's line this morning, almost an exact replica to what we're putting out there. So similar that Rome thinks there might be a mole in the company."

SARA NEY & MEGHAN QUINN

Oh. Shit.

I glance toward his office—he's fuming, sitting at his desk, head gripped in his hands, the tension radiating from his body palpable from where I stand. This must be killing him.

I don't blame him for being a moody bastard.

Given I'm heading up the marketing for his women's campaign, it's my duty to go in there and see what I can do.

Not because I hate seeing him like this.

Not because I want to comfort him, hold him.

But because it's my duty.

"Raincheck on lunch?"

Lauren scans her desk full of papers. "Looks like it. I'm so sorry."

I wave her off. "Don't be. I totally get it." Sometimes Rome is tyrannical, but it looks like today he has a good reason. "I'm going to go see if there is anything I can do on my end marketing-wise to help the situation. Thanks for filling me in."

"Good luck. He's been a complete bastard today. For a second there, I thought maybe he was different, a little happier, you know? He's been in a really good mood lately; even brought me coffee and lunch a few times this week. Me. I almost fell out of my chair the first time he did it. But today just reminds me of the man he really is."

I hide the smile that wants to play at my lips. I like to think that maybe I'm the reason he's been a little cheerier and happy, metaphorically loosening that tight tie around his neck. Right about now, I want to loosen it even more.

"Cut him some slack. I'm sure he's dealing with a lot right now." His stress level must be through the roof. "Text me when you can reschedule?"

Lauren nods. "I will."

I give the counter a few raps with my knuckles and throw a little wave at her with my fingers, pushing through Rome's heavy glass door without knocking.

Close it behind me, careful not to make a bunch of noise.

Keeping his head tilted down, he lifts his eyes and spots me. Letting out a long exhale, he leans back in his chair and tries to act as casual as possible, but I see right through him.

"I'm busy, Peyton."

"So I've heard." I make my way around his desk, set my purse down on the floor, and prop my body up on the edge, staring directly down at him. His cologne relaxes my nerves—just the smell of him does—the vulnerability in his eyes reminding me that he is, in fact, *human* despite the terse façade he likes to wear. I'm no longer an employee of his company, and have no cause to be intimidated. This passionate man needs some propping up. And I can at least do *that*.

His fingernails rake over his stubble as he makes no attempt to hide his blatant once-over of my body, his eyes lingering on my chest before they fall to my lips. Involuntarily I lick them. His eyes darken, become more sinister.

"It's best you leave, Peyton."

"Why?" My breath starts to pick up as Rome shifts in his seat, the V of his shirt falling open revealing the tan, smooth skin of his clavicle and collarbone—two of my favorite spots on a man's body.

"Because I'm *shitty* company. I need to get work done, and right now, you're a distraction."

"A distraction?" I mock surprise. "I'm here to see if there's anything I can do to help."

"You don't work here anymore; you're not obligated to stick around and help me." He licks his lips, reaches over to his desk, and presses a button. I know exactly what that button does. I've seen it done plenty of times when he has important meetings in his office. It tints the windows.

My heart rate picks up to a sprinting beat, my chest rises and falls, my breasts stretching the already tight fabric of my button-down blouse.

"I might not work in this building, but I work for you, Rome." And I thought we were becoming friends; I'd do anything to help my friend if I could.

"Do you? Did I officially hire you without knowing about it?"

Oh, wow—he's in a rare mood today; too bad he doesn't scare me like he scares everyone else in this office. Moody grouch—maybe I should start calling him Oscar.

"Stop taking your anger out on me."

"If I'm taking my anger out on you, I sure as hell would know about it."

My cheeks flame, but that doesn't stop my eyes from falling on his lap. Just a few feet away, I could easily just reach down and ease some of that anxiety he's feeling right now. Wipe away that furrowed brow; relax it a little.

Just a pull . . . a quick tug and *zip* down on the front of his trousers.

It would be so easy.

"Why are you really here, Peyton?" he grits out before standing and moving around his desk to pace the room, shocking me out of my reverie with his stern attitude.

I thought we'd had a breakthrough . . .

Shaking all thoughts of his crotch out of my head, I say, "You know why I'm here—to collect Lauren for lunch. Then she told me about Project Mountain. Since I'm in charge of marketing, even though for some reason you're denying it today, I want to know what I'm dealing with here."

"You want to know what you're dealing with," he mimics me and shakes his head, both hands drumming the wooden top of his desk. Fingers thrum the surface. "*We* are dealing with a titan of a company that seems to have stolen every ounce of the product line right from under my nose. They plan on launching a week before us."

Shit.

Rome is about to crack his teeth from the grinding of his jaw. This has been a huge project for him, the launch of a new branch for this company. A lot riding on this women's division, so to have to deal with his top competitor launching one before us, is pretty much a kick to the balls.

How the hell do I get my hands on that information from a competitor?

I chew on the side of my mouth, trying to think of a solution. "Then we should do whatever it takes to launch before them."

"We barely have a marketing plan," he huffs. "We can't launch a week before them. We have media to schedule, commercials to finish, an entire campaign to finalize."

"Good thing you hired me then," I say, walking up to him and pressing my hand on his arm, gathering the attention of those worried eyes. "I'm an evil genius."

He grips the back of his neck, his biceps pulling tightly on the sleeves of his shirt. "It's too much."

"I literally have nothing else on my calendar. My sole focus is Roam, Inc. We can *do* this, Rome. Trust me."

My thumb rubs over the soft hairs on his forearm. *God, his skin.* My insides are churning, the need to pull him into my arms, rub his back, let him know everything is going to be okay is far too tempting.

Rome studies my movements as I run the pads of my thumbs across his masculine skin; along the lines in his defined brow, his own hand still busy rubbing the back of his neck.

"Trust me?" I ask, my breath escaping with every blink of his eyes. I can't stop staring. I want him so bad.

My thumbs knead.

He takes a deep breath and slips his hand out of his pocket. When I think he's about to push away from me, he surprises me. He places that hand at my waist, gently pressing me against his wall—a familiar position I remember being in right before I left Roam, Inc.

"You want me to trust you?" he asks, his voice so low, it rumbles over every inch of my body, sending a wave of arousal through my veins. "I can barely concentrate when you're around, Peyton. I don't even trust myself around you. I don't trust that I'm not going to ruin the professional relationship we have. I don't trust myself not to peel that white blouse off your chest and suck your nipples into my mouth. I don't trust myself to keep myself from sinking so fucking deep inside you that you have no other choice but to scream my name. And I sure as hell don't trust myself to stay away from you, when all I want is to feel your soft skin against mine."

His hands are straddling my head, his eyes boring straight into my soul, his knee pressing between my legs.

I can't breathe.

I can't feel my bottom half.

I can't come up with one single word to say that will stop him.

I don't want him to stop, even though I know he should, even though I know we are bordering on crossing a professional line, a line we could never get back.

"Rome . . ." I breathe out, reaching out and fishing a finger around one of his belt loops.

He sucks in a sharp breath of air as his hips move closer. His forehead lowers, his breath just as erratic as mine.

"I . . ." He pauses and licks his lips. "I need help, Peyton."

Everything around me stills. *I need help, Peyton.* All pretenses are gone. It's just the vulnerable, worried CEO needing a strong advocate and business partner to steady him again. *Me.* God . . . he's so . . . real. Raw. *Incredible.* The lust I have for this man is put on hold as his words sink in.

He needs me.

For the first time since I've known him, he's asking for help and not in a boss-type manner, but with a hint of desperation.

This is the Rome no one else has seen, the Rome I knew was trapped deep down inside of him, only present in his most vulnerable of moments.

And I'm privy to see this beautiful man at his finest, raw, defenseless, and completely exposed.

"How can I help?"

Pushing off the wall a few inches, one of his hands comes to my cheek, and then he searches my eyes. "Have dinner with me, tonight."

"Having dinner with you is going to help?"

"Bring work." He lets out a deep sigh. "It's going to be a long night."

I nod. "Text me where. I'll be there and for now, I'll start moving up media dates."

His thumb strokes my cheek, his brow softening, the tension in his shoulders easing. "Okay."

With one final stroke, he pushes off the wall and gives me some space, some unwanted breathing room.

"I, uh . . . I have some work to do," he says, going to his desk where he picks up my purse and brings it to me.

"Then I'll give you some space." I take my purse from him, our fingers connecting for a brief second before I start toward his office door.

His hand goes to my back, guiding me gently to the heavy door, sliding down until it rests right above my ass. I squeeze my eyes shut as his chest falls in close behind me, his masculine scent invading me once again. Leaning over, his mouth to my ear, he says, "Thank you, Peyton."

He reaches in front of me and opens the door, ushering me through. When I look behind me, he's gripping the door and the glass wall, his gaze sharp and enticing.

Keeping his eyes fixed on mine, he says, "Lauren, please make reservations for Peyton and me at Number 9. Seven o'clock."

Lauren pops her head up and nods. "On it."

Never wavering, he says, "See you then."

And then he shuts his door, sending my heart into a tailspin.

Seven o'clock can't come soon enough.

CHAPTER TWENTY-TWO

ROME

I take a sip of my wine and lean back in the curved booth I'm sharing with Peyton, completely and utterly exhausted. We took a twenty-minute break to eat, but the rest of our time here has been spent nailing down all the fine details of the campaign.

Despite the fact that we're at a five-star restaurant in the heart of New York City.

It's been meticulous and time-consuming, but for the first time today, I feel at ease—and optimistic—and it's all because of the beautiful woman sitting next to me, sipping on a glass of red wine.

"How do you feel?" she asks, eyeing me, her gaze falling to my neck; the spot where my shirt is unbuttoned. Peyton wets her lips, mouth parted, eyes sparkling.

I stare, my own wineglass inches from my lips.

Sip your wine. *Drink it all, you fool.*

This woman just saved your ass. Do not hit on her—it's not professional. Jesus Christ—that's something Hunter would do.

Not me.

Then again, I can't think of a better way to *thank* her by taking her to my apartment and stripping her down bare so I can roam my hands and tongue and body over every last inch of her.

"How do you feel?" she repeats, assuming I didn't hear it the first time.

"I feel," I say it slowly, choosing the words. "Relieved."

"Really?" Her eyebrows lift in surprise. "Relieved?"

"Yeah, relieved." I nod. "You did good, Peyton."

"I . . . you don't know how much that mea—" She pauses and takes a deep breath, getting choked up. "Thank you. That means a lot to me, Rome. I worked my ass off for you once I left the office. I wanted to make sure that this was all going to be okay."

She really is amazing.

Why did it take me so long to see it? *Apparently because I didn't lift my eyes from my desk.* Something else this woman in front of me has taught me. Beautiful and intelligent.

"It shows, and I really can't thank you enough."

Smiling, she slightly tilts her head to the side and takes a sip of her wine, a playful look in her eyes that's making me feel a little uneasy, makes me squirm in my seat.

"What?" What's the look she's giving me? I don't want to misinterpret anything. I'm trying to be professional, but it's just so damn hard.

"Rome Blackburn, you are really nice when you want to be."

"You think I said all that just to be nice?"

"Well, no, but—"

"You did a damn good job. You are saving my ass, and possibly the company. You're really fucking good at what you do, and I'm pissed at myself for not seeing it while I had you at the office."

"What do you mean—not seeing it while you had me in the office? You mean . . . how good I am at my job?"

She's fishing for compliments, but I let it slide. I'm feeling so fucking fantastic right now I want to pick her up out of that chair and spin her around in circles.

Do I tell her that the job isn't the only thing she's good at? Maybe she's good at other things? Like making me feel like I'm not such a dickhead, after all? It bothers me now that employees tiptoe around me—and that they see me as unapproachable—more than it ever did in the past.

Everyone always thinks they can do a better job running a company; everyone thinks it's so goddamn easy having that many people depend on you for their livelihood.

It keeps me up at night.

That's why this bullshit with Project Mountain scared the living shit out of me. Sure, everybody thought I was pissed—and I was—but mostly I was out of my goddamn mind with worry. I can't lose those quarterlies to that company; I need them in my pocket, for *my* people. My employees.

"You're not just good at your job, Peyton—you're . . ." Shit. Why are the words getting lodged in my damn throat? What do I want to say? "You're good for me."

It's dark in here, but I swear, her face gets red. "I am?"

"Yeah."

"Define 'good for you.'" Her smirk is knowing, her fingers using air-quotes around the words *good for you*, and for once, I'm happy to oblige her with an explanation.

I lean forward, resting my hands on the table in front of us. Clasp them. "You make me want to be . . ."

Okay, so this isn't as easy as I thought it would be.

"Nice?" Peyton supplies hopefully.

"Uh, no." Not the word I was looking for.

"Kind?"

"Not *that* one either."

I laugh, then she laughs, and soon, we're both staring at one another like complete morons. Anyone watching would think we were love-struck fools. Because right now, I feel like one. Jesus, shoot me now.

"What then? How do I make you want to be?"

She's staring at me so expectantly, and I really want to say something profound; something damn good—but it's harder pulling emotion from an ass that hasn't spewed anything sweet or meaningful in ages.

"You make me feel . . . like I'm not a giant asshole."

Not the most profound answer in the world, but it resonates with her because instead of cringing from my choice of words, her face softens.

"I do?"

"Yeah, but I think that came out all wrong." I resist the temptation to run my fingers through my hair. "You make me fucking excited. You excite me."

"I do? Me?"

"You don't believe me?"

"No, I do. It's just that—no one has ever said that to me before."

"Then your other dates have been idiots."

"This is a date?"

My mouth gapes. *Is it?* No. Yes.

I look around at the surroundings, well aware that it's a sophisticated place, and we're at a secluded table. The lights are dim. The menu is sublime.

I invited her under the pretense of work, obviously—that's my MO. It's what I do. Work. Work. More work.

But if I'm being honest with myself, yes—there was some romantic intention when I had Lauren book this table, at this restaurant, and I do both Peyton and me a favor by not denying it.

"Yes. I guess this was like a date, wasn't it?"

Her eyes light up, this time not from surprise. They're excited and sparkly and alive—and beautiful.

"Wow," she says with a little laugh. "I can't believe you just admitted that."

"Why?"

"Because you're such a hard-ass all the time. You have way too much pride, Rome Blackburn, and sometimes you do things just to spite yourself."

That's probably true.

"So. A date, huh?" Peyton rests back in her chair, crossing her legs and shooting me a flirty look. "You couldn't just ask? You had to pretend we were only here for a meeting? So typical."

"We did have a meeting," I can't help pointing out, physically pointing to her portfolio and my notes.

"We've been doing nothing but meetings since I offered to take on this project and crush all competitors' skulls." Peyton pantomimes what she probably considers "crushing skulls" in her fist, grinding her left hand into her open right palm.

God, she's adorable when she talks trash. Or tries to.

Cute.

Sexy.

Self-conscious now because I'm watching her, Peyton ducks her head and bites her bottom lip, shying away from my intense gaze. But I can't help it. I want to suck on her lip and brush her hair aside and suck on her neck, too.

For starters.

We're through with our meal and when the waiter comes back with a dessert menu, I offer it to her. *You want?* I question her with my brows.

Do you?

No.

"I have a bottle of wine at my place."

My place, which is just around the corner—within walking distance. How convenient.

"Just the check."

"Very good, sir." The waiter nods, pulling a narrow, black leather folder out of his apron. Lands it on my side of the table, and without hesitating, I hand him my credit card.

"Dessert at your place?" Peyton asks. "Do you actually have any?"

"Not really." *I'm looking at it, though.* "Want to come over for a nightcap?"

She visibly swallows, brushes the hair falling over her shoulder to one side, and sits up straighter in her chair. "I thought you'd never ask."

CHAPTER TWENTY-THREE

PEYTON

We'regonnabang, we'regonnabang, we'regonnabang. I can't keep the chant out of my head. I just know we're going to—I can tell by the way Rome is watching me; like I'm the tastiest thing on the menu.

His hand singeing the small of my back, we walk the dark, damp streets of New York, dodging people the entire three-block walk to his place.

By way of necessity, because I'm wearing high heels, I grasp his forearm and hold steady after the first time my heel gets caught in a sewer grate and almost snaps.

Rome steadies me the remaining block.

One. More. Block.

My heart wants to vomit, it's fluttering so fast.

We're at a building with a doorman wearing a green jacket; he smiles, nods, and pulls the heavy door open with a flourish, ushering us inside the opulent lobby.

Somehow, the building too feels demanding; too high-end. Too glossy and cold, as if it has high expectations of anyone walking through the door.

I tilt my chin up.

Brace my back against the cool metal elevator walls when the doors open and we step in, riding to the top floor. When it dings and slides back open, Rome sheds his coat by the door.

I do the same, and hang it by the door, and turn to face him.

Just like everything else he does, he wastes no time focusing on what he wants and taking it with precise movements. Sure and confident, he walks to me, hands settling on my waist.

I back up until I'm pressed gently against the wall, his hot mouth settling on my neck just below my ear. He sucks on my earring, earning himself an eye-roll—the erotic kind, where my eyes damn near roll to the back of my head.

"Wanna tour of the place now, or in the morning?"

Whoa.

We're doing this.

It.

Banging.

"In the morning, after you feed me pancakes with lots of butter and syrup," I moan, luxuriating in the feel of his warm breath.

"I don't have any pancake batter," he murmurs back.

"Mmm. You better get some, or these clothes aren't coming off."

He rears back to study my expression. "Are you fucking for real?"

I laugh. "Yes. I want pancakes."

His grumble is hilarious. Sexy. "Fine. God, you're bossy."

"Mm-hmm." I pull his mouth back down, square on mine, opening for him so his tongue can slip in. It does, and mine dances with his, rolling. Twirling.

Wet and hot.

Kind of dirty, we lap each other up. *I am kissing Rome Blackburn.* Kissing. Rome. And it's even hotter, even better, even more intense than I thought possible. But now there is a need alive in me that I have to take. *Now.*

"Show me your bedroom."

Holy crap, did I just say that? That is so unlike me. I might think about saying things like that, but I've certainly never said anything like it out loud to a man before.

Nevertheless, Rome clearly likes it, because he reaches down, and before I know it, he's scooping me up and carrying me down his entry hall. Doesn't stop until he enters a dark room, bumping the outlet with his elbow and two bedside table lights flicker on.

They're dim—more mood lighting than for efficiency—casting a beautiful glow over his dark bedroom. It's just like I pictured it: large and imposing, with huge panoramic windows overlooking the borough. The sky is lit up from the city, and although the view is obstructed from all the tall buildings, it's still spectacular.

Concrete floors. Gray bed. White bedding, which surprises me. Black everything else. Stern and serious.

Cold and unrelenting.

Everything I thought he was before I got to know him.

I move toward him, fiddling with the blue tie around his neck, then loosen it until I'm able to lift it over his head, toss it aside, but close enough that I can use it later for . . . whatever reason.

"I've daydreamed about this forever," I whisper, fingers working the top button of his dress shirt—so stuffy for a date, but appropriate for a business meeting.

"Tell me." Are my ears deceiving me, or did his voice crack? "In detail."

"Well," I begin. "In my fantasy, I'm removing your tie like this, and I keep it nearby in case I want to bind your hands with it."

"Is that so?"

"Yes. Or . . . I can gag you with it if you give me attitude. Which we both know is the likely scenario here."

"You think you're in charge?"

I smirk. "Oh, Rome. I don't think I'm in charge here. I know I am. You might be the boss at work, but I'll be the boss of this bedroom."

I sound so sure of myself. So aggressive.

I love it.

Love the way he's looking at me, eyes half-hooded and lazy, liking the way I'm taking control.

I don't want to *dominate* him; I just want to do what I want with him . . .

"All right." His answer is low. Amused.

His eyes are so watchful still as I work the front of his shirt. The fabric is worn and butter soft, gliding through my fingers when I tug the hem out of his jeans, his breath hitching.

Sliding my palms under his tee, I touch his chest, tentatively at first. Then more confidently, working my way up his abs and pecs.

Mmm. One of us moans and I'm almost certain it's not me. Leisurely, I let my hands roam his upper torso, basking in his smooth flesh. He doesn't have much hair on his chest like I thought he would, just a light sprinkle across his hard pecs. It's light, barely noticeable, but there.

When I'm done exploring, my hands run under the shoulders of his shirt. Tug it up and over his head until it's free from his body and falling to the floor.

Rome Blackburn, standing before me with only his pants on is not something I thought I'd ever see. He is mine for the taking; putty in my hands.

My hands are trembling a little. I might talk a lot of shit about *banging*, but in reality, I'm not the most experienced in the world . . . I've only had a small handful of sexual partners. Like, three.

One almost didn't count, because we were in college, and neither of us knew any better. Fumbled around, pawing at each other. And I'm pretty sure he didn't even stick it in the right hole the first time.

I almost laugh at the memories, nervous laughter bubbling in my throat when Rome's serious, grey eyes catch mine.

His mouth twitches; he's amused. He doesn't know why I'm

laughing, but the sound of it makes him smile. My voice makes him smile.

"You like me," I simply state, tracing his bottom lip with the tip of my thumb. Back and forth, slowly, pad of my finger memorizing how soft his mouth is.

"I do," he says, which is so unlike him.

"I can't believe you admitted that."

"I can't believe it either. But you have my shirt on the floor and your fingers tracing my mouth and—shit. I just want to stand here and see what you're going to do next."

But he's lying.

He doesn't wait to see what I'm going to do next, because he's impossible and impatient.

His hands are at his sides—but not for long. They find my waist and skim my hips over the silky fabric of my dress, gliding up my rib cage. They snake around to the front and tug at the sash tied over my abdomen, slowly dragging it out of its loop. Pulling it so the sash completely unties, the dress parts, and my entire middle is exposed. Bra. Panties.

"Well, this is a fun surprise."

I'm full of them, I want to boast. But don't have the courage; plus, I would choke on my nerves if I tried to speak.

Instead, I gasp as the cool air from his frigid bedroom hits my body. I shiver, from Rome's hands and the temperature.

"Cold?" he murmurs, although he's more interested in his turn to explore. They rake up my stomach that's now covered in goose bumps, up to the lace trim on my red bra.

Yes, I wore a red bra. Yes, it's cliché. But it matches my dress, and hopefully, my mood. I needed to feel sexy tonight, so I could do all the sexy things.

Lace-covered courage, as one might say.

"I was cold, but not anymore."

His hands pass over my plump cleavage—*I'm disappointed*—not stopping until they reach the slope of my collarbone, gliding along there unhurried. It sends another shiver down my spine having his hands there. My skin is velvety smooth and tingles against his wanton fingertips.

"So beautiful," he whispers, inching closer. "So sexy."

His mouth finds the pulse in my neck and latches on.

"Don't you dare give me a hickey," I scold, pushing on his shoulders with the palm of my hands. It's useless; his body is a wall of masculine energy.

"But you need one." He laughs into my neck, the jerk.

"I'm serious, Rome. I have to hold my head up at work tomorrow. I'll die if anyone notices."

"You work for yourself; no one is going to rat you out."

"I will kill you." I pull back, glaring at him. "No. Hickeys."

He pulls a face. "You're no fun."

"Do you want me to give you one, instead?"

"Fuck, no."

"Then leave my neck alone."

When he does remove his mouth, I groan—it felt so damn good having his lips there—I'm rewarded when it slides up my jawline, the tip of his nose bumping my ear. Breathing warm breath into the shell, my eyes slide closed.

"Mmm."

I feel his mouth smiling at the same time his hands slide down my arms. Up again, thumbs hooking the cotton of my dress. Pushing it down my arms like I'd done with his dress shirt. And, just like his dress shirt, it slides off my body into a pool of red, liquid fabric, down to the floor.

Red bra. Red panties.

Nothing more.

He kisses me as I nimbly fumble with the buckle of his belt, then unbutton his jeans. Whirr the zipper down its track.

His cock strains against the thick fabric. I can feel it beneath my fingers as I pull the zipper along. Greedy fingers that want to feel it; greedy eyes that want to see it.

I'm glad he turned the lights on. I want to see all of him, every inch. My eyes cast downward—they simply cannot help themselves. I've only ever seen this man in a suit, jeans or shorts, and a T-shirt. Never even close to naked.

He's so laced up and stuffy.

Now he's bare and practically naked to my prying gaze.

Broad chest. Tan skin.

A stomach that dips into that glorious V into the waistband of his black boxers.

"Everything in this room matches," I can't help pointing out. What can I say? I'm a stickler for details. "The floor. Your bed. Your shirt. Your boxers. Do you do this on purpose?"

"Maybe," he teases back.

"Mmm . . ." is all I can muster, because I'm helping him shuck his pants and get them off his body.

Then, it's just the two of us.

Skin and lace and cotton briefs.

Hands and lips and tongue and a little teeth.

I want to be on the bed, so I take a few steps backward until the backs of my knees hit the mattress. Wait for him to guide me down, laying me flat on my back. I crab-crawl to the center; I'm not brave enough to pull down his underwear and give him a blow job—not yet anyway.

But he seems content to watch me recline on his stacked pillows—red panties against stark white—my dark hair fanned out, arms spread wide, inviting him to join me.

"God, you're sexy."

I crook a finger.

He comes.

Rome dives into my body, arms braced at my sides, tongue licking between the valley of my breasts. Playful. Sweet. My breath quickens when he lowers himself, settling between my legs, the hard length of him pressed into my core. It pulses.

Now, I shouldn't say this is the part where we dry fuck for a good ten minutes, but . . . this is the part where we dry fuck for a good ten minutes. Like teenagers. Rome moving over me, mimicking sex.

Digging the tip of his erection into the valley of my thighs, hitting the wet, hot center. My head tips back and I moan, biting my lip. All he's doing is rubbing himself against me, for God's sake.

We're still wearing underwear . . . and I love it.

God, it feels so good, and we're not even screwing.

"More," I whine. "Get these off."

Together we shove at his boxers. I've never seen Rome Blackburn so . . . desperate. Excitement shines in his eyes; he wants me bad.

And, dear God, his dick is ridiculous.

Big.

Thick.

Big and thick? *Stop repeating yourself, Peyton. You're about to bang your boss.* You're about to bang the man of your dreams.

Stop saying *bang*. It's not classy.

I try and focus on the task, and get out of my own headspace, but it's hard—I haven't had sex in two years, and his incredible penis is clouding my judgment.

Rome spreads my legs.

Inches down my body, peppering kisses on my stomach—it's not perfect, hardly flat—but he doesn't seem to mind. He seems to love it, licking my belly button and running his nose along my pelvis.

"So fucking sexy," he tells me for the umpteenth time tonight, and I stretch out beneath him, kind of like a cat lounging in the sun. "I've been wanting to get my mouth on this pussy for weeks."

"You have?" I squeak out in the unsexiest way, tipping my neck so I can see him better. I then watch as his mouth descends on my panties, sucking through the sheer, red nylon. His tongue flicks up and down the slit of my crotch, wetting the space between my legs.

Sucking.

He pulls the panties to the side and licks me clean up and down the middle.

"Oh, Jesus." My head casts to one side and I lay limply, like a rag doll. Legs spread by the width of his broad shoulders, his large palms splayed on my open thighs, keeping them open.

Open.

Hot. Wet.

Ready.

Rome's mouth sucks, fingers spread my pussy, and *oh God, I can't believe I just called it that word.* It doesn't take long for the nerve endings in my entire lower half to quiver; he is that good at this. *Someone get this man a medal.*

I grabble at his hair, grasping a handful.

"I don't want to come unless you're inside me," I protest when his mouth devours my clit.

"Shhh." Rome shakes his head, barely removing his mouth from where it's buried. "You will. Later."

Oh shit.

Oh shit, this feels good.

"Oh, God . . . yes . . . *mmm.*" My hips, of their own violation, begin a slow, steady rotation, and I raise them up, off the bed slightly when his teeth graze my clit. Just the barest hint. Just enough so I toss my head on the pillow and bite down on my bottom lip.

His flat tongue laps up my . . . "I'm gonna . . . oh God, don't stop doing that . . . right there, Rome, mmm . . ."

Nothing but incoherent thoughts course through my mind, body. Lower parts.

"Your pussy tastes too fucking good," he moans, coming up for air. "I need to fuck it. I'm gonna fuck this pussy."

Oh, Jesus.

I can't take the dirty talk; not from him.

He's stalwart and serious.

What do I even reply with? *Yeah, fuck me hard?* I'm not good at dirty talking—I've never really done it, and it feels weird and unnatural.

I try it anyway. "Yeah, Rome, fuck me." Then, even though I feel like an idiot, I add an extra, "Mmm."

The sound of my mmm drives him crazy, and he adds a finger where his mouth is. It hits the right spot, at the right time, and my hips come off the bed.

He pins them down, shoulders boxing out.

Glassy-eyed, I watch the top of his head. Watch his tongue and fingers work my pussy. The sight is as arousing as the actual act of him doing it, like sexual napalm.

Explosive.

Intoxicating.

I haven't had anyone go down on me in forever, and I'm getting high on watching Rome do it. So fucking hot.

My nerves quiver. Thighs tremble. Head rears back, hands reaching for the white sheets. I clench them, bringing the corner of one to my mouth, teeth biting down on the fabric.

"Oh God . . . oh . . ."

No actual words slip out of my mouth when I come, but my entire body is alive with pleasure, hitting me dead center, erupting like fireworks all through my nerves.

I'm incapable of speech. A little bit sweaty.

Spent.

"Oh no, you don't," Rome admonishes from down under, working his way back up my body, tugging at the sheer red bra cups. He pulls one down so my nipple pops out and lowers his head to suck.

One of his hands disappears beneath me, fingers working the strap until it's free, then pulling the entire thing off my body. Tosses it to the pile of clothes on the floor. Pushes my panties down while I languish on the mattress—fanned out and wanton— waiting to see what he's going to do next.

"You look like a goddess," Rome whispers into my neck, and I believe him.

"I love your body," is my contribution to the sex talk, my brain completely useless for stringing intelligent words together.

I can feel his stiff cock on my thigh, the pre-cum leaving a wet mark on my skin. Even though I just had an amazing orgasm, I want him inside me. Where he belongs.

He agrees, and then reaches across my body to the bedside table, yanking open the drawer unceremoniously and pulling out a box of condoms—the sight makes me blush, and my body is already on fire. Alive and on fire.

Still aroused—maybe more now than I was before, suddenly insatiable.

"God, I want you to fuck me so bad." I squirm on the mattress, twisting in the sheets, rubbing my thighs together. He makes me so hot.

"Yes, ma'am."

The condom gets rolled on, and watching it makes me bite down on my lower lip, anticipation coursing through my veins like it's the first time I've had sex.

Rome's bicep muscles flex when he positions himself over me, and my greedy palms land there, taking hold. I gasp when he reaches between us, grasping his dick and guiding it into my wet, slick heat.

One slow touch and then he pushes in a few inches.

"Jesus Christ, you're so fucking tight," he groans deep inside his chest.

"You like that?" I ask, eyes closing at the sensation of him sliding slowly inside me, inch by inch.

"I've never felt anything so good in my life," he groans again, louder.

"Wow. So many compliments." Why am I teasing him?

"You want to make jokes now?"

"I can't help it." I laugh. "Don't stop. Keep going."

"You couldn't pay me to leave this goddamn pussy."

Those words.

This man.

He pulls out, then pushes in, thrusting in . . . pulling out . . . nose buried in the crook of my neck, mouth on my pulse. Mine, for its part, hangs open.

"Shit, Peyton . . .," he moans into my hair. "Goddamn."

Yes, more. Say my name again.

He does.

"*Peyton.*"

Good old-fashioned sex, the best way there is—him on top, pounding into me, hard. The headboard begins to hit the wall and I concentrate on the sounds and sensations of it, alongside his moans that turn into soft, animalistic grunts. The sound of our sex.

Sweat on his brow.

The dampness between my legs.

I feel and hear it all.

And Rome was right; he is going to make me come again. I can feel it building . . . slowly but surely, the telltale clenching in my pelvis sending a shockwave up my spine, and I arch my back. Rome latches onto a nipple, suckling and it damn near makes me crazy.

"You're going to make me crazy." His voice echoes my thoughts.

"Good." That's what I want. "I want you to lose control."

He quickens his pace, thrusting harder. Deeper. Grabbing my ass with both his hands and getting as deep as he can go.

"Uhh," I moan. Because *mmm* . . .

"Peyton . . ." He groans my name again, and I know there will never be a time I forget the way it sounds leaving his lips.

"Rome," I whisper back, stroking his shoulder blades as he pumps his lean, athletic hips.

I'm so close. So is he. I can feel it in the way his body tightens, and his face morphs in awe when he lifts up to look at me.

Eyes locked.

Hips thrusting.

Bodies sweating.

It feels fantastic, everything I ever dreamed of.

"Fuck," he chokes out, strained and sexy.

And just like that, a rocket of pleasure shoots up my spine

hitting me so hard that my eyes squeeze shut, my back arches, and everything inside me feels like it's on fire as my orgasm takes hold of me.

"Jesus Christ." His hips pump harder, his lips land on mine where he kisses me relentlessly until he freezes and groans into my mouth.

I can feel him pulsing inside me, his orgasm consuming me, his heavy breaths consuming me.

Rome Blackburn is so freaking hot, especially when he comes and comes hard.

Blowing out a long breath of air, he collapses on top of me and then does the most surprising thing. Propping up on his elbows, he takes my face in his hands and strokes my cheeks with his thumbs before ever so softly brushing light kisses across my face. There is nothing urgent about them, just a reassurance that he's here, in my arms, filling every fantasy I've ever had.

And this will most likely be the end of me, because this is the Rome I saw, the Rome no one else could see.

Sensitive, sweet, and loving. *Intense.*

I sigh into the mattress, my heart beating a mile a minute. I'm not going to say it, but . . .

I think I'm falling for him.

CHAPTER TWENTY-FOUR

ROME

The sun is bright on my face as a light tapping continues to hammer on my shoulder. I squeeze the pillow tight, the feel of my silk sheets beneath me, rubbing at my morning wood.

"Hello. Anyone in there."

Peyton.

Goddammit Peyton.

My mind flashes to last night.

Peyton in my bed, Peyton in the shower, Peyton on the kitchen counter.

Her smell.

The way she tastes.

The way she fits like a glove against my body.

There's only one thing to say. She rocked my fucking world last night and not just with sex, but with how she opened *me* up.

I'm different around her, more vulnerable, more aware of my feelings. Not so much of a prick.

And even though I kind of hate to admit it given where we started, she makes me happy.

Groaning, I roll to the side and capture her between my arms, her brown hair a stark contrast to my bright white bedding. She laughs as I tangle us up and pin her to the mattress.

"That's not the proper way to wake up a man who gave you the best night of your life."

She cocks an eyebrow. "Best night of my life? How do you know it was the best?"

I dip my pelvis toward hers, my erection pressing against her stomach as I wiggle my eyebrows. "When you were coming on my tongue for the third time, you said and I quote, 'This is the best night of my life.'" I add a little facial expression impersonation where my eyes roll in the back of my head.

Laughing, she swats at my chest. "That is not what I look like when I come."

"How do you know? Ever look in a mirror?"

She squints, twisting her lips to the side. "Fine, if I look like that, then you look like this." She sticks her tongue out of her mouth, pants, and pulses her leg up and down like a damn dog.

I can't hide my smile or the laugh that pops out of me.

"So basically, you're comparing me to a dog."

"Pretty much."

I nod. "Fair enough." Gripping her hands, I pin them down and lower my head to her neck where I lightly lick the spot just below her ear and then work my way to her collarbone where I pause and smile to myself. Without warning, I suck her skin into my mouth and nibble.

"Rome!" she shouts, shifting beneath me. "Don't you fucking dare."

I suck hard and nibble.

"Rome, I'm not kidding."

I don't let up, making my mark and loving every second of it.

"I swear to God if you give me—" Her voice cuts off in a gulp as my dick slides against the juncture between her thighs. "Ohh," she moans, her legs parting open for me.

Last night, we had the awkward conversation about birth control and how she's on it, which only meant . . .

I glide my cock across her slit, slick and already wet.

"Shit, Peyton, you're so hot."

She doesn't say anything, instead she rocks her hips, her fingers entwining with mine, gripping onto me tightly.

I lower my head, our foreheads touching, our eyes locked on one another. Temporarily I unlock my hand from hers and grip my thick cock where I guide it in. Returning my hand, I keep her still as I fully insert myself inside her. Her face scrunches up right before she lets out a long breath, her entire body relaxing.

When her eyes open up again, glazed over and needy, I bring my mouth to hers in a heated frenzy. Our tongues clash, our mouths molding as I quickly begin to thrust in and out of her.

There is nothing slow about it. We are in desperate need of release despite the night we had.

My hips don't ease up, and when she wraps her legs around my waist, I bury myself even deeper, hitting her in just the right spot.

"Oh my God, yes. Right there, Rome."

I love how she talks to me, how she doesn't have any reservations about being vocal in bed. It's fucking sensational and turns me on even more. Sex with this woman is incredible.

"How close?" I grit out, my climax resting at the base of my spine, ready to rip through me.

There's something about morning sex that gets me off so much faster, and right now is no exception.

"I'm . . ." Her tongue sweeps across mine, her lips attacking mine before she pulls away and bites down on her bottom lip. A long moan escapes her as her pussy clenches around my shaft. "Oh. God," she practically screams, back arching. "Yes, Rome."

Grunting, I pulse a few more times.

One.

Two . . .

Fuck.

Three.

My orgasm tears through me as my balls tighten and I spill into her, pumping feverously until every last drop escapes me.

Christ.

I still. Press my forehead against hers, our noses touching, our breaths erratic as if we just ran a marathon.

Once our heartbeats start to slow down, Peyton finally says, "If you gave me a hickey, this little affair is over."

"If I gave you a hickey, it means you're fucking mine."

~

"That's cheating."

Peyton is sitting on my kitchen counter, in one of my button-up shirts, legs crossed, looking fine as fuck.

I shut the door with my foot and turn toward the kitchen, holding a steaming bag of food in my hand.

"You never requested I actually make the pancakes." I wink and set the bag next to her, only to spread her legs and slide my body between them, placing my hands on her hips.

Her hands fall on my shoulders. "I didn't think I had to specify."

"It's all about the details, babe." I place a quick kiss on her nose before stepping to the side to start unpacking the food.

When she doesn't move, I twist my head and ask, "Are you going to eat? Why are you just sitting there, staring at me like that?"

The smile that consumes her is so fucking overwhelming that I have to catch my breath when she finally says, "You called me, babe."

I lick my lips; look her up and down. She is a babe. There is no denying that.

"So?"

"Soooo," she carries out and pulls me back between her legs where she twists her fingers through my bedhead. "It's really cute."

"I'm not cute."

"You really are, especially when you get this little wrinkle between your eyes." She presses her index finger to my brow.

Sliding my hands up her thighs to her ass, I grip her tightly and bring my mouth to her jaw where I pepper her with kisses.

"Are you trying to distract me from my pancakes?" she asks, tilting her head to the side to give me more access to her neck.

"Is it working?"

"First calling me babe, now this, I would say maybe it is."

"Maybe? Or definitely?"

"Mmm . . ." she moans when I slip my hands under the shirt and move them up to her rib cage, just under her perfect breasts.

Fuck, I can't get enough of her. Every time we're in the same room, I can feel my need for her grow to an uncomfortable level, that if I don't take her right then and there, I might explode.

"Your skin is so soft," I mumble, bringing my hands to her breasts where I pinch her nipples.

Her head falls back, her hair floating down with her as her legs wrap around my back.

I twist and turn the little nubs between my fingers, working my mouth along her skin, desperate to make her come just from nipple play. She did last night, and it was the sexiest fucking thing I've ever seen, her head thrashing about, her pelvis thrusting up at mine, looking for relief of the pressure building until she came all on her own, my fingers plucking at her sensitive breasts.

I want that again.

I stroke my thumbs over the ends and pinch. Repeat the process over and over again until she's panting, her fingers gripping on the edge of the countertop. Her mouth parts open, her chest heaves.

Fuck, yes. She's so close . . .

I'm about to bring my mouth down on hers as the door to my apartment flies open, slamming into the wall, startling the ever-living fuck out of the both of us.

"Rome?" a panicked Hunter calls out right before he spots me in the kitchen, my hands up a scared Peyton who is now clutching onto me, arms wrapped around my neck. "Oh." A giant smile crosses over Hunter's face.

"What the fuck are you doing here?" I sneer, about to kill my best friend.

"I, uh, I thought you were dead or something." He pulls on the back of his neck, and that wicked smile is still on his face.

"Why the hell would you think I was dead?"

"Because" —he shifts on his feet— "you didn't show up to work. You're always at work. You missed a meeting. I thought maybe the whole Project Mountain thing got to you and you keeled over in your apartment. I didn't want you to be dead cold on your cement floors all by yourself."

I'm about to answer when Peyton turns her head, giving Hunter quite the shock when she shows her face. "Don't worry about Project Mountain, Hunter, I got it all covered."

He chuckles and nods his head. "You sure do, don't you?"

"You can leave now."

Standing on his toes, he eyes the bag on the counter and points to it. "What's in there?" He sniffs the air. "Pancakes?"

"Get. The. Fuck. Out." I point to the door.

Holding up his hands, he starts to back away. "You can at least say thank you for making sure you're not dead."

"Don't make him leave. He can join us for breakfast." Peyton flips her hair to the side.

The fuck he can stay. No way in hell is Hunter going to join us for pancakes. I have plans for breakfast, and they don't involve my best friend who can shovel a trough of food in his mouth and still be hungry.

"He's not joining us for breakfast."

Shutting the door. Hunter pats his stomach and walks toward the kitchen where he snags the bag and takes it to the dining table. "Grab napkins, bro, things might get messy."

Jesus Christ.

∿

"**P**ass the syrup." Hunter makes grabby hands at me as I lean back in my chair, completely and utterly irritated that he took over my morning and Peyton seems to be enjoying it. But every time she glances my way with that fucking cute and huge smile on her face, I can't really be angry. She's too gorgeous. *Happy.* With me. *And my idiot friend.*

I push the syrup toward him and watch him drench a stack of pancakes while popping a piece of bacon in his mouth. "I like your outfit, by the way, Peyton. Very *I had a lot of sex last night* look."

"Watch it," I grit out, pulling a piece of bacon off his plate.

"What? It's a compliment." He smiles and winks at Peyton who's blushing, the pink of her cheeks so goddamn endearing.

She fluffs the collar up and says, "Thanks. It's from Rome's hamper. Can you believe that? So chic."

Mouth full, he points his fork at her, brown syrup dripping off the ends and onto my two-thousand-dollar table. "Very becoming on you and the no bra"—he gives her an *okay* sign while turning his lips down and nodding—"nice touch."

I'm about to punch him in the damn teeth if he doesn't stop complimenting my girl.

Yeah, my girl. I left the hickey to prove it.

And he's right; the no bra is a really nice touch. It would be even better if fucking Hunter wasn't here cock-blocking, and I could get my hands back on her tits.

"Do you want to take your pancakes to go?" I ask, hinting for Hunter to leave.

"I'm good here. Thanks though." He halts his chewing for a second to smile at me. "So, when did this start?" He motions between us.

"Last night, actually," Peyton says cheerfully. "He acted like it was all business, but this lovable hunk had other plans." She nudges Hunter with her elbow and wiggles her eyebrows.

Hunter laughs. "You old dog."

Christ. I drag my hands over my face and let out a long breath.

"I think we're upsetting him," Hunter whispers, as if I can't hear him.

"I think it's because he was playing with my nipples before you interrupted us."

"Peyton, can you not?" I ask, wishing we could keep some stuff between her and me.

She shrugs. "What? Your hand was up my shirt when he walked in, so I'm pretty sure he put two and two together."

"Not true." Hunter comes to my defense. "He could have been massaging your breasts, totally different ballgame than nipple play." Hunter cups his hands for demonstration. "You see—"

"You're both fired if you don't stop talking now."

As if they're best friends, they both laugh and go back to their pancakes. Great, just what I need, Hunter and Peyton becoming friends. It's bad enough I have to deal with Hunter's antics. I don't need him looping Peyton in as well. What am I thinking? That's why they get along so damn well. They both treat me the same way already. *So little respect.* Cue the eye-roll.

"Got laid and still uptight, should have known better." Hunter shakes his head and then grows serious. "I'm going to assume since you weren't in the office at the ass crack of dawn, you've found a solution to beat Project Mountain."

I bring my glass of orange juice to my mouth, the condensation running down my fingers. "We did. Peyton did some impressive work."

"And you didn't want to hire her."

Peyton shoots a glare in my direction. Keeping her eyes trained on mine, she asks, "How much did he resist?"

"More than I expected, but he finally gave in, knew you were the best."

"Is that right?" she asks a little skeptically, but I put that skepticism to rest.

"You are. Hands down."

I speak with such conviction that I can tell when my confession registers. Her face softens and she sets down her fork.

Eyes fixed on mine, she says, "You're going to need to take your pancakes to go now, Hunter. I need to properly thank your friend for having so much faith in me."

Like a tennis ball, Hunter's head bounces back and forth between our staredown. He backs his chair away, taking his plate and fork with him. "Uh, I'll just take these dishes and return them later."

The door shuts with a click.

I tilt my head at Peyton who stands from her chair and sways that perfect ass toward me while unbuttoning her shirt, revealing an inch of skin at a time. *Fuck. She got Hunter to leave with few words. Now with even less, she's coming for me.*

I slouch in my chair and grip her hips when she reaches me. She drops the shirt to the floor and leans forward, pressing her hands into my shoulders. My hand glides down the slope of her back to her ass where I squeeze hard.

The smallest of gasps pops out of her mouth before she says, "Pull your pants down, Rome. I'm about to rock your fucking world."

Doesn't she know?

She already has.

CHAPTER TWENTY-FIVE

PEYTON

"Don't you dare turn your nose up at me."

"I'm not."

Accusingly, I point my finger. "You are so turning your nose up. I need a mirror, you should see your face right now."

"Stop."

"Rome."

"Peyton," he answers with that smooth and sweet voice that I know is made for only me. When he's talking to anyone else, there is more of a bite to his words, but for me, he has a different tone, and it does something to my insides that makes them all jumpy.

"Be honest, you're slightly scared."

He eyes the hot dog I just bought for him from the street vendor with the overgrown beard and dubious expression. We just spent the last two hours lounging and reading in the New York City Public Library, looking at all the art, and taking in the beautiful architecture. And get this . . .

Are you ready for it?

We held hands the entire time.

Cue inner girl squeals. I held Rome Blackburn's hand, fingers entwined, legit handholding with the occasional thumb rub on his end. It's such a simple thing, but it meant the world to me, because I've dreamt of being with this man for so long that I almost still can't believe it's true.

And not only are we together, but we've been straight-up monogamously dating for three weeks now. Three weeks of Rome calling me, texting me, sending me flowers.

So many flowers.

Would you ever think of Rome as a flower-giving guy? Me either, but he is. He also sends sex toys, real kinky stuff. That didn't surprise me.

I see him almost every night. Sometimes we talk about business, but most of the time we just talk. He told me all about how he started Roam, Inc. from the ground up like I'm trying to do with Fresh Minted Designs. He told me about his parents and his childhood growing up in Upstate New York and his dream to live in the city one day. He told me about his relationship with Hunter, and why he still loves him even though he drives him crazy most of the time.

I feel like I know more about Rome than I ever thought I would, and what's the best part about all of it? Apart from the mind-blowing sex? When I come into the office, he's all business. We talk strategy, go over mock-ups, and work like professionals. It isn't until he slaps me on the ass and kisses me before I leave that I remember we're a couple.

It's like I have the best of both worlds, and I still can't fathom how I made it all work. With a silly little email joke on my thirtieth birthday. Crazy how things work out sometimes.

"You know, I've lived in the city for years and never once have I ever stopped at a street vendor's cart and bought any type of food from them. Not even a drink."

"It's because you're a snob." I lift his hot dog to his mouth. "Now eat up, it's not going to kill you."

"The guy had cheese dangling from his beard when he served this to us."

I shrug and take a giant bite from my dog, savoring the flavors of the rich onions. "Hey, don't count the guy out. Cheese Beard really knows how to make a good hot dog. This thing is delicious." I lift the hot dog even farther and press it to his lips. "Go on, eat."

He doesn't open his mouth. Ugh, he really is a snob.

"Rome, it's good. Try it."

"I think I'm okay. You can have mine."

I place my hand on my hip, frustration hitting me hard. Not only is he a snob, but he's also stubborn. "Rome Michael, if you don't eat that hot dog right now, I will never give you another blow job again."

Just as the words come out of my mouth, an elderly couple decked out in designer clothing walks by, giving me the stink-eye. I give them a quick salute followed with, "Kids these days, right? Talking about oral sex in public, sheesh?"

They both make a disgusted sound and scurry away, clearly insulted by my crassness. Oh well.

"Was that necessary?" Rome asks.

"Don't change the subject. I will never put my lips on your dick again if you don't eat that hot dog." I run my fingers up his thigh. "And you know the kind of orgasm I can give you with just my tongue. Remember last night . . ."

How could he not? Last night was so incredibly hot. I took him in my mouth in the shower, made him sit on the little bench, and I blew him for what seemed like ten minutes. Every time he got close, I would edge him out, never fully letting him come until I was ready. I've never seen him so angry and turned on at the same time.

Groaning, he relents and takes a big bite of the hot dog, cringing like a baby the whole time. Slowly his face starts to relax, and I can see that he actually enjoys it even if he doesn't want to admit it.

"Good, huh?"

He purses his lips to the side, acting like the hot dog "ain't no thang" when we both know it's heaven on our tongues.

"It's all right."

Liar. I poke his side causing him to laugh as he tries to dodge my finger. "You're such a stubborn man."

Capturing my finger in his hand, he tugs me closer to him and places a sweet kiss across my lips. "I might be stubborn, but at least I'm your man."

So freaking true.

"When did you switch from hard-ass to softie?"

"I'm still a hard-ass."

I shake my head. "Not with me. It's like I hit a soft spot with you."

Growing serious, he brings his hand to my face and strokes my cheek with his thumb. "I hate to admit it, but you did hit a soft spot. I think you hit that soft spot the minute you wrote that first email."

"Yeah, made that soft spot turn hard, huh?" I wiggle my eyebrows at him. "Get it, I'm talking about your penis."

He gives me a giant eye-roll and takes another bite of his hot dog. I knew he liked it. "I got it."

"Just making sure, since you're so stiff all the time." I shoot my finger guns at him. "Hey-o."

Standing, he shakes his head. "I think it's time we went our separate ways now."

Not looking back, his jeans hugging him in all the right places, he takes off down the street without me.

"Hey," I call out, grabbing my purse and chasing after him. I loop my hand through his arm and yank on him to slow down.

Laughing, he leans down and places a kiss on my head before slowing down his powerful stride and enjoying New York City in the afternoon with me.

~

"W here are we?" I ask as we ride up a very long elevator.

"I told you it's a surprise," Rome answers, moving his hand to my hip and pulling me into his chest.

The only thing I know about our dinner tonight is he told me to dress sexy and to bring a coat.

So I spent the day primping my entire body, from head to toe —literally, got a pedicure—curled my hair in waves, stepped into my sexiest lingerie, and put on a killer black dress with a deep V neckline and a short hem that hits me mid-thigh.

And the heels I'm wearing, let's just hope I don't have to walk too far, because there is no way I'll make it.

The elevator above us dings, indicating we've made it to our floor. By the small of my back, Rome guides me out of the elevator and into what feels like an open room.

With an arm wrapped around my waist, holding on to me tightly, he undoes my blindfold and presses a kiss to the side of my head when he says, "Surprise."

It takes a few blinks before my eyes adjust, but once they do, I'm blown away. A span of windows greet me, revealing the beautiful New York City skyline at night. Lights twinkle for miles in front of me, the Hudson River just off to the side, reflecting the picturesque scenery.

"Oh my God," I gasp.

Taking my hand in his, Rome guides me to a small sectioned-off area where there's a table set for two, lit by candlelight, and a bottle of our favorite wine chilled and waiting to be opened.

I turn to him and wrap my arms around his neck. "Rome, I can't believe you did all of this."

He lightly kisses me, his lips lingering for a few seconds before saying, "Anything for you, Peyton." He kisses me again and then asks, "Do you want to go outside, take in all the scenery before dinner?"

"I would love that."

Still caught up in the romance of this night, it isn't until we're outside, staring at the busy streets of the city that I realize we're at the top of a monumental building.

"Are we at the top of the Empire State Building?"

"Yup. Rented it for the night for us."

"You're kidding."

He shakes his head, his lips sealed together.

"You seriously rented the whole building?"

He wraps his arms around me, warming me up from the cold breeze. "Not the whole building, just the touristy part. And afterward, you can have your pick of any souvenir in the gift shop."

"Oh, you really *do* know how to win a girl's heart, don't you?"

He chuckles into my ear, the sound so sexy, so Rome.

"I know how to win *my* girl's heart. Let's put it that way. How long have we been together now? A month? I have realized that whenever we do something, you always like to get a souvenir, even if it's just a sticker."

I lean my head against his shoulder and take in the dark abyss that rests before us, only lit up by what seems like little lights from where we stand. "I like to remember the places I go, the things I do."

"I think it's cute."

"I think it's cute that you think I'm cute, or that you even say the word cute. If you told me two months ago that Rome Blackburn would be referring to me as cute, I would have told them they were high."

"I don't think *you're* cute. Your personality yes, but you, no. You're sexy, hot, and drop-dead gorgeous."

Wow.

Considering how gorgeous this man is, it still amazes me that he sees me that way, too.

I rub my hips against his, making a low thrumming sound in the back of my throat. "You're good to me, Rome."

"Because I care about you." He turns me around in his arms and lowers his hands to my back where they rest. "I hate to admit it, but you've kind of wiggled yourself into my life."

"Why do you hate to admit it?" I stroke the stubble on his jaw, coarse and rough, just like him.

He grips me tighter. "Because I'm stubborn, and from the beginning, you've wanted to be with me and I had to succumb to the overwhelming feelings I had for you. It wasn't an easy pill to swallow."

He goes in for a kiss, but I palm his face, stopping him. "Care to rephrase that? It wasn't the most romantic thing you've ever said."

Chuckling, he kisses my hand and says, "Basically, you're a leech I can't seem to get rid of."

"Rome." I pull on the lapels of his jacket.

"Okay, sorry." He clears his throat. "You're a piranha—"

"I hate you." I start to walk away when he pulls me back into his chest and captures my lips with his. Smooth like silk, they glide over mine, nipping, licking, and sucking to the point that my knees start to go weak, and I am forced to dig my hands into Rome's biceps to steady myself.

When he pulls away, he softly brushes a strand of hair behind my ear, keeping his eyes fixed on mine. "You're special to me, Peyton, and I wouldn't trade this last month for anything. Not because you're killer at what you do, and not because you're fucking sexy as shit in the bedroom, but because you've genuinely put a smile on my face, and there aren't many people I can say do that to me."

Be still my heart.

This man has rendered me speechless, because no one has ever said that to me before. Has ever seen all of me the way he does. I swallow back tears, because even though the words are romantic and sentimental, praise from this man still stuns me.

I bite my bottom lip to keep it from trembling and run my fingers through his hair, framing his face with my hand. "You've been my dream man for so long, Rome, and . . . actually no. That's not right. You are even better—more magnificent than the dream I'd imagined. And the fact that I can stand here, touching you any way I want, and I have those beautiful eyes of yours giving me your full attention, it means everything to me."

He pinches my chin and pulls on my bottom lip with his thumb. "Keep saying things like that and we'll never make it to dinner."

"What's for dinner?"

"Your favorite, chicken pot pie."

I weigh my options. "Sex or chicken pot pie." I pause, giving it some real thought. "God, I'm so sorry, Rome, but I'm going to have to go with the chicken pot pie."

Chuckling, he takes my hand and leads me inside to *our* table. "Don't worry, I knew that would be your answer. The passion you have for a dinner pie is powerful. I know where I stand."

"If it were a casserole, we would be naked right about now."

He pulls a chair out for me. "What if it were quiche?"

"Ooo," I cringe. "Tough matchup. Let me get back to you on that. You know how I love a good quiche."

Hands on my shoulders, leaning forward, he places a quick kiss on my jaw and whispers, "I know all too well how much you like quiche . . . babe."

"Peyton, what the hell is taking you so long?"

I stroll down Rome's hallway, the concrete chilly beneath my feet as I make my way toward my man.

It was a long day full of rigorous work, prepping the launch of the new women's line in a few weeks, and it's taken its toll on me. I'm exhausted.

It could also be from the insatiable man sitting on the stiff couch, shirtless, in sweatpants—yes, Rome owns a few pairs—who about ten minutes ago came inside me with such a vicious roar that I was certain he was going to pass out. But nope, he's sitting in the living room, waiting for me to cuddle and watch a movie.

"I'm a little sore," I say, hobbling over to him.

His forehead creases, sharp brows pulling together. "Sore? From what?"

Slowly, I ease myself down next to him, feeling a little twinge in my back, only to settle on a rock-hard surface, and I'm not talking, Rome.

I hate his couch, so much. It's so uncomfortable. Everything about his entire place is uncomfortable, but to be fair in this little relationship, I suggested splitting the nights we spend in each other's places. My apartment, although not as fancy, is a hell of a lot more comfortable, with maybe a crazy neighbor problem that likes to scream a lot. Not Rome's favorite part about staying with me, but at least he can sit on my couch without cracking a hip. I've told him you get used to the yelling after a while, but he hasn't seemed to catch on.

Turning toward me, Rome assesses my body, strong gaze unwavering as he looks me up and down. "Why are you sore?"

I hold my lower back. "I don't know, maybe it was the acrobats you put me through on a daily basis."

Just in time, I see his face go from extreme concern to a lazy smile as he pulls me into his chest. "Babe, sex sore is different than real sore. Sex sore is something to be proud of."

"Uh, speaking for the guy who doesn't want to dip his entire body in Bengay right about now."

He nuzzles his nose into my neck, his soft lips playing along my skin. "Who says I'm not sore?"

"Me, I do. You're not the one taking the brunt of your hips." I turn my head and look him in the eyes. "Not to boost your already inflated ego, but you have some powerful thrusts, my friend, and when you have me contorted, driving in me like that, yeah, girl's going to be sore."

"Powerful thrusts, huh?" His smile stretches across his handsome face, and even though I want to roll my eyes at how happy he is, I can't. Because he's happy. I make him happy, and that right there is everything.

244

"Don't get too cocky, all right? There are things you could improve on."

I hide my smirk.

Clearing his throat, completely stunned, he twists me in his arms and says, "Excuse me? What do you mean I have things I could improve on? From the sounds coming out of your mouth when I'm buried deep inside of you, it doesn't seem like I have anything to improve on."

Casually I shrug. "You know, foreplay might be lacking."

"What?" He nearly jumps out of his seat, pushing me to the side so he can really look me in the eyes. "You're complaining about foreplay?"

Bringing my hand to my face, I examine my nails and nonchalantly say, "It's okay, Rome, some people show weakness in bed." I pat his leg. "I think you just need to realize that foreplay isn't office talk. I don't get turned on talking about emails and highlighters like you do."

He studies me, his eyes boring into my soul, looking for any sort of falter in my demeanor, and when he clears his throat, I can't hide it anymore. A smile peeks out.

His eyes widen—disbelief etched in them—and he takes the pillow from behind him and tosses it at me as he roars out of his seat. "Oh, you're in fucking trouble, babe." He's rounding the couch and pointing at me. "So much trouble."

I chuck the pillow back at him that he easily dodges by swatting it away. "What kind of trouble?"

Energized, looking sexy as hell as he bounces on his feet, the muscles in his chest flexing, rippling. "The worst kind of trouble."

Loving this super playful side of him, I sit on my knees and say, "Ooo, what kind of trouble?"

"Not the kind of trouble you're hoping for."

My face falls. "So, not like the kind of trouble where you punish me with your penis?"

Lips sealed shut, he shakes his head, no. "Nope. This is the kind where you don't get any penis."

"Ha!" I laugh. "I would love for you to try to punish me that way, Mr. Morning Erection."

"Watch. You'll be begging for my 'horrible' foreplay." He uses air quotes, his smile so brilliant.

"I never said horrible."

Picking up another throw pillow from a chair close to him, he tosses it at me. "Might as well have."

                                    ∿

For the record, when Rome sets his mind to something, he means it. I should have known this given his work ethic.

But clearly, I forgot who I was dealing with.

We haven't had sex in a week. A freaking week.

I'm about to lose my mind from the built-up sexual tension inside me. We're still sleeping in the same bed, trading on and off at each other's places. *It's killing me.*

Try sleeping next to Mr. I Sleep Naked, when all you want is his mouth on your body, his hands on your breasts, and his dick inside you, pumping like a crazed sailor on leave.

He's holding out on me, and it almost seems like it's not affecting him one bit. If I knew he wasn't one hundred percent committed to me, I would think he's getting some side action.

His hand must be really good at getting the job done.

Mine, not so much. It's nothing like the real deal that is Rome. He commands my body, makes me feel things I've never felt before and after, when he's cuddling me, nuzzling his nose into my hair, it's pure bliss.

I miss it.

And being in this meeting right now where I have to act professionally is slowly eating me alive, especially when he keeps lifting his eyes to look down my blouse that I might have popped open the top few buttons just for him.

"And everything is in line in production, ready to roll out?" Rome asks, flipping his pen between his fingers. He's sitting at the head of the conference table like he always does, wearing a navy-blue button-up shirt and light gray slacks. I watched him get dressed this morning and couldn't help but gawk at how tight-fitting his pants are.

"Yes, Mr. Blackburn," some guy says to the right of me. I can't remember his name to save my life right now, not when Rome is slowly chewing on the corner of his lip.

I swear to God he's doing this on purpose.

"Miss Lévêque, care to answer?"

"Huh?" I shake my head, eyes blinking rapidly. I was so not paying attention.

Rome's face turns stern, but there is a sparkle in his eye that tells me he's amused. "It would help if you would pay attention rather than daydreaming."

"Sorry." I clear my throat. "I haven't had a good week. What was the question?"

Smirking behind his pen, Rome says, "How are we with our partnership with Adventure Protein Bars and Fuelade?"

"All set. Contracts have been signed, and products have already been shot for ads."

"Good." He taps his pen on his pad of paper and says, "That's all for this evening. It's late, get home and get some sleep. The next few weeks are going to be trying as we narrow down on release date. I'll have Lauren type up the notes and send them out tomorrow." He stands from his chair as well as everyone else. I take my time gathering my things, knowing Rome is the last to leave the conference room.

Hands in his pockets now, stoic as ever, he watches his employees filter out of the room one by one. This was the Rome I fell for, the one who caught my attention. Business minded, relentless, and vastly intelligent when it comes to running a company. But the Rome I get to see outside of the office, that's the one I've become addicted to, and it's about time I feed my addiction.

I stand from my chair, push it under the table, and then meander my way to Rome who's studying my every move.

When I step up to him, he gives me a full once-over. "Haven't had a good week, huh?"

I shake my head, pouting my lip. "No, not at all."

Hands still in his pockets, he tips his body forward, getting close to me, and his cologne seeps into my veins, awakening everything inside me. "It would be best if you don't bring your personal life into the office, Miss Lévêque."

The giant ass.

I flip my hair to the side and clutch my notes to my chest. "It would be best if you didn't eye-fuck me during meetings, Mr. Blackburn."

The smallest smirk passes over his lips, barely reaching his eyes. "Don't unbutton your blouse like that, and I won't eye-fuck you."

Chest puffed, I say, "Stop trying to prove a point and fuck me already, Rome."

I'm trying to garner a reaction out of him, but he doesn't even bat an eyelash. Instead, he rocks back on his heels and says, "Nah, I'm good," and then gestures toward the door for me to exit.

I'm going to kill him.

Huffing, I walk past him only to feel his hand float to the small of my back and his body fall behind me, chest close, breath mixing with mine.

I pause in my attempt to leave as his hand moves a little lower to just above my butt. A sharp intake of air hits my lungs along with his cologne making me feel dizzy and turned on all at once.

My nipples pucker when his thumb glides over my back.

My lips part when I feel his chest touch my shoulder.

And my breathing starts to become erratic when his mouth lowers to my ear.

Ever so quietly, he whispers, "This whole week, this right here, this is what you call foreplay, babe. One thousand dollars says if I shifted your thong to the side and felt that delicious pussy it would be soaking wet."

Goddamn him.

Chuckling from my silence, he whispers again, his lips grazing my ear, "Don't ever fucking say I don't have good foreplay game, because you damn well know that I do. Scurry on to my apartment, strip down, and have your legs spread by the time I get there. I'm going to fuck you until morning."

I want to be the defiant girlfriend, the one that tells him to fuck off, but I am so beyond turned on right now that I nod and exit the conference room with one thing on my mind: deliciously hard, hot sex with Rome.

And I couldn't be happier.

CHAPTER TWENTY-SIX

ROME

"How was your day?" Peyton asks, looking pretty as fuck sitting across from me, her hair tied up in a tight bun, her dress accentuating her beautiful collarbone.

Not a single damn day goes by that I don't think about how lucky I am. What a lucky bastard I am who won the girl.

But here I am, Peyton across from me in a restaurant I wouldn't have caught myself dead in a few weeks ago, and yet I'm here for her because she's never been.

"Fine," I answer, looking around.

Stained glass chandeliers of all shapes, sizes, colors and themes hang sporadically from the ceiling. Dainty white chairs and tables fill the space while little pom-pom bullshit things dangle everywhere.

It's a little girl's dream.

My freaking nightmare.

"Isn't it so cute in here?" Peyton leans over and clasps my hand with hers. "Thank you for taking me here."

And when she bats her eyelashes like that at me, so fucking

happy, I have to swallow my pride and deal with feeling like a complete dickhead in the well-known NYC restaurant, Serendipity.

Giving in to her smile, I say, "Anything for you, babe."

She squeezes my hand and takes a sip of her water, humor in her face. When she lowers her glass, she leans forward and says, "You're so getting laid for this tonight."

"Oh . . . I know." I tip my glass toward her and then take a sip of my own. "By the way, I was thinking." I pause, feeling my nerves start to climb up my spine.

We've been together for two months now, we spend every night together, and once I left work today, it hit me. I had this overwhelming need to take things to the next step. On the drive here, I played the conversation over and over in my head—what I would say, how I would ask, but now I'm here in the moment, I'm freezing.

Me.

Freezing.

It's never happened to me. I've been in meetings where I've had to introduce a new state-of-the-art product and I've never had an issue, but right here, right now, talking to Peyton, I choke.

"Is there an end to that sentence?" She tilts her head to the side, studying me. "Rome, are you okay?"

"Yeah." I pull on my collar, trying to get air to my burning skin.

What if she says no?

What if it's too soon?

Is it too soon?

Christ.

The waitress puts a giant cup of frozen hot chocolate in front of us with multiple straws, the one and only thing Peyton wanted to try from here.

"Enjoy, you two," the waitress says before taking off, neither of us paying any attention to her.

"Rome, you look pale."

"Really?" I nervously laugh. "Huh."

Her eyes narrow, her mind probably reeling with possibilities. She sees me retreating, and she's not going to let it happen.

Scooting her chair to my side, she takes my hand and gently strokes her thumb over my knuckles, easing the tension in my shoulders.

"Okay, we can do this the easy way or the hard way. You can either tell me what you were going to say," her voice is soft and sweet, caring, "or I can bug you all night until you tell me."

Truth, she's done it before.

Knowing I need to nut up, I let out a big breath and look her in her beautiful, expressive eyes. "I think we should move in together."

Blunt, to the point, perfect.

Peyton's expression doesn't change. She barely blinks, and I think I shock the hell out of her until she says, "That's how you're going to ask me to move in? With a statement? It wasn't even a question."

She moves back to the side of her table and is shaking her head.

"Oh no, Rome. Not like this." She takes a big sip of the frozen hot chocolate and then grips her head. "Ooo, ice cream headache."

Uh . . . so, is that a no?

Eyeing her, completely confused, I ask, "Am I taking that as a no?"

She shakes her head. "No, I'll move in with you, but not until you ask properly."

Jesus Christ. *Women*.

I refrain from rolling my eyes. "Fine, will you move in with me?"

Eyebrow cocked, straw halfway to her mouth, she mocks me. "'Fine, will you move in with me?' Oh no, not going to ask with attitude. And don't bother trying to rephrase it tonight. You're going to have to think this over, make a grand gesture now."

"You're serious?"

She looks me straight in the eyes. "Dead serious." Then she

lifts a straw, plasters a smile on her face, and says, "Drink up, handsome, it's delicious."

What the hell just happened here?

∼

"Grand gesture, huh?" Hunter says, patting me on the shoulder as we enter the conference room for our Tuesday morning meeting. "Good luck with that."

"I don't even know what it means."

"It means you better look on Pinterest or something, get some ideas."

I adjust the sleeves of my suit and speak quietly as we enter the room. "I'm not looking on goddamn Pinterest."

Lauren shuts the door behind me, a knowing smirk on her face. She is the only one in the office who knows Peyton and I are dating, and only because she walked in on us making out once late at night. She forgot something at her desk, and when she saw someone in my office, believing I'd already gone, she checked to see who it was. To her shock, it was Peyton and me lip-locked with my hand halfway up her blouse.

I gave her a nice little gift card the next morning and thanked her for her discretion.

And I hate to admit it, but she's been super helpful when it comes to sending things to Peyton during the day, especially things like lunch and . . . quiche.

I scan the room, making sure everyone is here. Peyton doesn't come to these meetings, because they're more about what's happening for the week than strategic planning.

Just like everyone else sitting in their seats, coffee in hand, a dreaded look on their face, I hate these meetings, but it's necessary to go to them.

We always start with a round-table shout-out, so if someone has something interesting to say that pertains to the company, they can speak up.

Employees take that time to discuss if they used a certain product over the weekend or if someone reached a milestone working for the company, light and fluffy shit that I don't care about but I know helps the morale of the company.

I take a seat, cross my ankle over my knee, and nod at the woman sitting close to me. Andrea I think is her name.

"Start us off with the shout-out."

Smiling brightly, she nods her head and starts talking about the new women's line, how she used one of the sweat-proof long-sleeved tees, and how amazing it was and comfortable.

Okay, I like to hear that kind of shit.

Next, it's George. The only announcement he had was his wife made brownies again, and they're on the marketing floor if anyone wants any.

Lauren will be sneaking down later to snag one for me. Those brownies are lethal. I eye Lauren who gives me a conspiratorial wink.

And we go down the line. Some people don't have anything to say while others talk about meaningless shit until the shout-out stops at a redhead I've seen before but never in these meetings.

Who is she again?

Waving, she says, "Hi, I'm Sasha, and George invited me up to this meeting, because I have some rather interesting news to share." Her voice is fucking awful, all high-pitched and squeaky. The less she talks, the better.

"Go on." I motion with my hand.

Showing no nerves, she says, "You know how we had that leak this weekend over the line of hats in our women's wear line?"

Don't get me fucking started on that. Thank God I don't care too much about the hats. We have four options, and that's it. The hats aren't going to make or break the launch, but it was annoying as shit when Project Mountain announced a hat line yesterday.

"Yeah," I push her to go on.

"Well, I think I found the leak."

Okay, now we're onto something. She nods to someone who's

standing by the lights of the conference room. The room turns dark, and the TV screen lights up with pictures.

"I took these this weekend. I thought I was seeing things at first, but once I got closer, I was blown away."

The pictures are shit. It looks like a bunch of people sitting outside at a dog café, having breakfast.

But then she scrolls to the next one, and that's when my heart catches in my chest and my blood starts to boil. Immediately, Hunter's hand goes to my shoulder, trying to calm me.

Sitting, legs crossed, laughing with a cup of coffee in hand, is Peyton, dressed fucking professionally and talking to Lance Holiday, the CEO of Project Mountain.

What the actual fuck?

"For those of you who don't know, I took Peyton's job in social media at Roam, Inc. when she resigned. She's now working on our women's line and running the entire marketing campaign. So you can imagine my surprise when I saw her talking to Lance." She flips to another slide. They're both looking at a mock-up, and she's pointing at it while he's listening intently.

I feel physically ill as Sasha continues to flip through, picture after picture, every single one of them like a nail to my fucking heart.

How could she do this to me? To Roam, Inc.?

I know she was desperate for a job, but that desperate to betray me?

She was so passionate about beating Project Mountain, but has she been double-crossing me this entire time?

I don't fucking get it.

Pushing back from the table, I stand from my chair and say, "Meeting is canceled."

I storm out of the conference room and to the elevator where I rapidly punch the down button with my index finger. Heavy footsteps chase after me, and I don't have to look to the side to figure out who it is.

"Dude, there has to be an explanation."

"Like what?"

Hunter's silent, trying to think of anything to give her a get-out-of-jail-free card. I wish I was trying to think of the same thing, but all I can see are those damming photos. All I can see is the woman I have trusted with everything, smiling at someone I consider my biggest rival. No, I can't see an explanation at all. "I don't know, but before you blow up on her, why don't you take a second to calm down and try to think about this rationally."

The elevator dings and I walk inside, pressing the lobby floor button.

As the doors close, I say, "There is no rational thought in me right now."

"That's what I'm afraid of," he answers right before the doors close.

On the way to the lobby, I take my phone out of my pocket and shoot George a quick email, telling him to have Martha email those pictures to me ASAP. Within five minutes, while I'm riding in the back of my driver's Buick, I have the pictures in hand. All the way to the coffee house, I study the photos, looking through each and every one of them with a sharp eye, and no matter how hard I try, the only conclusion I can come up with is that she's trying to dick me over.

I just have no fucking clue why.

~

There she is, sipping her coffee, looking fresh and beautiful in her bright yellow dress and matching high heels, working diligently on her iPad and computer. For a moment, you would think she actually gave a fuck about my company. Or maybe she isn't working on Roam, Inc. stuff. Maybe she's working on Project Mountain.

In six strides, I'm standing in front of her table, staring down at her.

She startles and looks up. A smile spreads across her face, but then is quickly washed away when she notices my expression.

"Rome, is everything okay?"

I don't fuck around. I take a seat across from her and speak just low enough that we are the only two who can hear our conversation. "Tell me right now if you've been fucking me over."

"What?" She sits back as if I just slapped her across the face.

"Don't fuck around, Peyton." Her name feels like a swear word coming out of my mouth. "Just tell me the truth."

She folds her arms across her chest, becoming defensive immediately. "Excuse me, but first of all, you could greet me like a normal human being and say hello, maybe act like my boyfriend and press a kiss against my cheek, and then in a level tone of voice, you can explain to me why you're accusing me of, as you so eloquently put it, 'fucking you over.'"

I drag my hand over my face out of frustration and remove my phone from my pocket. I open the email with all the pictures and flash the screen in her direction.

She takes a minute to look at them and with an impassive face, just stares at me.

"Well . . ." I ask, giving her a chance to explain.

"Well, what? Seems like you've already drawn your own conclusion."

"What kind of conclusion am I supposed to draw? We've had a leak in the line. Just this weekend there was a leak, and it just so happens to be the same weekend you were caught with the CEO from Project Mountain."

There is so much anger raging inside me, that I almost forget we're in a public area.

When I see past my rage boiling inside and take a look at Peyton, it looks like she's about to cry.

Cry . . . because she's been caught?

Without a word, she packs up her things, stuffs them in her bag, stands from the table, not even giving me a second glance before walking out of the coffee shop toward her apartment.

Is she kidding me?

I waste no time in chasing after her.

The relentless people of New York City around us continue on with their day as I snag Peyton by the arm and pull her to the side, out of the way of people walking from point A to point B.

"Let go of me," she says, tears in her eyes.

"Just admit it," I reply. "Just fucking tell me so I can move on."

Taking a deep breath, Peyton finally looks up at me, water filling those eyes I used to love staring into. Right now, all I can see is betrayal. *How could I have been such a damn fool?*

"You want the truth?"

"Truth would be fucking nice right about now."

"Fine." She reaches into her purse and pulls out a file folder and holds it up to me. "This is a rundown on everything Project Mountain has for their women's line. They called me last week, wanting to meet up and talk about using my services. I thought it would be a great opportunity to scope out the competition. The idiots gave me everything they planned on doing. I spent the entire day yesterday and this morning comparing and contrasting both lines and highlighting sections you need to be concerned about, while offering solutions to combat them. I didn't say anything, because I didn't want to get your hopes up that we might finally have more than just a breakthrough on this. I was planning on giving it to you tonight." She pushes the file against my chest, forcing me to take it, as my mind starts spiraling in a million directions.

I don't know if I should start with 'I'm sorry,' or 'Oh, fuck.'

"It would have been nice of you if . . . No. I *cannot* believe you accused me of trying to fuck you over. You know me better than that."

I swallow hard. Fuck, I'm such an idiot. "Peyton . . ."

"No." She shakes her head. "I understand your passion for your business and the employees that work for you. I've known from the beginning that you value each and every minute you're working, but *never* would I have ever guessed you'd treat me as poorly as you have today." She fixes her purse strap on her shoulder, pulling it closer to her body. "I would have expected you, out of anyone, to have respected me and my business enough to know I would never do that to you. Never deceive you *or* put your business on the line."

"I didn't know what to think," I say quickly, trying to come up with anything to ease the hurt in her eyes and the devastation in my heart.

"You could have thought, 'My girlfriend really likes me. No—I think there is possible love there. So even though these pictures look damming, I *know* she isn't capable of something so incredibly awful. Period.'" *Love?*

My heart swells just as it's deflated by the look in her eyes.

"I'm sorry." I drag my hand through my hair. "I was caught off guard."

Leaning forward, she looks me dead in the eyes and says, "Then let me catch you off guard again. We're done, Rome."

"What?" She starts to walk off, but I catch her by the arm again. "Peyton, come on."

"No, Rome." She shakes her head, tears falling from her eyes that she quickly wipes away. She points to the coffee house. "Back there, where you first gave me the job to work with you on the women's line, it meant the world to me that you trusted me enough with this project. And yeah, I might have fallen for you in the process of all this. But what it comes down to is that you've never really trusted me."

"That's not true."

"No? Well, it sure as hell seems like it to me." She shakes her head. "Don't worry, I'll finish out my work with Roam, Inc., see through the launch of the women's line, but I'll only work with Hunter on it. When it's over, I'm through with Roam, Inc. Done."

My chest constricts, my body is numb, and for the first time since I started dating Peyton, fear takes over me. She's serious. She's really ending this, and fuck if that doesn't devastate me more than anything.

Fuck the business.

Fuck the women's line.

Fuck Project Mountain.

I can't lose Peyton, not after everything we've been through, not after I've . . . I've . . .

Before I can come to terms with my feelings, Peyton is walking down the sidewalk, not even bothering to look back at me.

I tell my feet to move, to chase after her, but for the life of me, I can't seem to listen. Because all I can hear are her words: *"We're done . . . I might have fallen for you in the process of all this. But what it comes down to is that you've never really trusted me . . . We're done."*

CHAPTER TWENTY-SEVEN

ROME

"It's called a shower," Hunter says, barging through my office and taking a seat in front of me, a folder in his hand. The dickhead has actually been doing my job for the past two weeks.

My job of working with Peyton, and I can't fucking stand it.

I know when every meeting occurs, when it ends, and the exact moment they part ways, because Hunter texts me the goddamn update every time.

Just getting to the coffee house. Short dress. She looks fine, dude.

God, she's so smart. She is really good at this shit.

What's her perfume? It smells amazing.

Did you know she paints her fingernails often? Today it's pink.

The way she bites her bottom lip . . . dude.

She gave me a hug goodbye today. Her tits pressed against my chest **okay hand sign emoji**

Oh and she sways her ass when she walks away.

I could seriously kill him. It's been like that for the past two weeks.

I know what she smells like, like fucking rain and sunshine. And I know she paints her nails. I've watched her do it wearing nothing but my shirt. And smart? Fuck, she's the smartest girl I know, so clever and astute. It's why I hired her. Not because of the emails or the flirting, but because she's damn good at what she does, and I needed her on my team.

Now I need her in my life. A permanent fixture.

I miss everything about her. The way she tests my patience or brightens when I walk in the room, or the way she moans my name when I'm thrusting into her, never able to get enough.

I love her ability to bring me to my knees with her quick wit, and I love that she knows when I need her to sit on my lap and let me hold her, breathing in her scent and empathy after a hard day.

I love her personality—feisty and intelligent—how it kept me on my toes. And I love her smile, her sultry eyes, and her full lips.

Christ . . . I . . . I love her.

Hunter raps his knuckles on my wooden top desk. "Uh, hello in there. Were you even listening to me?"

I shake my head and rub my hand down my face, the three-day-old stubble growing into an actual beard. "No, I'm not listening to you because whatever you're saying is probably going to torture me, and I don't want to hear about it. Just give me the notes and move on."

After every visit with Peyton, Hunter makes his first stop here in the office to torture me with details about how amazing Peyton is.

Newsflash: I fucking know, and I'm the dipshit who screwed it up.

"You're right." Hunter reaches into his pocket and pulls out a protein bar. Unwraps, chomps, chews. The crinkling sound makes me want to drive my head into the wall. "I would have told you that she looked sad today. Her 'I'm okay' façade has worn off, and she's lacking the brilliance in her eyes."

Fuck.

I can't handle the image in my head. A sullen Peyton, barely getting through the meeting, that spark she carries, dulled and masked.

Fuck, I'm a moron.

"She didn't even order a drink this time."

"What?" I snap my head at Hunter. "Why?"

"Said she wasn't thirsty or hungry. Didn't stop me from eating a croissant and licking my fingers afterward."

"Shit," I mumble and lean back in my chair.

Hunter exhales and props his ankle up on his knee. "Dude, what's stopping you from saying you're sorry?"

"I already said I was sorry, but she walked away."

"Don't be a moron. Of course she walked away. You hurt her, big time. And mind you, I told you not to blow up, and look what you did."

"Thanks for the reminder."

"Seriously though, what are you waiting for? You look like shit; she looks like shit. You clearly miss her, so go grovel at her feet."

"It's not that easy," I answer, staring at the wallpaper on my computer screen. It's a picture Peyton took of us at Serendipity. She's sitting on my lap, arm wrapped around my neck as I kiss her cheek, the smile on her face so gorgeous.

"Why not?"

"Because she wouldn't even say yes to moving in with me—"

"Because she wanted a grand gesture, not some bullshit statement that you guys should move in together." Hunter snaps his finger and lowers his foot, inching closer to my desk. "Pull up Pinterest. I bet we could find some good ideas on how to win her back."

"I'm not looking at goddamn Pinterest." I push back from my desk, and pace my office, rubbing the back of my neck. My mind whirls but not with ideas, with worry. What if I've waited too long? What if she doesn't want me back?

Head bent forward, completely deflated, I say, "I love her, Hunter."

"I know, so what are you going to do about it?"

Turning toward him, I eye my computer again, her infectious joy reminding me where we started . . .

"I think I have an idea."

Hunter rubs his hands together and leans forward. "Oh, my nips just got hard. Lay it on me."

I really need to get a new best friend.

~

Hunter suggested I clean myself up before I try to win Peyton back, and I think he was right, for once. I didn't shave, kind of liking the scruff, but I trimmed it up so it didn't look like a truck just dragged me down nine miles of bumpy road. I chose to wear a pair of black jeans and a gray V-neck sweater with a white shirt underneath it. Peyton always said she loves me in my business clothes, but it's my "street" clothes that really turn her on.

Fuck, I'm nervous.

I've never had to win a girl back. I've never been interested enough to put in the effort, but Peyton is worth every single second of my time.

Sitting at a restaurant across from the coffee house, I have the perfect view of her. Dressed in jeans and a simple blue sweater, brown boots up to her knees, she looks so good. The minute I laid eyes on her, knowing she's so close, I felt the beat of my heart wanting to erupt out of my chest.

Pulling my phone from my pocket, I pull up the email I put together and give it one more look, tweaking it until I'm comfortable.

I glance at Peyton again. Her nose is buried in her computer working diligently, a cup of coffee next to her. What did she get today? A latte? She favors those more, but when she's in dire need of caffeine, she goes for the espresso. Does she need caffeine today like I need it, to help combat the sleepless nights I've had?

Only one way to find out.

Taking a deep breath, I press send and wait.

CHAPTER TWENTY-EIGHT

PEYTON

This latte is doing shit for me right now. I should have gone with the espresso with five shots, because oh my God, I can barely keep my eyes open as I look over these ad copies. My vision feels blurry, and my mind is elsewhere—on a certain asshole who unfortunately captured my heart.

I press my hand against my forehead, trying to keep myself propped up through my drowsiness.

Okay, maybe I kind of wish he would come apologize again. Yes, I'm that girl. What he did was presumptuous and mean and the definition of his personality, but it still stung . . . because I thought I was different. I thought I mattered to him, that I could be someone he could talk to before jumping to conclusions.

I'm so mad at him, but I also want him.

I love him.

I hate everything about this.

Sighing, I take a sip of my lukewarm latte just as a new email pops up on my computer.

I set my latte down as I click on the preview, pulling up the email.

I don't recognize the email address at first, but when I take a closer look, my heart sputters in my chest, and my breath catches in my throat.

Hands Roaming Peytons Body.

Subject: I don't want to bang you . . .

With shaking hands, I scroll to the start of the email.

To Whom it May Concern (I mean you, Peyton):

You don't know how gutted I am writing this, but it has to be said. Because I can't fucking stand it anymore.

I can't breathe as tears start to well in my eyes, making it impossible to see the screen in front of me. This is almost word for word the first email I sent him as LSY.

I cover my mouth in awe, taking a deep breath to steady my nerves.

But . . . full disclosure, I would like it to be known that I have consumed zero alcoholic beverages before writing this. Yes, I might have had too many drinks in the last two weeks while trying to fill an empty void in my heart, but I can honestly say right now, typing this email, I am completely sober and pouring my heart out to you. For the record though, I've had five cups of coffee this morning to make up for the sleepless nights without you.

I think it's important to be open and honest with the one you love, don't you? And full disclosure, Peyton?

I love you.

And I'm finally being honest.

I like you so much, and it's clouding my judgment, making me do things I never would, like lash out at you and blame you for things that you'd never in a million years do. < - - Did you read that? Never in a million years do I think you would BETRAY ME. I'm a fucking asshole for even thinking it for a second, and I'm so fucking sorry.

I have a hopeless, foolish, school yard crush on you.

Did you know people around the office call ME a sadist? An egomaniac? An insensitive, arrogant prick? But you knew from the beginning that

267

my bark was worse than my bite. You gave me a chance to prove that I'm more than the man behind the desk with a tie cinched tightly around my neck.

For once, you were the one who put a smile on my face. You were the one I wanted to impress. You were the one I wanted more than anyone else.

And as long as we're being honest, that blue sweater you're wearing? With the low-enough V that I can see the swell of your breasts? It really makes me want to ask you a very important question . . .

I don't want to bang you . . . I want to love you if you'll let me.

~~Love,~~

~~Sincerely,~~

ALWAYS Yours

Postscript: Look up.

Look up? What the heck does that mean?

I wipe the tears from my eyes and lift my head to find Rome standing in front of me with a white box in hand, the other hand stuffed in his pocket, looking nervous but so sexy in his sweater and jeans.

Oh God, I forgot how handsome he is.

"Hey babe," he says gently, taking a step forward. And there it is, his cologne waking me up for the first time in weeks. Before I can say anything, he drops to one knee in front of me and holds out the box. "Open it." His intense eyes are intent on me, soulful and hopeful all wrapped into one.

With shaky hands, I lift the lid of the pastry box to find my favorite quiche at the bottom and written on the top with a key taped below it, it says, "I can't live another day without your hugs and 'quiches.' Will you move in with me?"

Like the girl that I am, I cover my mouth, and tears continue to fall from my eyes. He sets the box on the table and takes my hands into his, never moving his eyes from mine.

"Peyton, I'm so goddamn sorry for what I said, for not trusting you when I know I should have. You mean everything to me, and not because of all the incredible work you've done for me, but because you're so beautifully intelligent and witty and make me so fucking happy. I can't imagine another day without you by my side." He kisses my hand and says, "Will you forgive me and please move in with me?"

Unable to hold back my excitement or keep him waiting, I nod my head and chuckle as he pulls me into his chest and hugs me until I feel like I'm about to break.

Sighing into my neck, he kisses my cheek and then whispers, "I love you so fucking much, Peyton. I'm sorry I hurt you."

Out of my mind with joy, I hug him even tighter and then pull away. I point my finger at him and say, "Don't do it again. I don't forgive easily."

He chuckles, the sound no longer foreign to my ears. "Never."

Gripping his cheeks, I bring his lips to mine where I place a soft, gentle kiss on them and say, "I love you, Rome, and I can't wait to share a home with you, but . . ."

"But?" He cocks a brow at me.

"But we're not living in that concrete jungle of an apartment you have."

Smiling brightly, he says, "Don't worry, I got the apartment two floors down. Fresh and new for the both of us."

"You're such a good man."

"Good for you."

He captures his mouth with mine and even though we're in the middle of a coffee house most likely making a scene, I don't care. He was known as a sadist and an egomaniac, and a tyrant, but I knew deep down, he was a soulful gentleman with an alpha tendency that was going to bring me to my knees.

And guess what? He's all MINE.

When he pulls away, he sighs and rests his head against mine. "God, I love you."

"I love you too." Twisting my lips to the side in a smile, I add, "And by the way, I can't live another day without your hugs and 'quiches.' Clever, Rome. Very clever."

He shyly shrugs. "Who knew Pinterest could help win your girl back?"

EPILOGUE

HUNTER

I can't even look at those two. They're so disgusting.

My two friends; the one I've had for half my life, and the other because, well—he fell in love with her, and she's fucking cool. I couldn't help but become her friend.

She's irresistible, and I fell for her too, only I don't get to bang her.

Rome does, the lucky bastard.

On the outside, Peyton looks like the girl-next-door, and I wouldn't have pulled her from a lineup if I were trying to find a date for him. Brunette when he preferred blondes. Petite when he'd preferred tall.

She's the opposite of everything he thought he wanted.

Not that he thought he wanted *any*one, the fickle bastard.

Then she had to go and say she wanted to bang him . . .

Cheeky little shit.

"Why are you just standing there? You look weird." Peyton's sweet but insistent voice interrupts my musing.

"I look weird?"

"Yeah, you look lost in space—and if you're not careful, you're going to drop that dresser right on your foot." She taps hers impatiently.

"And if you do, don't think for one goddamn second you're claiming that injury on my homeowner's insurance." Rome gives me a bump with the other end of the heavy, mahogany dresser that's going in their new bedroom.

We're in their new apartment—just two floors below the one where Rome was living before—and Peyton has us doing the heavy lifting.

"Give me some credit, asshole." I heft the heavy wood, blowing out a little puff of air. "Where are we putting this? I'm about to bust a nut."

Peyton laughs, pointing to the large wall adjacent to their king-size bed. "Right there would be good; center it against the wall." Her hands make a *more that way . . . to the right . . . just a little* motion, then she gives me the universal sign for stop. "Perfect."

Hey. I'm all for the bastard moving in with the love of his freaking life, but how the hell did I get roped into moving all their shit on my only weekend off?

He owes me.

I hate this bullshit; I'd rather pay some college kid a hundred bucks to come heft this crap in my place.

Man—sometimes it sucks being such a good friend.

Rome leans his ass against the dresser, crossing his ankles and arms. Studies me. "What are you doing tonight?"

It's Saturday.

"I don't know. Maybe I'll go out. Get a drink or three."

Peyton's brows go up. "No date?"

I laugh. "What, you think I have a list of chicks on speed dial ready and raring to go every weekend?"

"Whoa," she says. "I was just asking. No need to get defensive. And for the record, you shouldn't go out and drink alone."

I usually don't. But somehow, after spending the afternoon with these two disgusting lovebirds, the idea of going home to my cold, dark apartment holds no appeal.

And she's right; I shouldn't go out drinking alone.

That's just taking *loveless and lonely* to the next level, and I'm not ready to visit that place in purgatory.

Yet.

Forget it.

So I paste on a smile like I always do. "Are you kidding me? I have the ladies lined up when I walk in the door; I won't hurt for company."

It's a lie, one I always tell so they'll get off my back and leave me alone about dating.

It's Rome and Peyton's favorite new pastime, besides public displays of affection and learning how to play racquetball together.

They should stick to chasing balls and leave my love life the hell alone.

"Don't lie, Hunter; you talk a lot of shit, but we all know you're full of crap." Peyton is smug. "You'll probably go home and watch a Lifetime movie."

Close. It will probably be something on the CW.

"She's kidding. We literally don't give a shit what you do tonight."

"Rome. Be nice." She fixes her beautiful face on me and I squirm. I hate when she does this. "What you need to do is stop screwing around and—"

"Find myself a nice girl, I know. Blah, blah, blah. You've told me this a million times."

Peyton doesn't look affronted in the least. Rather, she looks *knowing*.

Always with the smirk.

"You know," she begins slowly, scooting around the couch and making her way to the kitchen. It's warmer than Rome's old one—neutral tones and dark navy accents—with stainless steel appliances and tons of natural sunlight. "Rome's sister is coming to town, maybe—"

"No," Rome and I shout at the same time.

Rome's girlfriend looks back and forth between us. "What did I say? You didn't even let me finish my sentence—"

"The answer is no. It doesn't matter what you were about to say."

"I was just going to say she's coming to town, and wouldn't it be nice if they—"

"No."

Peyton scrunches up her face in a way that's become familiar. "What's wrong with her?"

Nothing.

Absolutely nothing is wrong with Rome's sister, and that's the fucking problem.

Bailey Blackburn is the opposite of what's wrong; she's everything that's right, and I shouldn't go near her with a ten-foot pole.

I'm shocked Peyton would suggest it.

"The last time I saw Bay, she was on a feminist crusade with some college buddies, had sworn off men, hacked off half her hair, and wore purple lipstick."

But.

I've seen her accidentally online and, well—Bailey Blackburn has fucking changed. A lot.

She's sexy as hell. Delicate. Feminine.

Clever as shit.

Once or twice I've *accidentally* studied the photos she posted of herself in a swimsuit on a recent trip to Hawaii. I mean—the post popped up, and I had to fucking stare. It's not like I went looking for the damn thing.

"Yeah, no. She's a thorn in my side."

Liar.

"Oh. Well, never mind then. We can find someone else to show her around the office."

Come again? "What do you mean, show her around the office?"

Peyton avoids my question, a smile growing. "Rome didn't mention it?"

"Mention what?"

My partner and best friend shrugs, and I want to smack him. "She's moving home and needs a job."

"And a place to live," Peyton pipes in, getting a pan out of the cabinet and setting it on the stove with a clink.

"First we'll worry about the job." He shoots her a look, then focuses it on me. "I'm going to put her to work at the office, doing random things. Maybe even some field testing."

Field testing.

That's my department.

I refuse to give them the satisfaction of a reaction. "When?"

"Sometime next week. She's driving in from Colorado."

"What was she doing in Colorado? What year is she?"

I thought she was in college.

"She's been working for The Rockies doing sports marketing, but she's been homesick, and I told her if she ever wanted to come back, she'd have a home here."

"And she's homesick," I deadpan.

"Yup."

"Wait. Is she even old enough to have a job?"

Rome looks at me like I'm a fucking idiot. "She's twenty-six, dipshit."

Oh.

Well.

"Parlay, dude—I didn't know. I thought she was nineteen."

"You're such an idiot." Rome laughs, unable to stop himself. Christ, it's good to see him happy and smiling.

"Kids. When did they get so big?"

"Don't let her catch you calling her that. She's good at her job, highly respected."

"Does the kitten have claws now?" I joke.

Rome frowns. "Don't let her catch you calling her that, either. She'll literally claw your eyes out."

Noted.

I lean against the back of their new sectional, processing this information.

Rome's sister Bailey is coming home, and she'll be working at Roam, Inc. I can handle it—it's not like I'm in love with her or anything.

In fact, she's the one who was in love with me, not the other way around.

I mean—she was like, twelve, but still.

Love is love, and love knows no age.

Especially when you're twelve years old . . .

Bay was crazy, following me everywhere. Blushing when I'd talk to her directly or say her name. Giving me gifts (gum, mostly, and other cheap shit, like candy). Made me damn uncomfortable, but I was sixteen and she was younger, and I knew nothing about women, let alone impressionable, sensitive girls.

She was infatuated with me for one summer.

Until I told her to piss off and leave me alone, in those exact words.

She told me to fuck off.

I smile at the memory of the fire in her eyes, fueled by her humiliation.

She hated me after that and I don't blame her.

I was a pompous little prick, who acted like a dick.

Bailey Blackburn. Who would have thought?

And she's coming home . . .